NUMBER FIVE n+1 WINTER 2007

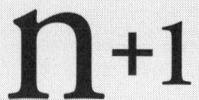

DECIVILIZING PROCESS

THE INTELLECTUAL SITUATION

1 **Against Email**
We are all spammers now

3 **Whatever Minutes**
"I'm in the Louvre!"

5 **The Blog Reflex**
Blog me with a spoon

7 **The Porn Machine**
Twelve-inch laptop

9 **The Decivilizing Process**
Everyday emergency

POLITICS

13 **My Predicament: A Fable** BENJAMIN KUNKEL
Murderous, bloody, full of blame

16 **Note from Cape Town** GEMMA SIEFF
Post-apartheid of the mind

PROLIFERATION

IMRAAN COOVADIA **Dr. Atomic** 21
A love story

BASHARAT PEER **Papa-2** 37
Growing up among the militants

NANCY BAUER **Pornutopia** 63
Don't look, touch

REBECCA CURTIS **The Near-Son** 109
A short story

IMMERSION

ELI S. EVANS **The Television Diaries** 75
Real World: Milwaukee

MARK GREIF **Anaesthetic Ideology** 91
The meaning of life, part II

KEITH GESSEN **Torture and the Known Unknowns** 119
We're only humint

JOSHUA GLENN **The Argonaut Folly** 137
Band apart

REVIEWS

MEGHAN FALVEY **On Dowd, Flanagan, Hirshman, Kipnis** 149
DANIEL ALBERT **On Flying Cars** 155
CARLA BLUMENKRANZ **On Not Chick Lit** 159

LETTERS

Bissell contra Batuman, Atlantic Yards, et cetera 167

NUMBER FIVE
WINTER 2007

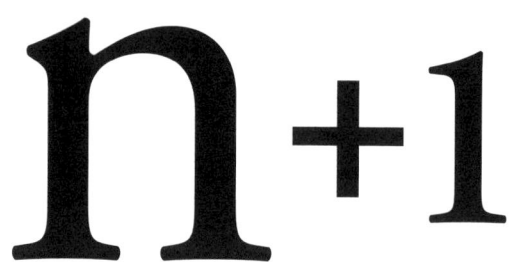

n+1 is published twice a year by n+1 Research, 195 Chrystie Street #200, NY, NY 10002. Single issues are available for $11.95. Subscriptions for $20 (two issues); in Canada, $25; other international, $30 (surface), $40 (airmail). Subscriptions and correspondence to the Editors, Park West Station, P. O. Box 20688, NY, NY 10025. Manuscripts will not be returned. Please correspond before submitting. *n+1* is distributed by Ingram, Ubiquity, Armadillo, and DoorMouse in Canada. To place an ad in *n+1* contact editors@nplusonemag.com. *n+1*, Number Five © 2007 n+1 Research. ISSN 1549-0033. ISBN 0-9760503-4-X.

Editorial Board
KEITH GESSEN
MARK GREIF
CHAD HARBACH
BENJAMIN KUNKEL
ALLISON LORENTZEN
MARCO ROTH

Design
DAN O. WILLIAMS

Photo Editor
SABINE ROGERS

Editorial Assistant
CARLA BLUMENKRANZ

Business Manager
ALEXANDRA HEIFETZ

Special Projects
GREGORY ROTHSCHILD JACKSON
NIKIL SAVAL

Copy Editors
SAM FRANK
EMILY VOTRUBA

Circulation Manager Emeritus
ISAAC SCARBOROUGH

WWW.NPLUSONEMAG.COM

THE INTELLECTUAL SITUATION
A Diary

IT WASN'T EASY FOR US, getting back from Juneau. The airports—when we flew—made us take off our shoes. You can't talk to anyone on the Greyhounds anymore—when we rode—since all the passengers now have other entertainments to amuse them. In every filthy burg along the way it cost five bucks in Kinko's just to check our email. Fifty solicitations for prescription drugs without prescription and fifty "urgent" alerts from MoveOn.org. And then, of course, we need to write all the people we failed to write while we were chained to that oil rig in Prudhoe Bay. And all the people we met on our journey across America. And all the people we've ever known. We hope they're not mad at us. But then—why aren't they writing?

AGAINST EMAIL

IN THE EARLY DAYS OF THE INBOX, IT AFforded the naive human organism a certain pleasure to receive an email. *Ah, someone thinking of me...* So a note or two of companionship whistled through the lonely day. Thanks to email, the residual eloquence of a moribund letter-writing culture received a rejuvenating jolt of immediacy. As late as the late '90s and early '00s, during the last days of dial-up, it still felt nice to send and receive the occasional squib, to play an epistolary game of catch with some friends. Sometimes you would even forward a joke, a larky practice that nowadays seems an unconscionable crime.

For it has lately become clear that nothing burdens a life like an email account. It's the old story: the new efficient technology ends up costing far more time than it ever saves, because it breeds new expectations of what a person can possibly do. So commuters in their fast cars spend hours each day in slow traffic, and then at the office they read and send email.

Correct emailing practice does not exist. The true mood of the form is spontaneity, alacrity—the right time to reply to a message is right away. But do that and your life is gone. So you reject the spontaneous spirit of email; you hold off replying for hours, days, even weeks. By then the initiatory email has gone stale, and your reply is bound to be labored. You compensate for the offense with a needlessly elaborate message. You ask polite questions to which you pray there will never come an answer. Oh, but there will.

Of course you could always reply gruffly, and in lowercase. Moreover, you could refuse to reply at all except where some practical matter was at issue. But Western civilization has always reserved for correspondence its most refined gestures of courtesy, and a memory of the old days persists. Over email, you can be in touch with so very many people—and make each one mad at you. And they *are* mad at you, your former friends, because no more efficient vehicle for the transmission of rashness and spleen has ever been devised than the email. Nettled by something—often something imaginary, since no one's tone comes across quite right, over email—you lash out instantaneously. You hit SEND and it's too late. It's too late because it's too soon.

Email is good for one thing only: flirtation. The problem with flirtation has always been that the nervousness you feel in front of the object of your infatuation deprives you of your wittiness. But with email you can spend an hour refining a casual sally. You trade clever notes as weightless, pretty, and tickling as feathers. The email, like the Petrarchan sonnet, is properly a seduction device, and everyone knows that the SUBJECT line should really read PRETEXT.

But one has many correspondents, and few if any lovers. Individually, they're all decent people; collectively, they form an army marching to invade your isolation and ransack your valuable time. Nietzsche declared that one should set aside an hour a week for reading letters; anything more was toxic. And now we read in the paper where Gloria Steinem is complaining that she spends *three hours a day* replying to email.

America, most efficient country on earth, is in fact a nightmare economy of squandered time. Our economic system condemns people to work in offices and send email; that's what they do there. (And in order to cover their asses, they cc everyone about everything.) Then they go home and take with them all the work they were supposed to be doing all day. Their revenge upon those of us who don't work in offices? To send us email from nine to five.

We too have sometimes been the have-nots in the email economy. In the role of supplicant emailer, we have labored to achieve the impossible right tone: so winning that others will have to write back, so casual you can pretend it doesn't matter when they don't. The whole thing is painful all around. And this, finally, is what must be understood: email, which presents itself as a convenience, a breeze, is in fact a stern disciplinary phenomenon. You must not stray too far from your desk. You must be polite, you must write back soon. And yet in order to strike the right note, you must not write when too giddy, angry, tired, or drunk. Always at the disposal of email, never, except guiltily, at the disposal of your moods.... It fits our phase of capitalism: the collective attitude is casual, natural-seeming, offhand; the discipline is constant and intense.

One now recalls those early days of sparse email traffic much as the cokehead recollects the first bumps of powder snorted sweetly up his nose. How quickly pleasure turned to compulsion and unhappiness! Nothing was left, in the end, but anxiety (*who am I forgetting to reply to?*) and guilt (*I know who*). And yet the compulsive emailer, addict of the insubstantial, is ultimately even worse off than the substance abuser: no clinic for *him* to check into. Western civilization has become a giant inbox; it will swell and groan but never be empty till it crashes.

Our sole consolation is the prospect of doom. For a while, email, in its efficiency, had seemed to serve very nicely the means of production and their owners. But lately, the business pages report a dialectical reversal whereby the means of communication overwhelm the means of production, so that the class of owners and managers can hardly do or even supervise any work; they can only discuss, over email, the things they should be doing. Sabotage and slowdown—old techniques of worker resistance—have become impossible to distinguish from white-collar office jobs. Yes, it may be that all of us together, tapping out ephemera at our keyboards, will bring down this civilization once and for all. But not before human flesh has turned to spam.

AT LEAST, WHEN WE finally get there, the New York winter sunshine is the same. You see your breath in the glitter, and people are still out, all bundled up, in Union Square. So not everybody's sitting home and emailing! There's still hope for us.

"I'm just looking for somebody to talk to," says a plaintive, kindly voice, its possessor's back to us, sitting on the steps.

Boy, so are we. "Hello!"

Our new friend unhappily moves the cell phone from his face, points at it. "I'm, um, talking to my friend?"

"Ah," we say. "Aha."

We are a ghost.

WHATEVER MINUTES

WESTERN CIVILIZATION SPENT 2,500 YEARS trying to get people to shut up. The armies of Alexander the Great were amazed to see their leader read a letter from his mother silently—because he alone knew how. After the dawn of Christianity, centuries upon centuries admired the ability *not* to vocalize, not to talk. Silence was an achievement. It is remembered of Saint Ambrose as part of his piety. It signaled an intensifying inwardness of belief, a world of individual privacy, a different mode of thought. Thus humans were gradually quieted—as part of the civilizing process.

The new etiquette eventually installed the calm of the library, the hush of the museum, the rustling anticipation of the concert hall. First, silence overtook the audiences watching dramas or musical comedies in the gaslit theaters of Paris, Berlin, New York; eventually, the new ways moved into the hinterlands. You could say it helped make the modern self. But then you don't have to believe in such just-so stories to feel that being quiet around strangers, except when having a conversation *with* them, does define a certain relation of kindness or respectful attention *to* them. As a child, when you stood near a stranger, talking loudly but not talking to him, you were taught by your parents to feel self-conscious—as you learned to put yourself in the shoes (or heads) of those accidental listeners, who might want quiet for their own reasons.

Now we have entered an age where technology has ways of making you talk. Not to anyone present—nor in ways that acknowledge your surroundings. We know now that people will answer cell phones in the library and the museum, and place calls, too. "I'm at the library!" They'll talk through whole transactions in a store. It's rude; it's insulting; nobody likes it. Then, annoyed, we do it too, phoning our friends and using our free Whenever minutes to complain. Alexander started the silent era of the West; Nokia will finish it.

Rudeness isn't the real issue: it's that we are building a new world, and consequences will follow. On a bus or a train, there is a competitive pressure not to be the only one without a friend to call when snow has caused delays. All of us deplore the yapping, and most of us join in. And the change reinforces truths we may have thought we already knew—but that, in fact, we never knew like this. Everyone may always have cared infinitely more about his friends and relations than about his temporary neighbors on a bus or in a store—just as he should. But he never could *show* it before. And it is this *showing* of mutual uncaring, of complete separation even among neighbors in public, that can gradually change your attitude about all sorts of things.

Civilization takes a turn. Not in the sense that talking on a cell phone while you pay for groceries is *uncivilized*, as in, uncouth, ignorant of the rules that still exist. The point is that it is *decivilizing*, undoing practices of civilization as fundamental as using silverware to eat. Or alternatively civilizing, if you like, because it doesn't send us on a straight path backward (as if we were going to eat with our fingers or read by whale-oil light) but deflects us into something new that no one intended or wanted in advance.

Some people, who just like human communication, may defend the cell phone for its end to loneliness. We'd rather not be lonely, either. We like noise OK; we aren't the ones who shush people talking during the movie previews. Valéry missed the days when he could smoke his pipe and carry his walking stick into the Louvre—when he could act naturally among his fellow spectators and not be so worshipful. But Valéry's kind of public freedom has nothing to do with a development that makes people talk in the museum while teleporting them outside of it. The steady stream of words coming out of our mouths—with cell phones, and voice recognition, and the babble of new advertising and printing styles and culture—becomes a substitute simultaneously for interior monologue and for formal conversation with listeners all around us. The two effects, for the individual, of the cell phone's contribution to the decivilizing process are *ceasing to be able to be alone*, and yet *refusing solitude without entering into company*.

This leads to the loss of one of the great comforts of modern urban life, not accounted for in the vast sociological literature on anomie: the fraternity of solitude. Sometimes you eat dinner alone; sometimes you do your grocery shopping alone; often you'll ride the bus alone. At such times, in a city, there are always other people who are dining alone, shopping alone, sitting in their bus seats alone, in exactly the same situation. The fraternity of solitaries is always there for you to join. Pynchon imagined a society of "Inamorati Anonymous," solitary anti-love and anti-company people who send letters through a secret network, simply to assure one another they are there. Go into a restaurant now, sit near a fellow single diner, and you will see him dial his cell phone during the appetizer and talk through to dessert. The only choices you have are to pull out your own phone or listen in.

From literature to advertising, we've developed a cultural style of ceaseless babbling. Never mind the endless self-interruptions and elaborations of needlessly footnoted fiction, talking copyright pages, and the rest; we got used to that, and it was sort of in the spirit of a warning. But even Burger King has now stolen the text-happy style of *McSweeney's*, so you are fed grease by some whimsical garrulous spirit of the paper sack and the napkin. Talking toys chat to children trying to learn to think silently. Talking heads on twenty-four-hour television say as quickly as possible the first thing that comes to mind, in order to make room for the next first thing. The heads melt into one another, without any quiet for new thoughts, just as the toys start to record what the infant child babbles, to play it back. Even my dinosaur becomes Me. But who the hell is that? When you eavesdrop on cell-phone conversations, you learn who people are by what they are saying to their friends: "I am now doing one thing. I am now doing another. I will report them all and notice none." And in effect this mode of constant self-report can be summed up in a single phrase: "I am on the phone. I am on the phone. I am on the phone."

∘ ∘ ∘

WE DO THE ONLY THING we can: pick a black Texas Instruments pocket calculator out of the trash can on the corner, wipe off the frost, press it to our ear, and start talking as loudly as we can. Now maybe we'll fit in. There used to be so many crazy people in New York, talking to themselves. Now it's the sane ones talking to themselves, until they turn to reveal their glowing blue earpieces—like android implants.

"Brothers and Sisters!" A man is up on a soapbox, it's like the old Union Square. "Fellow revolutionary workers of Manhattan!" Kids are pushing through the throng to hand out broadsides, looking up with naked admiration at the bearded orator shouting hoarsely. "They call us revisionists, followers of Bernstein, traitors to Marx. But this is the true Marx, brothers and sisters! This is our day! We have been expelled from the CP-USA, ostracized by the Spartacists, thrown bodily out of debates at the public library! But Karl Marx told us the system would undo itself by its contradictions, and we are in the final stage—not from the efficiency of exploitation, but the inefficiency of email! The poison is in the system, my comrades! We only need to bcc it!"

Having said this, the fiery revolutionary descends from his perch. "But how will we know how to break the chains?" the people shout.

"Read my blog!" says the man. "I only have an hour up here to regale you with true wisdom—before the cops interrupt the development of the critique. But online, I have twenty-three more!"

THE BLOG REFLEX

PAUL VIRILIO ONCE PROPOSED AN INTRIGUingly reductive account of world history. Progress was merely the history of speed: in warfare, infantry gave way to chariots, then horses, then tanks, and finally air power (used, er, to bomb infantry). He also coined the phrase "endo-colonization" to describe the accelerating attempts of states and corporations to exploit, as thoroughly as they have the earth, the last available frontier, our minds.

Shoot-outs, flame wars, the gold rush, and the transcontinental railroad all meet in the so-called blogosphere, as the various news corporations, frightened by the flight of readers and consequent loss of ad revenue, aim to recapture the great prize of our attention. But why are we so eager to bless their pages with our hits? The fast-moving history of technology here meets—as truck meets armadillo on the highway—the slow-moving history of thought. Kierkegaard wrote, "Our present age is one of advertising and publicity." That was in 1846! The perfect subject of this new epoch in world history was the newspaper reader, paralyzed by endless information. Sustained passion gave way to momentary enthusiasms. Kierkegaard had a homey analogy for what it was like to live in this state of constant mental stimulation: Imagine a grandfather clock that strikes at random intervals. You can't tell time by it and yet you begin to live in constant anticipation of the next random chime. In this way, Kierkegaard's present age (still ours) ironically fulfilled the messianic promise that "time shall be no more."

A more recent fantasy of revolution was that, hooked up to newswires, all this information at our fingertips, we'd get mad as hell and not take it any more. Instead, people took up blogging. Information would be linked, not to the body politic, but to—links! And more links! Links links links! Readers could now be writers; but was this all that was meant by seizing the means of production? "Citizen journalists" could monitor the professionals from the margins. This, at least, was one much-lauded aspect of blogging, and it was somewhat real (except that the best early news blogs were mostly written by professionals challenging other professionals). Then, of course, like all technological developments, blogs fell prey to existing market forces and inequalities of means, especially time and money. Capital beat out the citizenry. The same reactionary lunatics who dominated talk radio entered the blogosphere. Entrepreneurs like Nick Denton seized the chance to become the Murdochs of the new medium. Advertisers started prospecting in their wake, and the fragile human mind caved in.

A corollary to Virilio's theory of history was that each new stage in technology gave rise to new accidents. To understand the technology, you also needed to anticipate the accidents. When writing first developed, ancient philosophers feared it would destroy human memory; to write anything down was to put yourself in the position of that guy in the movie *Memento*. And this wasn't totally wrong. Also, letters: they had a funny way of getting lost or opened by the wrong people. The first accident in writing came about when a king was instructed to "kill the bearer of this letter." Fortunately, the intended bearer could read, too, and sent someone else in his place.

The accident waiting to happen to bloggers was most visible when they turned their attention to literature and ideas. The hope had been to democratize the intellectual sphere. Freedom of the press is for those who own one. But now all you needed was a laptop and some time on your hands. The idea was especially attractive in light of the consolidation of media holdings and the destruction of intellectual life in the '80s and '90s, when people began to work longer and harder for less, available public spaces and quiet cafés dried up, and argument in the academies gave way to "respect."

The blogs salved this ennui and created nourishing microcommunities. Yet criticism as an art didn't survive. People *might* have used their blogs to post the best they could think or say. They *could* have posted 5,000-word critiques of their favorite books and records. Some polymath might even have shown, online, how an acute and well-stocked sensibility responds to the streaming world in real time. But those things didn't happen, at least not often enough. In practice, blogs reveal how much we are unwitting stenographers of hip talk and marketing speak, and how secondhand and often ugly our unconscious impulses still are. The need for speed encourages, as a willed style, the intemperate, the unconsidered, the undigested. (Not for nothing is the word *blog* evocative of vomit.) "So hot right now," the bloggers say. Or: "Jumped the shark." The language is supposed to mimic the way people speak on the street or the college quad, the phatic emotive growl and purr of exhibitionistic consumer satisfaction—"The *Divine Comedy* is SOOO GOOOD!"—or displeasure—"I shit on Dante!" So man hands on information to man.

One thing cannot be denied: Lit-bloggers are the avant-garde of 21st-century publicity. They represent a perfection of the outsourcing ethos of contemporary capitalism. The savvy readers of our age are already suspicious of advertising from above, from the cartel of publishers, weekly book reviews, and entertainment-industry executives. So why should publishers pay publicists and advertise in book supplements when a community of native agents exist who will perform the same service for nothing and with an aura of indie cred? In addition to free advance copies, the blogger gets some recognition: from the big houses, and from fellow bloggers. Recognition is also measured in the number of hits—by their clicks you shall know them—and by the people who bother to respond to your posts with subposts of their own. The lit-bloggers become a self-sustaining community, minutemen ready to rise up in defense of their niches. So it is when people have only their precarious self-respect. But responses—fillips of contempt, wet kisses—aren't criticism. They can only reinforce, they can never change another person's point of view. So much typing, so little communication . . . It's incredible. A bottomless labor market exists in which the free activity of the mind gets bartered away for something even less nourishing than a bowl of porridge. And you can't dine off your inflated self-respect and popularity—not unless you get enough hits to sell advertising.

THE REVOLUTIONARY HAS left behind a pamphlet. Opening up the cheaply inked pages, blackening our fingers, we figure it will contain the usual articles on Chiapas and a "police riot" in Detroit. Instead, it's one lingerie-clad model after another, plus hung studs in banana hammocks, in advertisements absent a single phone number or in-call/out-call promise—but all with web addresses. So this is how our modern Bakunin hopes to speed the poison along. We're not sure it's going to work.

THE PORN MACHINE

FREUD'S FAVORITE SEXOLOGIST HAVELOCK Ellis unleashed the dignified term "autoeroticism" on the world in 1899. The date was fitting, for the century that followed was nothing other than the triumphal march of masturbation—from Freud's Dora to Joyce's letters to Nora ("Are you too, then, like me, one moment high as the stars, the next lower than the lowest wretches?") and Leopold Bloom on the beach ("And then Mr. Bloom adjusted with a careful hand his wet shirt"), to Kinsey and Masters and Johnson and back to Molly Bloom, yes yes yes, and Anaïs Nin of course and Eve Kosofsky Sedgwick claiming that the sisters in *Sense and Sensibility* were masturbating (poor Jane Austen—you understate a few things and this is what they do), and then Ginsberg masturbating while his mother died, and Portnoy, and Woody Allen ("Now you're knocking my hobbies!"), and that movie where Cameron Diaz had semen in her hair the whole time. Most touching in this procession is the extent to which male and female masturbation went hand in hand, so to speak, into the bright masturbatory future. Even radical feminists, who stressed the female right to self-pleasure in the face of male sexual incompetence, graciously extended the olive branch on this one point. For wasn't the masturbating youth just as defenseless in our culture as the objectified, sexualized female? At one point the feminist writer Lonnie Barbach even suggested that men's propensity to ejaculate before their female partners had achieved orgasm was the result not of selfishness but of an oppressive anti-masturbatory regime that taught boys to come as quickly as possible so as to avoid detection by their parents and schoolmasters. Now this—this was solidarity. Masturbation had achieved the height of its moral prestige.

Then the internet happened. It freed workers from office buildings by connecting them to a worldwide network for the instantaneous transmission of large image and streaming files. You see the problem. Office workers, no longer chained to their desks, become chained, as never before, to their computers. And now, when their personal emails are read and their work emails read and written and cc'ed, and finally they can get up and go for a walk, pornography lures them back. To the painful postindustrial syndromes of carpal tunnel, repetitive stress injury, and chronic eye strain is added Masturbator's Thumb.

This is confusing. The work machine is also a porn machine; the porn machine is also a work machine. Work enters everything. And therefore porn becomes, in its way, a revenge. In the midst of a productivity boost of the sort that comes along once in a century, workers are indulging, in record numbers, in the least productive human activity of all. What does the working masturbator really imagine, in his heart of hearts, as he watches, in super slow motion, the "cum shot" onto the face of his favorite porn star? Does he, too, imagine coming onto someone's face? Or doesn't he rather dream of coming onto his computer screen (possibly breaking it), and freeing himself, once and for all, of both labor and porn? But this would be hard to explain to his bosses. He'll do what he can. *Masturbation*, then, is the workers' sabotage!

Or it would be, if they did it at work. Instead you get the bind of the modern freelance masturbator, the liberated individual who tries to "work from home." Some years ago it was worried that with the advent of virtual offices and virtual relationships, everyone would simply sit in their apartments, in their pajamas, blogging. Instead the public squares, the coffeehouses, the tea lounges, are teeming and brimming over, they are overflowing with the freelancers, with their laptops, their coffees, their BlueZone headsets. Are they there to talk and argue, to bask in the company of others? They are not. They update their MySpace profiles, they IM their high school friends. But they are *not looking at porn*; for the mere price of a coffee, they are basking in their fellow cafégoers' supervisory gaze. "In Military Schools the walls themselves breathe their surveillance of homosexuality and masturbation," wrote Foucault, disapprovingly. In cafés, too, the other patrons breathe this surveillance—for which, says the masturbator, thank god. Or, rather, thank you. The masturbator drops a dollar in the tip jar.

We have freed masturbation from the stigma of the centuries. But who will free us from masturbation? Even the figures often cited for male masturbation, once so liberating to the guilt-ridden teen, begin to feel oppressive. Kinsey has 92 percent of men masturbating. Koestler, in his *Encyclopedia of Sexual Knowledge*, has 85, 90, 93, and 95 percent! But what if you don't want to? The genitalia, Freud once wrote while discussing early sexual development, are "destined for great things in the future." This is not what he had in mind. So hold on, you brave hearts. You 10 percent, 8 percent, you 5 percent—hang in there you stalwarts, you rebels, you diamonds. Just wait a minute, you weirdos. We're coming.

Luddite Song
[traditional]

Chaunt no more your old rhymes 'bout bold Robin Hood
His feats I but little admire
I will sing the Achievements of good old Ned Ludd
The Hero of Nottinghamshire.

He broke the new Looms; it was only a start,
He'll catch your cell phones in a dragnet,
Melt down all your SIM cards like the Calf of Gold
And erase your hard drives with his Magnet.

The wireless waves breaking like surf round
your heads
He'll snare in his chapeau tricorner.
The Boss may forbid him to shoot the router
dead,
In that case the Boss is a goner.

Yes, Ned Ludd arises to heed a demand
He would free you from slavery for leisure
There's only one thing he cannot understand—
Those chains you retain for your pleasure.

THE DECIVILIZING PROCESS

GRADUALLY THE ELEMENTS ADD UP, AND THE most trivial devices may someday become the most important things. Voice recognition, if it ever does all its proponents promise, will make the work we do at our computers continuous with everything else we do, the talk on phones, the talk in meetings, the commands we give to car dashboards to turn down the air conditioning, the instructions we give to our children. As the specific addressee of any set of remarks becomes less important, in the midst of more and more babble, it will become more and more difficult to remember the special status of listening human beings, in the confusion of shouted orders. This is where one starts to enter the realm of science fiction. But just such science fictions of endless, constant communication and control by voice are now being advertised to those who can afford them.

Maybe it's time to reintroduce an old distinction between savagery and barbarism. In their loincloths and bowing to rain gods, savages were people without advanced technology. Barbarians, in contrast, were people *with* technology. Plenty of it. But they gained it without maintaining the values that created it. They sacked the cities, pillaged the countryside, moved onto the estates, and used the mosaic baths and the wine cellars as long as they could. We can try to remember: the world has eliminated most of its savages, but it smiles on barbarians and says they have the most advanced civilization in the world. We in America created the technologies ourselves. And we ourselves misuse them.

The separation of technology from science was one fateful step, and science from philosophy a second step, and philosophy from the search for a moral life a third. And the steps lead down, while the buildings rise and the missiles fly. Thus it became possible for a nation that doesn't believe in Darwin to elect an ape as its President, and equally possible for that ape, who doesn't believe scientists about the warming of the earth, to call for engineers to build a missile shield in outer space. Our new technologies always open the possibilities to the best, and somehow open the floodgates to the worst. The benevolent uses of the phone, the internet, the weblog, email, and so forth, ride like bits of cork on a great tide of waste.

What's odd about so many modern technological improvements is that they are achievements of human liberation in their *emergency* uses, and they decivilize in their *daily* use. The cell phone came into people's lives as a kind of walkie-talkie or emergency radio of infinite range and convenience. If you were stuck on the highway, needed to report a mugging in progress, or had to tell a friend you'd be late, you were saved. Fifty minutes a month was too much for such purposes, and the early calling plans didn't go much past that. And yet the plans that now offer 700 minutes of talk, plus free nights and weekends, or unlimited calling altogether, are still not enough. The internet was going to keep emergency communications up if the rest of the civilian grid went down. Even the blog, the log *on* the web rather than the log *of* the web, arose for people who had to speak their minds, in diaries—we do miss those early blog diaries—until, with the proliferation of links, the true online diaries seemed to disappear. Gradually, the decivilizing process, by this array of devices and images that we employ upon ourselves, will undo our thoughts, our speech, our fantasies. That's an emergency, too. Only who do you call about it? +

Paper Monument

A semi-annual journal of contemporary art

New York Must End
The Painting of Triumph
Peter Nagy from New Delhi
Clocking Out
The Price of Nothing
Terminal Degrees
+ projects and reviews

First issue available Spring 2007.
Published in association with n+1.

Subscriptions:
$20 per year, $10 for a single issue.
$16/$8 for n+1 subscribers.

www.papermonument.com

Paper Monument
1085 Willoughby Ave #401
Brooklyn, NY 11221

JEAN RAY, *FROM BENEATH AN OIL DERRICK*, 2005,
COLOR DIGITAL PHOTOGRAPH, 10½ X 8". COURTESY OF THE ARTIST.

POLITICS
Memoranda

MY PREDICAMENT: A FABLE

I DON'T LIKE BEING A SPIDER. EXCEPT FOR rash moments when my web's been struck and I scramble automatically after my prey, hissing and excited, my venom up and my jaws parted wide—perhaps I'm even smiling—I don't like being a spider at all, generally I experience the same contempt for spiders as do the other creatures of this terrible world. Of course there is pleasure, too, in rearing up on all four of your legs and sinking your jaws into the victim you have just seized with two or four of your hands (sometimes only two hands are necessary and the other two can shake or pump in triumph), there is pleasure or self-forgetful joy likewise to be had in bundling a white moth or black fly in winding-sheets spun from yourself, and what animal does not like a feast, a feast, in the case of us spiders, enjoyed in the air? And then I am simply too glutted with blood to think what I am and regret what I do, days of torpid fullness follow, I doze in my web and ride the breeze, there is sunshine in flood all around me, I close my eyes and listen to the gurgling process of digestion. But when my consciousness revives and begins to raise itself above these facts, the old guilt returns—ancient guilt in spite of my youth—and I know myself for the thing I am, and resolve to let myself starve.

Often—I say often although I have only eaten on three or four occasions: a spider of my species is not a large creature, especially not during the first and likely the only year of his life, he doesn't require too many victims—often after I have eaten and digested a victim, and after my consciousness has sluggishly revived and my mental and bodily quickness resumed, I become frantic with self-loathing and race back and forth across my web wondering what I might do by way of expiation or suicide. It was like that after I ate the white moth in the spring, and it was like that all over again just last week, when I finished digesting the butterfly. Whatever my guilt may have lost in intensity since the white moth, due to habit, it regained when I thought of how beautiful and delicate the wings of my butterfly had been, and how delicious, light, and crisp as I ate them, and how poignant the look of supplication in the dying butterfly's eyes—the look in the eyes of a creature you are devouring is like nothing else, they look at you as if you were a god. I'm sure a cruel spider would enjoy this sight, a hungry spider like myself merely wipes his mouth with one or two hands and ignores it while he can. Until, that is, he is sated and revived, and somehow the pleading look remains before him, although the pleading eyes have been devoured.

After my first meal on my own (whether I had eaten before in the company of my mother and siblings is something I'm not quite sure about), I immediately vowed never to eat again. I couldn't tell whether I was surprised or unsurprised by my ravenous behavior, but it didn't matter, I was appalled, and with quick repentant hands I undid my web where it was secured at one corner to a branch across this narrow ravine, then undid the other far corner where it was fastened to another such branch, and I rode the collapsing structure as it sank to the ground. I will wander through the woods, I thought, until I starve, or else I'll scurry beneath the falling foot of some large animal, positioning myself just so in order to be smashed. I was very distraught as I wandered over the red dirt and fallen branches, underneath green or skeletal fallen leaves, drifting and straying first in this direction, then in that one, with no destination or even direction in mind, except of course my death. And it wasn't too many days before I began to weaken and stumble, I would pause and several limbs would buckle, I would grow dizzy and lose track of the sun. I am dying, I thought, I will be dead, then dry, and then dissolve in the rain. And I believe I was glad as the day dimmed, or my eyesight did, and I lost hope of finding—what I did not want—anything more to eat.

But one evening I saw a small ignorant green beetle shining and crawling, like an ambulatory jewel, in the dimness before me, not two inches away—and I charged after him, knowing he was food. With his hard shell and quick legs, the beetle escaped me, and I was left behind gasping in exhaustion and remorse. You have no self-control! I said to myself, and I experienced the despair of the creature who evidently cannot will himself to die. A spider's mother tells him and his siblings so little as they set out scrambling away on top of one another—there is very little I remember my own mother saying anyway—and I didn't and don't recall her warning us of any plants poisonous to spiders or of any generally fatal locations in which to install a web, fatal to the spider that is. (She spoke of the seasons, nothing else, and seemed mostly to be raving to herself.) So I didn't know what to do, it occurred to me that had there been a stream nearby I might have drowned myself. But there was none.

I reasoned that possibly the world would be safer from me if I were restored to my web. So with what was left of my strength I leaped to a low branch, and then another, and before long I had draped the rudiments of a web between the branches of some low scrub trees. The web was so weak, and composed of so few strands, that I didn't see how any small creature, unless very unlucky, could bumble into it, or how any large creature could be even temporarily restrained. And so I dangled weakly from my weak web, fainting in and out of consciousness, and in a trance of hunger and guilt awaited my starvation. And in those bygone days of the advancing spring, I was still so new in this world that it took me truly by surprise to notice, one day, how my guilt and remorse, if not in the least my hunger, were draining away—to be replaced by anger and desire. Yes, anger, desire, and hunger were all chanting, I noticed (while the chant grew louder), in endless concentric rings in my brain, and I discovered that instead of wanting to die, I wanted to kill and eat and live. All at once I repented of my penitence: I wanted to eat and eat, I wanted one, two, many creatures to gorge on, and I wanted this as if my prey had somehow offended me and I required vengeance, or as if my desire were lust and to eat therefore would be sex, public, an orgy.

Spiders do not chuckle—we are confined, for sound, to hissing—but it was with a sensation of smug and almost chuckling good humor, in spite of my weakness, that I set about expanding and reinforcing my web to the point of ideal fatality. Then, at the center of my web, I hung and waited. I hung and waited there and hoped I could command the necessary strength if some living creature—no mere breeze-detached leaf, as sometimes happens—blundered into my web. And I did have the strength, when it came to that. For she did blunder, the poor plump little fly, several long days later. My entire web hummed and shook, I scrambled in the direction of the blow, and my jaws were wide as I reared above the struggling creature.

ANOTHER WEEK and I was dangling from my tattered web and praying—leaning out from the web and actually praying with my four hands—that nothing would come my way. Please let me starve, I prayed, to no one of course. I am so sorry, I apologized, equally to no one, nature as a rule is a solitary condition, and we spiders are even more solitary than the rest. But at length my vivid guilt began to turn vague again, hunger enfeebled my mind and conscience, and that angry desire of mine that now I know so well returned, fusing itself with hunger, and for a second time I substituted for my resolution to starve a fresh resolution to glut myself on whatever blood I could. Just imagine, I said to myself, how you could feast from season to season on the body of one large creature, a dog, a man, a horse... Just imagine how fat and large you yourself, a pale little spider, might grow! The next victim, however, my most recent, was in reality the butterfly: its wings were stained glass in appearance, in texture and lightness more like a meringue. And its eyes...

I hate myself.

I do.

Not that there aren't times of respite, times of peace. There are times when I am so faint with hunger, and my mind so nearly blank, the sac of my belly so light and empty, that in a strong breeze I simply ride and sway on the air, nearly torn down—nearly but not yet thrown down to the ground—and at such times, with the web at its limit, billowing as far it can, I hardly even know that I remain myself, only that I am alive, and the world is. My own life fades out, but life itself remains: blue sky, red dirt, green world, streaming in a blur. And yet these spells are short. Now it's morning again and the air is still. The air hangs still, the birds query and trill in the trees, light flays the dew from my web, and I know very well that I don't have much time before anger, desire, and hunger combine again. I could resolve at this moment never to attack what hits my web again, but that would be lying.

What can I do, now that I know my nature? Of course I may yet starve accidentally, you do see here and there dry spiders hanging askew from torn webs. And then there is the coming season of fall that I have heard of, when the temperature somehow drops lower in the day than even now at night and, unimaginably, the trees shake off their leaves. A cold event called a frost would seem to promise my death—except perhaps for another warning I recall.

I have few enough memories of my mother, my siblings, our birth. And whether the image I have of falling on and eating one of these siblings is a memory or comes instead from bad dreams is something I just don't know. I do, however, remember the general hissing of tiny fleeing spiders, and the louder articulate hissing of our mother. She was clearly surprised to be a mother to so many young, and she raved in particular about her surprise at being a mother again. Did one of us ask her what she meant by this, or did she go on raving of her own accord? I don't remember, my childhood is so dim. But from what she kept saying, to us or to herself, I gathered that she'd expected the previous year, her first, also to be her last, since it seems we live in a region where something called a killing frost has always been the rule. But our mother burrowed underground, last fall, in what she thought would prove her grave, and then to her great surprise emerged heavily pregnant, several months later, in the springtime air. To this accident it would seem we owe our lives. So she said, lying on her back and raving: she'd climbed from her hole, lay on her back, and given birth to us all, and was surprised to be alive again. And now of course I wonder whether I too will survive my first year. I hope not—and know that soon I may be hoping that I will.

I could not discern my mother's attitude toward being a mother again, except to see she was surprised. (So was I surprised, to be born.) And I remember almost nothing else about her, except her raving surprise—that and the pale color of her body, and her very blue blue eyes. After all, so little in nature is blue: those eyes of my mother, the wings of certain butterflies, and then of course the sky.

—*Benjamin Kunkel*

NOTE FROM CAPE TOWN

IN 1995, A YEAR AFTER THE END OF APARTheid, South Africa's new government formed the Truth and Reconciliation Commission. Disgraced officials met face to face with their victims, offering up their sins in exchange for amnesty. Not everyone got off so easily. Eugene de Kock, the architect of apartheid's secret police force and an executioner responsible for thousands of murders, spoke to the commission despite serving a 212-year prison sentence.

The psychologist Pumla Gobodo-Madikizela spent several months interviewing de Kock in his cell at Pretoria Central Prison. In her book, *A Human Being Died That Night*, she describes being by turns charmed, repulsed, drawn in. Something de Kock says makes her want to comfort him—and she reaches out to touch his "clenched, cold, and rigid" hand. Later, he informs her that it was "'my trigger hand you touched.'" She notes then how he splits himself into sections, corralling his bad acts into a discrete part of his body, and concludes that she must do the same: "It was through 'splitting' that I too … had managed to separate the evil deeds from the doer … [to] embrace the side of de Kock that showed some of the positive elements of being human."

This splitting mechanism has its roots in apartheid—what Gobodo-Madikizela calls a "compartmentalization of South African thinking."

> There were two South Africas: white and black. Similarly, there was the public world and the private world, the open and the covert. And they were rigidly separate.... White South African bystanders were able to live with the brutality against blacks because it was being carried out in relative secret, in that "other world." Everyone engaged in an "apartheid of the mind."

ONE WANTS, POST-APARTHEID, to be able to frame South Africa more cohesively, but what's happening now that the barriers have come down simply feels schizophrenic. The sweep of the view from Silvermine Reserve; tourists buying farm-stall watermelon *konfyt*; teams of manual laborers in their distinctive blue jumpsuits; a man left for dead on the shoulder of the road, having been robbed of his prosthetic leg: it won't, it cannot, cohere. The splitting going on today is not so much about race or public disclosure as it is about time: the newness of this democracy versus the welter of memory, and its bitterness. Mandela deferred the reckoning for a while. He acted as a stopgap, his promises of a gorgeous future made credible by his ancient face.

Now AIDS has distorted time, but in a different way; it has retroactively poisoned the hopeful past. It stayed dormant, or at least unobtrusive, during those first euphoric years, until it erupted everywhere at once. Government ministers began dying at 40 of "TB"—but TB was an opportunistic infection caused by AIDS, something the newspaper obituaries never mentioned. HIV transmission was stealthy—covert, to use Gobodo-Madikizela's term—and its silence implied a national hex, or worse. It didn't seem much of a stretch to think of the disease as apartheid's latest iteration. It was killing only black people, after all. Perhaps disgraced Boer officials and American pharmaceutical companies had conspired to make condoms spread the disease? And condoms were oddly slimy; many men preferred "dry sex," wherein a woman used herbs, soil, or salt to desiccate her vaginal lining. Condoms dulled sensation—you didn't eat candy with the wrapper on—but if you slept with x many virgins, you might get rid of the virus. Hence the spate of baby rapes, unthinkable yet easily explained. Health minister Manto Tshabalala-Msimang urged everyone to get well via a robust diet of beetroot, garlic, and olive oil; a gentle-looking lady named Sonette Ehlers patented a device called Rapex, a female condom fitted with tiny barbs.

I WAS IN CAPE TOWN this past August during Women's Week. The newspapers issued lists of outstanding South African women—Antjie Krog, who wrote so memorably about the Truth and Reconciliation Commission; human rights activist Fatima Hassan; Minister of Environmental Affairs Rejoice Mabudafhasi—alongside outrageous statistics of rape and domestic violence. American postfeminism was also on offer. My cabdriver, a Cape Coloured woman named Ilene, had been, excitingly, a finalist in an *OK!* magazine competition modeled on the American television show *The Swan*. One lucky entrant won a free array of plastic surgery. "It wasn't a beauty contest," Ilene explained. "It was an ugliness contest. I know I am fat, but they want you worse than just fat. The ones they chose, they were so ugly they gave you a *skrik*. And all of them said they hated their noses. The *OK!* judges *want* you to hate your nose. My nose is fine and sits neatly on my face." I confirmed this. "So they didn't choose me: there wasn't enough to cut."

Cape Town was still experiencing fallout from the sensational trial of Jacob Zuma, former deputy president and head of the National AIDS Council, and before that a heroic anti-apartheid leader with Mandela's ANC. Zuma had been acquitted of raping a family acquaintance who was also an AIDS activist, and HIV positive. There was not enough evidence to determine whether the sex was consensual; Zuma himself admitted it was unprotected. His accuser had a raft of past rape claims; she'd also worn a skirt above the knee. Zuma, in his defense, cited effective last-ditch measures (a shower afterward) and binding tribal roles ("In the Zulu culture you don't just leave a woman in [a state of arousal], because if you do then she will... say that you are a rapist"). Zuma's political persona relies heavily on such invocations of his Zulu heritage. To his detractors, his acquittal symbolized a descent into tribalist politics and showcased the government's incompetence. His supporters countered that he was a scapegoat, the girl a liar and a whore, and who was to say she had HIV anyway? (I wondered if he already had HIV—and this explained the unsafe sex.) After yet another Zuma trial, for corruption, he would lead his supporters in the rendition of an old anti-apartheid anthem, in which the singer calls for his machine gun. Outside this courtroom, protesters called for Zuma's accuser to be stoned.

Meanwhile actual stonings were occurring on the major motorways—the N1, the N2, the N7, the R300. A Kuilsriver man had died. Skittish drivers ran red lights and looked heavenward as they approached overpasses: bricks sometimes fell from the bridges. They talked about the menace in line at Pick & Pay: "It's township kids playing Kill Whitey. Urchins with rocks while you wait at a traffic light—but not your typical smash-and-grab." In the past, someone would take out a window to snatch the briefcase or handbag left on the front seat. But in the recent cases there was no theft: the shattered glass was the point. The police put up emergency phone booths along the N2 route, but it turned out the phones didn't work.

Savvy South Africans don't rely on landlines, of course; they all have pay-as-you-go mobiles. My grandmother's maid Nomisa used hers to call one Thursday, to say she wouldn't be coming to work: her granddaughter had died in the night. Nomisa has worked for my grandmother for thirty years. When I was a fussy child visiting in the summers from America, she remembered the ways in which I was particular, leaving out the sliced tomatoes from my salad or sandwiches because I hated the stray seeds. (This kindness embarrasses me when I think of it today.) I wrote a story for my sixth-grade teacher describing exotic Nomisa, with her Xhosa intonation, strong forearms, smell of yellow soap, stiff housedresses in pastel colors: salmon, seafoam, powder blue. Her housedresses are unchanged, although she's put on weight in her hips and middle. She still has strong forearms, but does not smell of yellow soap—I think I stole that detail from Carol Ryrie Brink. And now she calls my grandmother "Gran" rather than "medem."

Nomisa's 21-year-old son showed great promise—good looks, good marks in school—and had gone on to an IT college. (As is fairly common practice, my grandmother pays his tuition and so has an investment in his success; her letters to me usually contain some news about him.) Nomisa didn't approve of his girlfriend, a township girl, extremely pretty but unemployed. The girlfriend got pregnant and my gran said pessimistically, "There goes his future." But when the baby was born, and all three were living with Nomisa in her tiny, tidy, government-issued house, everything felt different. They named her Lelethu, which means *She is ours*.

In the daytime, Lelethu stayed with her maternal grandmother, who decided earlier that week that she seemed unwell and took her to the township *sangoma*. He threw the bones and administered herbs. Lelethu writhed through the night; in the morning, she had stopped breathing. Nomisa thought the treatment's toxicity killed the child; her other grandmother claimed she was sick and would have died anyway. The nurses at the local clinic said it was impossible to determine cause of death. They swaddled her and turned her over to Nomisa, who had funerary rites to arrange and pay for.

In this age of AIDS, funerals are the subject of black humor among blacks and the source of complaints among whites—domestic servants attend too many. When Zuma was exonerated, and his supporters wanted to humiliate his political rival, the imagery of interment was ready to hand: they staged a mock funeral for Thabo Mbeki, with a paper cutout of the president's head affixed to a child-size coffin.

THIS WAS ALL VERY DIFFERENT from the Cape Town I played in just three years ago, which at Christmastime was a city of beachy insouciance. I skirted surfers and bluebottles in the sea at Muizenberg, drove through the lush vineyards of Franschhoek and Paarl, did shots of Amarula liqueur on the strong dollar. My American friend Nick was studying abroad at UCT that year, and he hiked Table Mountain on acid. On New Year's Eve, I went with my trendiest cousin to a club called Eclipse in Heritage Square, where we paid a 700-rand fee to enter a torch-lit space full of people with very few clothes on. There were eight or ten extremely beautiful black South Africans and eighty or a hundred slightly less beautiful white ones. The music—house beats and richly textured strings—thrummed up through our calves. Soon I was drunk, and a blue-eyed man with a creased face stopped me to talk. Did I know that I was an Indigo Child, the harbinger of everything resplendent in the next world? Had I heard of synchronicity? He offered me a tab of Ecstasy. Above us the club's performers, every one of them black, balanced exquisitely, dressed in spangled spandex and navigating the tightrope with their strong toes.

That feels long ago. The crime spike has made people jittery and sad. My grandmother would not allow me to walk six blocks to return a rented DVD, nor to unlock the car by myself: "You don't know how to look around." Nadine Gordimer, the 82-year-old novelist and Nobel Prize winner, was recently robbed in her home in Parkhurst. She handed over cash and jewelry, but was locked in a storeroom after she refused to give up her wedding ring. No one wants to feel disillusioned, but "it's been ten years."

On the other hand, ten years isn't a very long time, and the country is still in flux. The government's Black Economic Empowerment initiative has begun to invert the hierarchy of the workplace. Black couples, young and ultracoiffed, tip valets along the waterfront. (White kids, unable to find jobs, are leaving South Africa to work as masseuses on cruise ships and ski-lift operators at Vail.) There is electricity and clean water in the townships, and recently an emboldened deputy health minister promised there would soon be a comprehensive new HIV plan. And the nonspecific buoyancy one feels here, which comes from the height of the sun, the unrushed rigmarole of greeting a stranger, the things sold at the side of the highway (boxes of hyper-pigmented fruit; intricate toy cars woven from telephone wire)—that's still intact. *Kwaito* blasts from battered combis and taxi vans, and the schoolchildren inside, immaculate in ironed uniforms, bounce in their seats to its snug rhythms.

HERE IS J. M. COETZEE in *Youth*, the second installment of his memoirs, speaking about the apartheid era: "Between black and white there is a gulf fixed. [There] lies an awareness on both sides that people like ... himself, with their pianos and violins, are here on this earth, the earth of South Africa, on the shakiest of pretexts." This "shakiest of pretexts" has collapsed now, and without a civil war. But the situation is deteriorating (Coetzee for his part lives in Australia). South Africa is still the richest country on the continent; it is also the whitest. The gulf between black and white is more than ever a gulf of money, and if it does not close quickly enough the country could turn into Zimbabwe. Meanwhile people are dying and dying, and all the things that made the ANC great when it fought apartheid—its militancy, its cultural pride, its ability to keep a secret—make it, in the face of AIDS, ineffectual or worse. *Matsatsi a loyana*, says a Sesotho proverb: *Days are not the same.*

—*Gemma Sieff*

MAY DAY STADIUM, PYONGYANG, SOUTH KOREA, 2005
SATELLITE PHOTOGRAPH. COPYRIGHT IMAGESAT INTERNATIONAL N.V.

DR. ATOMIC
Imraan Coovadia

THE AIRPORT IS DESERTED at two in the morning, Pyongyang time. A tractor stands on the apron behind an unroofed, unpainted cargo container. It hisses into life as he passes into the custody of the ground guards. The turboprop, which has brought him all the way from Karachi, spins down its engine. He looks back at the aircraft. The red bulb mounted above the wing has been his companion through six hours of uneven sleep. Now it blinks, and turns off. The phalanx of guards moves him through the terminal, past rows of Formica desks and tables. They square up on the main road, in silence.

The doctor is accustomed to his hosts' reticence, to their military demeanor. He knows not to speak until spoken to. This doesn't happen until he's deposited in the backseat of an old Zil limousine that must date from the Truman administration. His translator's is the first voice he hears on the ground in North Korea. Joon Sung-Lee looks hardly a day into her twenties. She sits beside him as rectilinear in her posture as an oil rig. With her plum brown eyes and rectangular haircut, she owns a postbox mouth which opens and closes, he notices, without implicating her stiff face. You could place a message on her tongue and never be able to retrieve it.

He also notices the epaulettes on Joon's blouse, which signify military rank. Everyone he meets, in North Korea, is an officer in one or the other war-making organization. His conclusion is that North Korea is an army camp, not a country, but even an army camp has the right to benefit from the technology he brings in his suitcase. In Pakistan, a girl as eerily beautiful as Joon would be a TV presenter. It's fortunate that the doctor gave up on courting women thirty years ago, although there's still an ample measure of gallantry in his manner. He's not sure it will be noticed by his companion. Here, north of the 37th Parallel, Joon is the curved iron side of a scimitar.

They speak in English.

"You are in good condition, Doctor? They looked after you properly on the flight?"

"Oh, I'm extremely well," he tells her. "I even managed to sleep on the plane, which is usually difficult for me. But I took a tablet, an Ambien, and managed a good few hours." He looks out at the snow-dusted roads of Pyongyang. Cement monoliths rise above the intersection. In their facades not a lit window is to be seen. The Zil has downtown to itself and ignores traffic signals. "Perhaps it's the side effect of having a good conscience. The sleep of the just, I believe that's the right phrase. Since we're going to be together a lot this weekend, perhaps you could call me just SQ—short for Saif Qader Khan, of course. I picked up the nickname during my years at the Technical Institute in Munich. The Germans, they're real ones for nicknames." He sees less than nothing flicker across her countenance. "Look, if you like, continue to call me Doctor. Only please remember that my doctorate lies in the field of nuclear engineering. I'm not the person to consult about your aches and pains."

The doctor has told the very same joke, if you can dignify it with the term, a hundred times in his life. Joon, like other North Koreans, doesn't acknowledge his words with a smile. She dips her head, doesn't pick up the conversation until they get to the hotel. The doctor doesn't object. Joon is a serious person who is dedicated to serious business. Splitting the hydrogen atom, fusing two heliums, is a serious enterprise. Truth be told, his own lack of seriousness troubles the doctor. An easy temper is something expected of Pakistani men of a certain class. The Khan men are generally lighthearted, a low-voltage charm. But no one's so charming as to change Joon's demeanor. It's not unusual. The doctor knows that his clients clam up the moment he deviates from the expected script—Libyans, Iranians, and North Koreans alike.

Joon walks him up to his room at the Fraternal North Korea Supreme Guest House. She walks ahead of him and he observes the revolver holstered in her belt. He imagines the cling of her underwear beneath her tight green pants. She unlocks the door and sends him into the hotel room in front of her.

"You should be comfortable here, Comrade. We have selected the best available room in the entire capital for your refreshment. Your bags should be up in a minute. Tomorrow, if it suits you, I will collect you bright and early." She smiles for the first time since they've met. She shakes his hand good-bye. "We are going to a soccer game."

THE ROOM IS SMALL, CLEAN, SPARTAN. A washbasin springs from the wall at one side. The window, half closed by a blind, opens on the back of the hotel, where he sees several tanks of gargantuan proportions anchored in the disused parking lot. The cylinders loom into the afternoon of the streetlamps. He observes the flash of a lighter as two sentries share a cigarette. Obscurely running through his mind is the warning from a World War I movie... three on a match. While he waits for the luggage to be delivered, the doctor begins his exercises. It's vital to keep up, at his age. First come the pushups. Then he does yoga routines—breathing, bending, and mental discipline.

By the time they turn up with his suitcases, the doctor is almost done with the memory game he plays to maintain his powers of concentration, a game he learned from a former German colleague, one of the few men with whom he had a meaningful exchange during six years in the Federal Republic. He finishes first, and unpacks, stretches out his jacket and trousers. The clothes in his bags have been meticulously refolded, his documents refiled; as he expected, everything has been searched, presumably photographed. It's almost a relief to know that his visit is running smoothly. Nobody in the proliferation business should expect privacy, or even want it. Indeed he would have been disappointed if the Koreans were any less thorough than his female minders in Tripoli.

A TWELVE GUN SALUTE INTRODUCES the First Eleven of the International Soccer Brigade of the Democratic People's Republic of Korea. The players, in their red and gold uniforms, filter onto the pitch while the barrage continues in the stands. Army helicopters swing over the stadium, pivoting awkwardly around their tails. They carry long red banners which unfurl from their infantry bays.

Today Joon arrives in a softer uniform. She looks less like a tank commander, the doctor reflects with pleasure, and more like an air hostess in a red scarf, stiff red blouse, and woollen red stockings. She escorts him through the official's gate at the stadium, brushes against him as they take their seats on a wooden bench above the bleachers. The lines still filing into the stadium are spookily well behaved and quiet, quite unlike any large group of people on the subcontinent. Very few Korean children, it seems, have come out. As for the weather, it's brisk and sterile, perhaps because they're high above sea level. The cold air, from what he can judge in this stadium in the center of town, is unpolluted.

Half a lifetime ago the doctor visited the Eastern European cities—Warsaw, Berlin, Prague after the Spring, Timișoara under the Ceauçescu regime. Those streets were choked by buses and fumes. North Korea's environment is far purer. The doctor admires purity above all things. It's what interests him about the atom, about yoga and calisthenics, about vegetarianism, about the life of the Prophet. Sure, he's not much of a religious man. He doesn't fast during *ramzaan*, doesn't go to mosque on Fridays. But if you do happen to be a religious man, the doctor believes and has often remarked, then it becomes you to be a fanatic. He's an engineer, after all. If you do have convictions, it is incumbent on you to take them to the logical extreme. For this reason the doctor appreciates the evident fanaticism of the Koreans.

The national team is winning by two goals to nothing at halftime. The visiting Cubans mount a ragged defense in the last quarter of the game, and then a counterattack that stalls with a failed shot at goal from the far left-hand corner. The Cuban forwards miss on the rebound. Their defenders flunk a long pass, and the Cuban goalie stirs into action only after the ball has landed squarely inside the net. The doctor loses interest. It's obvious the Cubans, who took a game off Brazil in the Americas Cup, aren't on top form in Pyongyang. It makes sense. You don't want to try too hard when you're visiting a dictatorship. Perhaps it's a courtesy they extend to each other.

The doctor inspects his fellow onlookers, and formulates the idea that the height of a Korean man rarely exceeds five foot five. They tend to have compact frames, big muscular arms, and muscular heads. Many of the Korean women, in another country, even if it was Pakistan, would be viewed as distressingly thin. Here they look properly proportioned. In a matter of a day, the doctor tells himself, a visitor becomes accustomed to any permutation of the human shape... to a mortuary, an Auschwitz, a radiation ward, an army camp disguised as a nation state.

"I hope you've enjoyed the match, Doctor."

He waves his hands. "Please, my dear, 'SQ'"

"SQ then. How do you like the victory of our illustrious team over our Cuban brothers?"

"I like it very much indeed. Your team plays very well on the offense, from what I can tell. To be honest I'm not a football man. Even in Munich I never quite picked up the bug. Back at home I watch cricket, if anything. But I can say for certain that your players are superb. They totally outgunned the Cubans."

But Joon has another item on her lecture list. They're always teaching the foreigners, these North Koreans…

"Doctor, do you see the difference between our socialist athletic contests, which are healthy, fraternal competitions without the negative influence of material incentives, and the utter corruption of the Western sport-industrial complex where multinationals like Coca-Cola and Marlboro exploit the players to promote their own commercial interests?"

The doctor's in a surpassingly good mood. He says, "Oh, Joon, I believe your team, and their Cuban visitors, have far more real incentive to perform up to scratch."

She smiles, and it's Hiroshima. Just yesterday it was unthinkable that Joon, behind her postbox mouth, would be comfortable around him. Today she behaves like the daughter of a family friend. Like other Korean women Joon doesn't wear makeup, although it seems almost as if her lips are pinked. She leans into him, out of the wind, when the audience erupts into a chorus at the successful conclusion of the game. Two socialisms have been vindicated.

The doctor decides that half the charm of North Korea, at least for him, is the hope that things that are rigid will melt. There's so much to melt on this end of the peninsula—the disciplined expressions of the hotel staff and their military manners, Joon's harshly composed face in which, in mirage, he identifies moments of tenderness, and, of course, in two days' time, the landscape around the test site forty miles west of the city at Kon Wilshen where Western satellites and earthquake detectors cannot penetrate. The atom has been the true love of his life, he thinks, because it is the enemy of everything solid, everything permanent.

° ° °

THEY ARE INVITED TO DINE with the triumphant team. Joon takes him by the hand into the changing room. They're honored guests. The players, already scrubbed, are arranged in a reception line to receive them. Steam from the hot showers still hangs in the corridor. Water swirls freshly into the floor drains. The doctor shakes hands with a series of young, dark-haired men who seem to have applied generous quantities of curious-smelling foot powder.

At dinner the doctor's in a radiant condition. He toasts the players, praises the landscape and the orderly character of the society, works his hand into Joon's. He's always been affectionate toward the young. In Pakistan he has trained a cohort of young men, and one woman, in the intricacies of nuclear engineering. They are poised to go out into the world, circumstances permitting, and confer the benefit of atomic arms on nation after nation. That great benefit is national pride, cultural pride, the pride of legitimate self-assertion. It's false to call his students nuclear *mujahideen*; they're freedom fighters, for all religions and political systems. For too long the international system has been organized and dominated by a handful of governments. Atomic pride, dispensed liberally by the doctor, will bring that colonial epoch to a finish. In a sense, in one sense, he is... but he doesn't allow himself to complete this thought.

Nothing he tells himself would be disagreeable to his hosts, in all probability, but obviously no one can speak openly about his purpose in visiting Korea. The conversation in the mess, a converted barracks, is stilted. The players must have conventions to talk among themselves, whereas for a foreigner they have no template. The doctor seems to be the only outlander anywhere in Pyongyang, with the exception of the hapless Cubans. His cover, sketched by Joon, is that of a visiting expert in the field of sports medicine. Through Joon the players ask him about Pakistan. Inevitably he finds himself explaining cricket to them—overs, wickets, one-day matches, the tradition of the Ashes. It's as close to comedy as his time in North Korea permits. The Libyans, with their boiling-kettle temperaments and their ostentatious hospitality, not to mention Qaddafi's cadre of female ninjas, were the more entertaining hosts.

The lights tremble now and again as the electricity fluctuates in the barracks. Dishes of meat and noodles go around the table, followed by small bowls of kimchi, mashed potatoes, diced eel and radish, anchovies, spinach in some kind of red oil. In an expansive mood, the doctor tries everything, pronounces on everything, and likes everything he tries. He watches Joon out of the corner of his eye. She enjoys herself, too. Finally, someone produces a bottle of liquor from a tog bag under the table. People go quiet. The alcohol is contained in a jam jar covered by a disk of red paper. One of the players brandishes it beneath the doctor's nose. He laughs.

Joon translates. "He asks, can he offer you some of this refreshment, SQ?"

The doctor is careful to be as amused as the players. "What is it I am being given, may I enquire?"

"It's *yuju*. Korean horse-milk wine. It's very concentrated, and it's made only in people's backyards in the countryside, when they have a horse to spare. I must inform you that the players will be extremely disappointed if you don't try a glass. These men are risking execution."

"That makes me doubly sorry to be forced to decline," he says. "I never dreamed you could milk a horse. It's not that I am opposed to them drinking. Please, tell them to drink and be merry. It's just that my doctor, my medical doctor, has forbidden me to partake on health grounds. Otherwise, he tells me, there isn't more than a year left in this sorry organism of mine." He places his hand on his chest as if he's taking an oath. "My pecker... I'm sorry, my ticker, my heart, you understand. Would you translate that for me, and tell them to go ahead, for my sake?"

"I'm sorry to hear that, Doctor."

Joon explains to the team. He's pleased that they seem to take his injunctions sincerely. The jug of *yuju* circulates from hand to hand. The shots, executed as precisely as the barrage over the stadium, bring stinging red circles to the otherwise chalky complexion of the drinkers. Joon herself drinks only for show, although, like the doctor, she is affected by the atmosphere of revelry. The players throw a ball from one side of the long room to the other. They swear, bringing a blush to Joon's cheeks, they tell jokes in Korean. Crockery is broken. One of the men slips underneath the table and goes to sleep with his head on a pair of boots. A window is shattered so that the cold night suddenly surges into the badly lit room.

They need music. The manager, a Mr. Kim, goes out to his car, doubled over laughing. He returns with a record player and a selection of albums. Soon the place is filled with popular Korean songs as well as Sinatra, Stevie Wonder, and the Four Tops. Joon declines to dance with one of the forwards, but she nods her head and moves her shoulders.

Through the broken window, Mr. Kim notices a canvas truck parking on the opposite side of the street. It's mounted with a loudspeaker. They suspect it's a police patrol. The room undergoes a phase transformation. In seconds the record player is hidden in a locker. What remained of the liquor has been poured into a drain. Joon sweeps the broken glass from the window into a scoop. Nobody emerges from the truck but the party breaks up anyway. One player washes his hair under the cold-water tap. The others go home to their unheated houses, their Party-selected spouses, their canned United Nations food rations, and their exultant memories of the day's game.

The end of festivities disappoints the doctor. He's been the presiding deity of the party. Joon, who knows a little about his background, has started to call him "Dr. Atomic" under her breath. Somehow the manager, Kim, overhears her. The players are delighted by his new moniker. As they trickle out they embrace Dr. Atomic. Under the influence of *yuju*, they're unexpectedly emotional. Though sober, the doctor is also. It's not unusual for him. He has an open nature, is easily affected. As a child he wept copiously before each school morning, and again when the patrolling *ayah* deposited him in his mother's arms in the afternoon.

The Zil returns them to the hotel downtown. Sitting in the back with Joon, the doctor imagines that they are a couple gliding through the streets on their way to some romantic destination. When Joon walks him up to his hotel room, past the brooding security men, the doctor sits on the bed and begins to cry. Is it joy? Is he overwhelmed by the prospect of the weekend? Is it a delayed result of jet lag? He can't explain to her from behind his curtain of tears. Joon embraces him. He stops crying for a moment, as if to catch his breath, then the crying comes back with renewed intensity. Her thin body burns on his skin. Her cheap deodorant bewilders him.

They stay there, one sitting, one standing, until Joon bends down, unties his laces, and removes his shoes. The gesture moves him still further. Working up, she rapidly undresses him. Once he's naked he allows her to seat him between the sheets. Joon pulls off her own top and lies down beside him. They make no further approach to each other. They sleep back to back in the enormous hotel bed. Her frame, hardly touching his own, is half his width. The doctor wakes up during the night. His attention wanders through the window where clean dry stars, in a firmament rinsed as clear as a child's eye, stare down on Pyongyang. He turns around so that his face is buried in Joon's back. The dry starlight echoes at the back of his vision and into his dreams.

N EXT MORNING IT IS AS IF NOTHING has happened between them, which is best because there's plenty of work to be done. In preparation the doctor submerges himself in a bath for a quarter of an hour. He soaps his hair, trims his eyebrows with scissors, releases a dollop of Vicks ointment into the hot water. By the time he changes, Joon is back in a new outfit. He's disappointed to find that she's retreated from the previous afternoon, with a Mao-style cap, a severe khaki shirt, and dungarees. Nonetheless she reminds the doctor of Audrey Hepburn. She kisses him on the cheek, and retreats to a safe distance.

"We must be ready for a big day, Doctor. We have a very long itinerary. Look, I can show you." She unfurls a printout and runs through the items with a pen. "First, we travel to Kandiriya Plant. Now, the location, of course, is a number-one state secret. The imperialists across the border would love to have that information, in order to control Korea. We cannot afford to take any risks. Therefore, for this part of the journey, we will have to blindfold you. Assuming everything goes well, we have scheduled the most exciting opportunity of your visit, your appointment with our Dear Leader. He knows the particulars of your mission. He's heard a good deal about your accomplishments, and he has expressed a particular interest in meeting you."

The doctor beams. "I am also looking forward to it... extremely. Joon, I have read many interesting things about the Dear Leader. You know, many years ago, when I was still young, I had the privilege of listening to his father speak, in Kuala Lumpur. The impression he left was one of immense power, and insight. What an inspiration! You may not believe it to look at me, but as a youngster I was pretty senior in the International Socialist Friendship League." He wants to touch her face. He's nostalgic for his long-ago student holiday in Malaysia, nostalgic for a young man's heart. "But that was those days."

The morning brings the half-forgotten joys of work. He takes pleasure in being able to do his job and bring his knowledge to bear on the infinite details of running a modern reactor. At home, nowadays, the doctor has little to do, less to contribute, since his protégés have taken up positions.

Plus, the logistics of the Pakistani nuclear program have gone beyond the purview of any single man, no matter how talented or experienced. At Biwalhapur, the young engineers who did their dissertations under him now keep the breeder reactor shipshape. They manufacture plutonium under watchful batteries of anti-aircraft missiles, ready to round on intruding Indian aeroplanes. At Kohanip, the generation of physicists whose careers he mentored seals ounces of the potent plutonium into cheese-shaped steel casks.

The work goes on day and night. Whether he, as a single person, lives or dies is immaterial—the production of atomic rockets continues. What did Khrushchev say? *We're making rockets like sausage.* National pride knows no limits. In Pakistan, just as much as Hindu India, the missiles are worshipped as gods in street festivals. He, the humble engineer, is worshipped in Pakistan as a creator of gods. One and a quarter billion souls, a quarter of the earth's population, have been endowed with dignity by him and his Indian counterparts. Their task is accomplished. His task, at home, is accomplished.

Whereas in North Korea he can be of service. The Koreans are still learning. They're building pride. There are kinks in their procedures. Joon and the doctor are brought to the swimming pool filled with heavy water that stands at the heart of the reactor. The doctor recognizes his own design. The Koreans got the schematics from Libya, but there's no substitute for a designer's wisdom. Not everything in the world can be translated onto paper. The staff send one of their number along with the doctor. He's a gruff fellow who has one technical question after another. Khan fields them all successfully, yet the man seems angrier after each response. It's a consuming exercise. There's scarcely time to admire the tanks of fissile material which glint far beneath the water's surface. He wants to show off in front of Joon, but the opportunity doesn't arise.

They go up to the control room. Like identical chambers in Pakistan and Libya and Iran where the doctor has spent many hours of his life, the place resembles the cockpit of a MD-11, a resemblance that isn't accidental. Clocklike gauges and dials populate the walls. The center of the room is taken up by a bank of machines. The doctor knows that it contains transistor arrays copied from a Siemens device. Levers connect to the pneumatic beds underneath their feet. A steam pressure valve below the main window is the doctor's particular contribution. He's proud of the thing to this day. The design is borrowed from the hatch of a World War II–era British submarine. In an emergency, God forbid, opening the valve will entomb the reactor in a lead casket.

The doctor jokes about a meltdown. He knows he shouldn't, but he's suddenly as frivolous as a child. As before, his mirth falls on deaf ears. He and the engineer go back over the difficulties the Koreans have experienced. They tinker together, write on the schematics, run calculations on the old vacuum-tube mainframe in the back of the control room.

By one o'clock the mechanism has been recalibrated and a new batch of plutonium emerges from the swimming pool. It's encased in a steel and concrete ball. Only in the doctor's imagination does the sphere gleam with dazzling blue light. He's thinking of Čerenkov radiation, invisible to the naked eye. Ultraviolet Čerenkov radiation passes untouchably through steel and concrete, through endless lengths of water and space. He knows that Čerenkov particles pass ceaselessly through his skull, through Joon's, and then out through the roof, through the moon, and far out into the Milky Way. If some being broods at the core of the galaxy, he thinks, it's more likely to notice these flashes of radiation than anything the Egyptians, the Greeks, or the Jews have contributed to the species.

PERHAPS BECAUSE THE AFTERNOON went well, the audience with the Supreme Leader comes to pass. But to arrive at court requires certain adjustments; the Doctor loses his translator. Joon leaves him in another, newer Zil limousine which draws up outside the reactor. She promises to meet him before his flight the next morning. He doesn't believe her and remains discontented throughout the long drive.

He's alone almost for the first time during a Korean day. The car has been furnished with a television set which shows the single, government-run channel. There's a full bar he addresses only to pour himself a glass of tonic. The driver is separated from him by a smoked-glass partition through which the doctor hears the occasional crackle of a radio set. They glide past an airbase through bales and bales of fog. The doctor thinks about Joon as long cement trenches on the outskirts of a town give way to smoldering wet power stations and acres of industrial plant, then to bare hillside, and finally to a series of fortified gates.

At each gate they stop and their credentials are checked. A guard rolls up at the driver's window, scowls, reads their papers, checks with the next position, scowls again, and waves them through. Nothing else moves on this road. The Glorious Leader, it seems, is better protected than the Glorious Atomic Weapons Program. They halt at the side entrance of the palace, where, as the doctor is hurried into the door, snow drops out of a boiling black sky. Inside it's warm and protected. A platoon of men in black uniforms marches the doctor along a red-carpeted hall, then up and down staircases and into a glass-paneled booth, where he is frisked by a female soldier. An elevator drops him a hundred feet into the earth, a hundred feet of safety from an atomic blast.

The doctor finds himself suddenly alone in a gigantic living room. Couches hulk around the walls. There are love seats loaded with cushions, and even a jacuzzi closed off by a thick plate-glass lid. A huge flat-screen television occupies one wall. Along the other walls are shelves, holding CDs and DVDs, alongside framed movie posters. The doctor recognizes *Casablanca*, Marilyn Monroe in *Some Like It Hot*, and *Andrei Rublev*, and *Nostalgia*. And there are more movie posters in Japanese and Chinese script. The Glorious Leader, he has been told, is a fan of the cinema. The doctor thinks of the contrasting realities and fantasies he's seen in these busy last few years—the half-reality of Pakistan, the made-up realities of Libya and Korea, the silky realities of the Hollywood and Bollywood flicks he dislikes, and the ultimate, final, unappeasable reality of the atom.

His reverie is interrupted by a train of scantily dressed women who precede the Glorious Leader. They're colorful, done up, transfigured by jewelry and perfumes like no other North Koreans. It's as if they're from a different world, a television universe. They hobble around him on high heels, peck him with faces buried deep beneath cosmetics, and return to their master. The Glorious Leader, who is also the Dear Leader and the Illustrious Leader, reminds the doctor of Elvis Presley. Kim the Second seems to be wearing thick makeup, an apricot-colored foundation. His proportions are strange, too. From the great Mongolian ruff of his fur coat sprouts a gigantic head.

They speak through one of the women who acts as interpreter. Unlike Joon, this lady's English is conveyed in a strong French accent, in fact a Parisian *lycée* accent. The woman holds hands with Kim while she translates, as if they're new lovers. All the women seem to be connected to Kim in this way. It's odd that at the very heart of the North Korean army-state is a cell bound together by love. But the doctor is not one to dwell on an irony. His work, his atomic pilgrimages, brings him face to face with too many such complications.

The Leader exchanges words with his representative. "The Dear Leader wants to know, if your stay in the Democratic People's Republic of Korea has been a comfortable one? If anything more could have been done to increase your pleasure?"

"Oh, it's been very pleasurable. Put your mind at rest."

"Good." She turns to Kim and then back to the doctor. "We have tried to show you the best of everything of which Korean socialism is capable. True luxury and true joy, according to the Dear Leader, is only possible under the socialist system, because we fulfill real human needs, not invented ones, as in the imperialist West." She pauses for a moment, waits on the Leader's next sentence. "Dr. Khan, you have benefited the laboring masses of Korea more than you can imagine. Our gratitude is unshakable."

"Oh, I do what I can. I only do what is in my power."

The doctor is waved onto the sofa while the Leader and his party settle around him like a flock of starlings. Kim keeps his coat on. The man's thick black hair, the doctor sees, is speckled with dandruff. More pleasantries are exchanged. Then the occasion moves beyond the doctor, and the translation of the conversation ceases. A chocolate cake is sliced and does the rounds on a silver platter.

One of the women sets out a flask and a small bucket of ice. Drinks are poured. The doctor tries to decline but, literally, no one will hear of his refusal. The cold yellow brandy goes down his throat the wrong way. He concentrates on the Glorious Leader's haphazard stream of what must be questions, remarks, elaborate jokes in Korean, and anecdotes. Kim's words light up among the women as if they're so many matches tossed in their midst. Some of the Leader's companions seem to be playing a socialist version of charades. Others put on a Motown CD. Several of the women dance with each other.

It appears that the Dear Leader has ordered the translator to settle in the doctor's lap. He doesn't protest. She slings herself into the curve of his arm so that he can just smell the tang of the brandy on her breath, perhaps on his own breath. He senses the swell of her breasts close to him. The doctor has no idea what to do with such a helping of woman.

"The Dear Leader wants to know if there is any act, any commodity, which our country can provide, to better demonstrate our gratitude? Any little favor? The sum of money that we negotiated beforehand has, the Leader assures you, already been deposited in your Geneva account. But is there some personal request, Doctor?"

An idea occurs to him. "Since you mention it, I wouldn't mind a chance to spend tomorrow with Joon before I go." He sees her face darkening and he knows it's hopeless. "You know, the young lady who served as my guide and interpreter around Pyongyang these past few days."

The woman transmits his request to the Glorious Leader. Kim listens, nods, shakes his head, then glowers over at the doctor. After a minute he turns his interest back to the women of his entourage. It's the last point of contact between the doctor and the guiding intelligence of this vast army. And it's been squandered. The translator stands up. A glance at her features tells the doctor that she's also translating the Leader's sudden frost.

"We're very sorry, Doctor. The doctrine of the Illustrious State forbids the use of a deceptive notion of individuality. Any relationship you have developed with Joon Sung-Lee, or may want to develop, you can continue with any of the women who are present tonight."

But the doctor has his own pride to match Korean pride, and atomic pride. "In that case, my dear," he tells her, "perhaps I will retire for the evening, if possible. I have a long flight ahead of me to Karachi."

THE DOCTOR'S LETTERS TO JOON are never acknowledged, never returned, although he writes to her once a month for the next two years. He's a rich man. The North Koreans have been more generous than the Libyans and the mullahs of Tehran, perhaps because they recognize the ultimate value of his contribution to their cause.

There's no further personal communication from his onetime hosts, but they do send him a DVD of the first test explosion carried out on Korean soil. The doctor takes the disc over to his nephew's house in Karachi to watch the footage. It's beyond imagination. An enormous yellow blast front sweeps across the range of the camera. Flame and heat blossom into the sky. It's a vision of the end of the world. The doctor still takes consolation in his life's work, in dispensing pride to Pakistan and Libya, Iran, and now North Korea. What other man has done so much? And with what poor material! He comes back in his mind to the report on BBC News concerning the fate of the North Korean soccer team. After losing to Japan, all the players and the manager have been brought up on charges of anti-socialist drunkenness, and executed.

    The doctor imagines twelve unmarked graves set, perhaps, behind an industrial site on the periphery of Pyongyang. He wonders if Joon's makes a thirteenth. His attention returns to the television set, a fifty-inch monstrosity he bought for his nephew, the fruit of his new riches. Atomic pride has dissipated in an enormous cloud of gravel and dust that hangs over the plateau. The sun has turned dark and cold through the haze. On the frozen mountainside, where there are no longer any buildings or fences, pride has gouged a great black vault into the ground which, he calculates, must be nine hundred meters in diameter. +

JAVEED SHAH, *PAPA-2 I AND II*, 2007,
COLOR DIGITAL PHOTOGRAPHS, 4½ X 4". COURTESY OF THE ARTIST.

PAPA-2

Basharat Peer

I WAS BORN IN WINTER IN KASHMIR. My village sat at the edge of a southern mountain range. Paddy fields, green in early summer, golden by autumn, surrounded the cluster of mud and brick houses.

In winter, snow slid slowly from our conical tin roof and fell on our lawn with a thud. My younger brother and I made snowmen. The footprints we left on our lawn would blur slowly, like pleasant memories, and when our mother was busy with some household chore and our grandfather was away, we would rush to the roof, break off the icicles, and mix them with milk and sugar to make ice cream. We would slide down the slope of the hill overlooking our neighborhood or play cricket on the frozen waters of a pond nearby. Sometimes my grandfather would scold us on his way home from work. As a schoolmaster, he was dreaded as if he were a military or a paramilitary man—not only by his own grandchildren but by every child in the village, and at his familiar bark the cricket players would scatter and disappear.

On those cold afternoons, Grandfather sat with most men of our neighborhood on the shop fronts. They warmed themselves with portable firepots called *kangri*, gossiping or discussing how that year's snowfall would affect the mustard crop in spring; though my grandfather had a job in a government school, like most other villagers he depended on agriculture to supplement his income. After the muezzin gave the call for afternoon prayers, the men left the shop fronts, fed the cattle at home, and gathered in the mosque. Almost everyone prayed at the mosque in winter—it was a warm place.

My family's house was by the roadside. We would stare out at the tourist buses passing by. Multicolored, the buses carried people from faraway places like Delhi and Calcutta and also many *angrez*, the word for "English" and our only word for Westerners. I would later learn how to tell exactly where they came from. They were interesting; some had very long hair and some shaved their heads. Some rode big motorbikes and at times were half naked. I once asked a neighbor who worked in a hotel, "Why do the *angrez* travel and we do not?" "Because they are *angrez* and we are not," he said. But I worked it out. They had to travel to see Kashmir; we lived here and did not need to travel. We waved at them; they waved back.

KASHMIR WAS THE BIGGEST of the approximately 500 princely states under British sovereignty as of 1947. It was predominantly Muslim but ruled by a Hindu maharaja, Hari Singh; his counterpart was a popular socialist leader named Shaikh Abdullah Mohammed, who sought an independent Kashmir. When British India was violently partitioned into India and Pakistan, both Singh and Shaikh Abdullah sought time before deciding Kashmir's fate. In October 1947, however, tribesmen from the North-West Frontier province of Pakistan, supported by the Pakistani army, invaded Kashmir, forcing their hand; Singh decided to join India, and Shaikh Abdullah, who was a friend of the new Indian Prime Minister, Nehru, supported him. In January 1949, the fighting stopped after the UN endorsed a ceasefire line. It still divides Kashmir into Pakistan-controlled and India-controlled parts, and is now known as the Line of Control (LoC).

The agreement of accession that Hari Singh signed with India in October 1947 gave Kashmir great autonomy. India controlled only defense, foreign affairs, and telecommunications. Kashmir had its own constitution and flag; the heads of its local government were called the President and the Prime Minister. Gradually, this autonomy disappeared. In 1953, India jailed Shaikh Abdullah, who was now Kashmir's prime minister, after he implemented a radical land reform and gave a speech suggesting the possibility of an independent Kashmir. In the following decades India installed puppet rulers, eroded the legal status of Kashmiri autonomy, and ignored the democratic rights of the Kashmiris. Shaikh remained in jail for twenty years, after which he finally broke down and signed a compromise with the Indian government. Twelve years later, in 1987, the Indian government rigged state elections, arresting opposition candidates and terrorizing their supporters. An opposition polling agent named Yasin Malik crossed over into Pakistan with some friends and began to receive arms training.

The next year, at the age of 12, I was sent to boarding school in a small town, Aishmuqam, seven miles from my village. I was terrible at sports and spent long hours in the library reading British and American adventure novels. In December 1989 I returned home for the holidays. That month, a group of Kashmiri militants led by Yasin Malik kidnapped the daughter of the Indian home minister. It was the beginning of the militant phase of the Kashmiri independence movement.

Instead of the regular village gossip people talked about militants, freedom, and processions. Indian troops opened fire on a demonstration in Srinagar, killing dozens. After prayers and before the recitation of *darood*, people made spontaneous speeches and shouted slogans of *aazadi*—Persian for independence. In retrospect, it seemed that Shaikh Abdullah was a traitor. In Srinagar, mobs tried to dig up his grave.

One day a young man from our village who worked in Srinagar gave a speech at the mosque. He grabbed the microphone and shouted, "*Kabiran kabira!*" The slogan meant, "Who is the greatest?" But no one understood. None of us spoke Arabic. He shouted again and there was silence—then the adolescents in the last row began to laugh. Embarrassed, the young man explained that in reply to the slogan people were supposed to shout, "*Allah o akbar!*" (God is great.) He shouted again, "*Kabiran kabira!*" He was answered with a hesitant, awkward "*Allah o akbar.*" For about a year after, we teased him.

THAT WINTER BEGAN MY POLITICAL EDUCATION. It took the form of acronyms: JKLF (Jammu and Kashmir Liberation Front), JKSLF (Jammu and Kashmir Students Liberation Front), BSF (Border Security Force), CRPF (Central Reserve Police Force). To go with these I learned new phrases: frisking, crackdown, bunker, search, identity card, arrest, and torture.

That winter, too, busloads of Kashmiri youth went to border towns and crossed over to Pakistan and Pakistan-administered Kashmir for arms training. They returned as militants carrying Kalashnikovs, hand grenades, light machine guns, and rocket launchers issued by Pakistan. The whole of Kashmir was on the streets raising slogans of freedom. WAR TILL VICTORY was graffitied everywhere in Kashmir; it was painted alongside another slogan, SELF-DETERMINATION IS OUR BIRTHRIGHT, on the brick wall of my school building. In the lunch break between math and English class, my friends and I shared stories of militancy. Someone would have seen a militant and he would tell us how the militant styled his hair, what clothes and shoes he wore, and how many days he said it would be before we had our freedom.

The best story was about the magical Kalashnikov. Made in Russia, a gift from Pakistan, it was known to have powers greater than Aladdin's lamp. "It is as small as a hand and shoots two hundred bullets." "No! It is as long as a cricket bat and fires fifty bullets in a minute." "My brother touched a Kalashnikov, he says it is very light. He told Mother that he wanted to become a militant. She cried, and Father slapped him."

My roommate Pervez told me there were many militants in his village and they wore beautiful green uniforms. One afternoon, we were in the football field when a militant passed by. Even our snooty games teacher went up to him, smiled, and shook hands. Encouraged, we gathered around. "Can we see your gun, please?" Pervez said. He was the center forward, beaming in his blue tracksuit, and he could not resist asking. The militant took off his loose *pheran* and showed us his gun. "We call it Kalashnikov and Indians call it AK-47," the militant said. We clapped. From then on we all carried our cricket bats inside our *pheran*s, in imitation and preparation.

The next morning before the school assembly, the seniors told us not to chant the Indian national anthem. "We are Kashmiris and now we are fighting for independence. We cannot go on chanting the Indian songs, even if the principal might like us to." The principal, Gulab Chand Sharma, was a tiny man from Rajasthan. He liked to eat raw peas and practice yoga. At the assembly, the students refused to chant the Indian anthem. Gulab Sharma was hurt. He talked about the Indian struggle for freedom from the British and how a lot of the students who had joined it had paid the highest price. Pervez, who stood next to me, simply giggled.

Some months later, a group of seniors boarded the local bus to Srinagar and from there took another bus to a northern border town, Kupwara. There they met representatives from the militants. Some were sent back because they were too small, but others crossed the high snowy mountains (they are part of the Himalayas) of the Line of Control. They trained in small arms and returned to fight the Indian armed forces. I was 14, too small to go, but how I longed to join them. We had to fight for freedom, and every man who died fighting the Indian armed forces was a martyr for Kashmir. Like most Kashmiri youngsters, apart from the usual daydreaming of girls, I also began to daydream of dying.

IN 1991, A SECOND COUSIN OF MINE, Tariq, crossed the Line of Control.

Tariq's younger brother, Shabnam, attended boarding school with me. In his dorm room Shabnam listened to Sadaa-e-Hurriyat (Voice of Freedom) Radio, which was based in Muzafferabad, the capital of Pakistan-administered Kashmir. Every evening the separatist radio station ran a show featuring separatist songs, interspersed with propaganda and messages from listeners. There were constant stories at the time about boys being killed, losing their way, being arrested by Indian patrols—and we were also beginning to hear stories about the torture of young men in Indian custody, particularly in a place called Papa-2. And so when a militant-in-training wanted to let his family know how he was, he requested a song, and a message was played along with it: "Tariq Peer from Panzmulla village of Islamabad likes the program and requests this song be played." Huddled around the radio, his family and relatives heard the song and the message and knew he was safe.

Around a year after he left home, Tariq returned. There was an enormous celebration, like the one we had when my father returned from Hajj, years earlier. Shabnam served *kahwa*, carrying a samovar from one guest to another. Tariq sat on a velvet-covered cushion like the ones Kashmiris use for bridegrooms; relatives and friends filled the room. Tariq's father, my uncle, was there also. He had once been the chief of security for Shaikh Abdullah, the great prime minister. He found it hard to accept the fact that Tariq had crossed the border and joined a militant group without his permission.

On this day, Uncle sat next to Tariq without speaking. The militant talked; the police officer listened. So did the room full of people, as if Tariq were Marco Polo back from the New World. He told us how he and his friends had met a point man from the militant group at the crowded Batamaloo station in southern Srinagar. There they boarded a bus for the north Kashmir town of Baramulla. The driver played Bollywood songs, and the passengers talked about the militant movement. Some passengers recognized Tariq and his friends as boys heading for the border and smiled at them. On the road from Srinagar to Baramulla there were neither checkpoints nor patrols. (The Indian military presence in Kashmir was just about to increase exponentially.)

Tariq and his friends spent the night in Baramulla at a stranger's house with two more groups of young men waiting to cross the border. Next morning they all boarded a bus to Kupwara, the town closest to the LoC. The ticket collector refused to accept a fare from them. Kupwara teemed with such young men and boys. Tariq and his friends were introduced to a man who was to take them across the mountains. Such men, known as "guides," were often natives of the border villages who knew the terrain well. Wearing rubber shoes, carrying rucksacks full of clothes and food, they left Kupwara in a truck.

Two days later Tariq was in Muzafferabad. He was taken to an arms training camp. For six months he trained in small arms, land mines, and rocket-propelled grenades.

He hiked back home in early spring when the border mountains were still covered in snow. He was bolder on his way back; he carried a bag full of ammunition and a Kalashnikov. The trek took three days. The ammunition bags were heavy. Tariq and his fellow guerrillas lightened them by burying food packages and some bullet magazines in the snow.

They had an encounter with Indian paramilitaries near the border town of Kupwara. Three of them were killed. A bullet grazed Tariq's leg, tearing a hole in his trousers. Later, Shabnam showed me Tariq's bullet-torn trousers, like an athlete displaying a trophy.

After that night, Tariq could only visit hurriedly, stealthily. Soldiers often knocked at my uncle's door, looking for him, beating my uncle and my cousins, telling them to ask Tariq to surrender. I saw him for the last time in August 1992, near my uncle's house, on a plateau that served twice a year as the *eidgah*, the ground for ceremonial Eid prayers, and otherwise as a cricket field. On this day, August 15, it was used to celebrate Pakistani Independence Day. Shabnam and I sneaked through the crowd to the front row. Militant leaders made fiery speeches in favor of Pakistan and raised separatist slogans. We stared at the militants in their green uniforms holding their rifles. They performed military stunts and sang battle songs to a clapping audience. A militant leader raised the Pakistani flag. His men fired their Kalashnikovs into the air. I still remember one of their songs:

Iqbal ke shaheen hain,
Hizb-ul-mujahideen hain

We are Iqbal's falcons
We are the Hizb-ul-mujahideen.

Then someone said the army was coming, and the gathering dispersed.

ONE AFTERNOON I WALKED with four boys from my dormitory to a nearby village looking for guerrillas. We wanted to join their ranks, cross the border into Pakistan, and fight for Kashmir. We soon found a group of youths dressed in fatigues, assault rifles slung on their shoulders. They were tall, handsome, and armed. The four of us in our school uniforms—white shirts and gray trousers—introduced ourselves and hesitantly told them our story. The white badges on their green uniforms read JKLF.

"We want to join you," I said.

The commander, a lean, stubbly youth, laughed in my face. "Go home and grow up, kids!" His tone was patronizing. I was up on the internal politics of the independence movements and said: "If you do not take us with you, we will join Hizb-ul-Mujahideen." Hizb-ul-Mujahideen was one of JKLF's ideological rivals. The guerrillas burst into laughter again and walked away.

The JKLF commander we had approached turned out to be a former student of my grandfather's. Not long after, he ran into my grandfather in the market and told him about my intentions. A meeting was called at home. My grandfather, my parents, and my uncles held long discussions. Grandfather was furious. He wanted to come to my boarding school and set me right once and for all. My father argued against it. One of my uncles, a bank manager in his early thirties, was dispatched instead.

My uncle was an interesting man. He wore his hair a bit like John Travolta in *Grease*, and he had a distinctive English accent, picked up during a friendship with some German tourists. He wore loose baggy denims and checked shirts. He arrived at my school while I was in math class. One of my friends had a few minutes earlier shown me a silver gray Chinese pistol he was hiding inside his jacket. "Got it from the SLF," he whispered in my ear. Students Liberation Front was the student wing of the JKLF; its members often stayed in our hostel. My classmate intended to show the pistol to the teacher because he loathed the man for beating him when he couldn't solve his sums. Then there was a knock at the door. The teacher went out and returned to tell me my uncle was here.

Uncle and I went to my room in the hostel. He had brought an elaborate lunch from home. "Your mother made it for you," he said. We talked about my studies. He said my family dreamt of seeing me in the Indian Civil Service. "I know you will do us proud," he said. "I met your school principal and he had great things to say about you."

He went on to paint a romantic picture of the colleges and universities in New Delhi. "Man! You would have a great time there. Two more years and we will send you. Your father and I were talking about it last night." He wanted me to come home with him for a few days. I agreed happily, unsuspecting. We left the school premises and walked to the nearest bus stand. A scrawl of graffiti on the wall of a house nearby read: WAR TILL VICTORY—JKLF. "So that is the group you want to join," my uncle said, smiling. I was startled. I denied everything. He shook his head slowly. He said, "We know it," and then he told me about the meeting waiting for me at home.

When I arrived home, my grandfather made me sit next to him. He talked about the excitement of the day I was born—and how I ran back home on the first day of school. He recalled how, inspired by my Superman comics, I once jumped from the first-floor window. My younger brother had helped me tie my *pheran* like a cape. I broke my right arm.

My grandfather fixed his watery green eyes on me. "How do you think this old man can deal with your death?" he said. "You don't live long in a war, son."

My grandfather, the dreaded headmaster—who was proud that nobody in our village lit a cigarette or raised his voice in his presence—had tears in his eyes. He was pleading with me.

My father returned from work. He was carrying several books; they turned out to be commentaries on the Quran in English. He said, "You must read them. The commentaries will make you understand Islam and also improve your English. You must also read the Bible, which is again a very good way to improve your language skills." Father went around in circles, talking about the Biblical and Quranic versions of the story of Ishmael and his father, Isaac. He connected their story to an anecdote from the life of Prophet Muhammad about the obligation of children toward their parents. Then he began talking about my intentions of joining a militant group. "I would say that maybe you should read and think about it for a few years and then decide for yourself. At that point I will not say that you should or should not join any group. From what I have read I can tell you that any movement that seeks a separate country takes a very long time. It took India many decades to get freedom from the British. The Tibetans have been asking for independence from China for more than thirty years now. Czechoslovakia has its freedom now, but it was already a country. And even that took a long time."

He continued to argue that rebellions were long affairs, led by educated men. "Nehru and Gandhi studied law in England and were both very good writers. You have seen their books in our library. Vaclav Havel is a very big writer. The Dalai Lama has read a lot and can teach so many things to people. None of them used guns but they changed history. If you want to do something for Kashmir, I would say you should read."

I did like reading, especially in my father's library. I first saw Sartre's *Iron in the Soul* and *Nausea* on his bookshelves, next to Nehru's *Discovery of India* and the Orwell novels. Yet reading had hardly enabled him, a government bureaucrat, squeezed between two powerful foes, to help Kashmir.

A few days later, as I was leaving to go back to school, my mother took her scarf off her head and laid it at my feet. "Please don't try that again," she said and hugged me. She was crying. A head scarf is a symbol of honor in Kashmiri society. It is the most desperate act of pleading to lay your headgear at somebody's feet. In my world there was no argument more powerful than that. I could not walk over my mother's scarf to an arms training camp.

I REMEMBER THESE ARGUMENTS VERY WELL NOW, all this time later, not only because they were so dramatic, and because I had never seen my family in such a state, but also because I was, secretly, so relieved.

The next winter, I was home again for vacation. One cold morning we did not hear the predawn call for prayers. Instead, the muezzin announced that the Indian army had cordoned off the entire village and all the men were ordered to assemble on the grounds of the local hospital by six. The muezzin, Gul Khan, was a tiny, aging farmer who lived in a brick hut next to the mosque; few responded to his early-morning calls for prayer. But announcing the crackdown gave his voice the power to move the entire village. Within minutes my family had gathered in the kitchen.

A small, reluctant crowd began the short journey toward the hospital compound. The women had been ordered to stay at home so they could open the doors of every room and cupboard. I was worried about my mother and my aunts. Kashmir was rife with stories of Indian soldiers misbehaving—a euphemism for molestation and rape—during crackdowns. I walked behind my father.

Heavily armed soldiers stood along the road and shouted at us to walk faster. Another group asked us to pull out our identity cards and raise our hands. Within seconds a queue formed at the hospital gate. There were no distinctions of age or social status or class, no line drawn between the farmhand and the judge. There were just two long parallel rows of raised hands—the right, clutching an identity card, held a few inches higher than the empty left.

After the identity checks we were asked to sit on the cold ground, which had a few leaves of grass left on it. An army officer ordered all guests and visiting relatives to stand in a separate group. Then they walked in a queue past an armored car. Every man had to stop near the window and show his face to the Cat. The Cat was a masked Kashmiri, probably from a neighboring village, who had become a collaborator. He was supposed to know who in my village was a militant or a supporter—and it was possible that if he didn't know, he would simply point out a nervous or hostile-looking youth to please his masters. Most people passed the test; some were hustled away to the residential quarters of the doctor, which had been converted into an ad hoc interrogation center.

Over the next few hours we formed queues and walked past the Cat. If he raised his hand, soldiers pounced on the suspect and took him away to the doctor's quarters. My turn came. I stood facing the Cat. His eyes stared out at me from behind his black mask. My heart galloped. The Cat waited for a moment and told me to move on.

I joined my group on the ground. But Manzoor, our neighbor's son, was taken away for interrogation. His arrest made everyone in our group nervous; his father was tense but silent.

Manzoor's family used to run a hotel in a nearby tourist resort, but after the fighting began and the tourists stopped coming to Kashmir, they had locked the hotel and opened a grocery shop. On the days of general strikes, which happened more and more frequently and closed down the schools, Manzoor manned the shop. He was a gregarious teenager. Occasionally the militants passing by would stop to buy something from his shop or simply to sit and talk. Manzoor loved the attention he received and flaunted his position. Word seemed to have reached the Indian army.

Now two soldiers came toward us. "Is there someone called Basharat Peer here? He is a ninth standard student." They had the name of my school. I stood up. "Come with us," one said. "But... I am a student," I protested. "We know," the soldier said. "We just need you to identify somebody." They walked me to the interrogation center. I followed them, not turning back to see how my father and grandfather were reacting. We entered the three-room building. I had been there many times; the doctor was a family friend. I was asked to sit in a tiny storeroom. The soldiers slammed the doors behind me.

Every two minutes, I looked at my watch. I heard the shrieks of the boys in the other rooms. Over and over I heard the words: *Khodayo Bachaav!* (Save me, God!) and *Sir nahin pata*! (I don't know, sir!) I muttered all the prayers I had ever known. About two hours later the door opened violently. A pair of soldiers pointed their guns at me. I stood up. My face must have been white with fear. I thought it was my time to shout the words I had been hearing. But they did not hit me or take me to the other rooms. One of them began questioning me.

"Which group are you with, KLF or HM?"

"How many of your friends are with the group?"

"Where are the weapons?"

I was not a member of any militant group and that was my answer for all his questions. I showed my identity card again and again, repeating: "I know nothing, sir! I am a student, sir!"

"Come on, tell us. You know we have other ways of finding out."

"I know sir! But I am only a student!" I pleaded.

"Think harder. I will come back in a few minutes," said the interrogator and left. The other soldier stood there in silence. I tried to persuade him that I was telling the truth. "Talk to the officer when he returns," he said. The interrogator returned and the same questions and answers were repeated. "All right," he said. "Do you know Majid?"

"Yes sir!" I said. Majid was a boy in my class who was visiting relatives in my village. He was not connected to any militant groups, as far as I knew. "He is in my class," I said, and followed with information about Majid's father—his name and profession, and the name of their village. I also mentioned that he had relatives in our village. The interrogator looked at me for a moment and said, "All right! You can leave." I thanked him profusely and walked back to join my group. My father and grandfather rose. I hugged them. My father said, "Did they beat you, commander-in-chief?" Grandfather's eyes were moist; he threw an arm around my shoulders and said nothing.

Manzoor too was released after a while; he was limping and bruised. His father forbade him from manning the grocery shop. Later that day, when the crackdown was lifted and the neighbors and acquaintances who had come to ask about my welfare left, my father gave me his shaving set. Traces of a mustache and beard had begun to grow on my face. Indian soldiers were particularly suspicious of anyone with any kind of facial hair. It felt awkward, but with directions from my father I managed my first shave.

A YEAR LATER, IN 1993, my parents insisted I join a college in India, hundreds of miles away. They had the money to send a child there, which was not true of everyone's parents, and so I went. I studied at the Muslim University of Aligarh, a few hours from Delhi. My generation of Kashmiri students was sent there because the university and the surrounding town had a sizable Muslim population; in other parts of the country, an ugly xenophobia had developed against Kashmiris.

Eventually I moved to Delhi and became a journalist for an Indian news site in 2000. I lived in a run-down student neighborhood in south Delhi; landlords in better neighborhoods had turned me away because I was a Kashmiri Muslim. But I learned to ignore these irritations. India had opened its economy in the early 1990s. Round-the-clock channels broadcast the news, and the number of magazines was growing. Young anchors and reporters asked tragedy-struck people questions like "So how does it feel?" in their fake American accents. I saw Pamela Anderson's breasts.

The newly moneyed capital of India prided itself on its special DJ nights, malls featuring Marks & Spencer showrooms and Nokia outlets, and the belly dancers performing in its luxury hotels. Thousands of

Toyotas ferried call-center executives for night shifts at the suburban BPO offices, among them a flatmate of mine, a boy from a small southern Indian town, who had been told to jettison his traditional name, Sateesh. He would tell me about his job and begin acting out his calls: "Hi! This is Jack Smith calling from JC Penney!"

India was grotesque, and fascinating. While the virtual courts were being introduced to expedite cases for the rich, thousands of poor people wasted years of their lives in prisons waiting for a hearing. A few hundred meters from the luxury hotels and the multiplex theaters, the urban poor lived in mud huts. Online matrimonial sites received a million views a month, while a few hours from Delhi lovers could be killed for being from different castes. The elites bragged about being a nuclear power, yet the laborers in the uranium mines didn't have enough protective clothing and lived with radiation-related sicknesses. A few hours from the technology parks of Hyderabad, thousands of farmers committed suicide after failing to repay their debts. Every summer and winter more than a thousand homeless people were killed by extreme heat and cold; meanwhile fancy suburbs with names like Beverly Hills grew around every major Indian city. In the noise and chaos of this India, I might have forgotten Kashmir—might have turned it into a place I visited every two or three months as a reporter—but I could not. The Kashmiri body count appeared almost every day in the newspapers; Kashmir was the text and subtext of my professional, personal, and social worlds in Delhi.

IN 2003, I DECIDED TO RETURN TO KASHMIR.
The nature of the separatist militancy had changed. In the early '90s, the secular groups had been dominated by the pro-Pakistan Hizb-ul-Mujahideen. By the mid-'90s the pan-Islamist militants from Pakistan had taken over. They did not mingle with the population like the Kashmiri militants. Especially after 9/11, their presence in Kashmir won India major diplomatic credit with the West. Any criticism of Indian policies in Kashmir could be rebutted with the argument that an officially secular and pro-globalization India was fighting Islamic terrorism. The jihadis also believed in suicide bombings, which the Kashmiri militants had avoided.

The Indian military presence in Kashmir now numbered more than half a million. Around three thousand Kashmiri and Pakistani militants were fighting them. Srinagar was a city of bunkers, armored cars, and soldiers with assault rifles. Road patrols and checkpoints had become as much a part of the Kashmiri landscape as willows, poplars, and pines.

In November 2003, a few days after Ramadan, I took a walk from the center of Srinagar past a colonial mansion painted blue and white. Its architecture was of a dying style, a blend of Kashmiri woodwork and British mock-Tudor. A plaque on the gate read: UNITED NATIONS MILITARY OBSERVER GROUP FOR INDIA AND PAKISTAN.

A short walk from the UN office lies Gupkar Road, a well-bunkered and well-patrolled neighborhood of government offices and the residences of ministers and bureaucrats. Until the late '80s, passersby marveled at the buildings and the splendor of their surroundings. But from the early to mid-'90s, people dreaded Gupkar Road. It was the road to Papa-2, the most notorious torture chamber in all of Kashmir. Hundreds who went there did not come back. Those who returned are wrecks.

Papa-2 is a large mansion built by the pre-1947 dynastic ruler of Kashmir, Hari Singh. In the late '90s, a top government official renovated the building and made it his residence. Before moving in, the officer called priests of all religions to perform exorcisms. Now the building was the home of a state government minister, and a friend had gotten me permission to visit. I was supposed to be interested in the architecture.

Soft, honey-hued curtains hung on the windows of the minister's room on the first floor. A brown bedspread covered his bed; books on law and literature filled the book racks. My guide, a local man my age, pulled the curtains from the windows; clear, bright light fell on the mementos and awards resting on the shelves. A carpet woven with verses from the Koran hung from one wall, and a canvas by the Indian painter Raja Ravi Verma adorned the other. There was a woman in the painting; the colors were red and brown. I looked studiously at the chairs, the sofas, the tables, the ceilings and whitewashed walls.

My guide was silent; he knew what it was about. Finally he spoke. "This was Papa-2, brother! This was Papa-2."

AN HOUR LATER I WAS IN THE CITY CENTER, Lal Chowk, talking to two friends about my visit. "Where can I find someone who has been at Papa-2?" I asked.

"Ask anyone on the street. Half of Kashmir has been there."

"Or just walk up to Maisuma, you will find ten guys who have been there."

I walked past the soldiers and policemen and turned toward the J&K Liberation Front office in the nearby separatist neighborhood. A group of young men stood outside the nondescript building. "Papa-2?" A brief silence followed. They asked each other: Were you there? "No. I was in Rajasthan." "No. I was at Kot Balwal." "No. I was at Gogoland." "No. I was in Ranchi." Names, pouring out in their young voices, identified a whole geography of Indian prisons. They were all about my age. "Shafi was at Papa-2." "Irfan was there." "And Irshad was at Papa-2." "Sayeed was there too." In less than five minutes I had six names. "Shafi will be home now," said one of the young men, Abid. "Let us go." We walked through a labyrinth of lanes. Abid stopped to greet a few men on the way. He asked them whether they had been at Papa-2. Some talked about their friends who had been in Papa-2; others talked about other jails and other torture chambers.

Finally Abid stopped at a crumbling two-story house. He knocked.

A woman's voice asked, "Who is it?"

"Abid here. Is Shafi around?"

"He is at the mosque," the voice shouted back. "Wait here; he shall be back any moment."

A few minutes later we saw a tall, frail, bespectacled man in his early thirties limping toward us with the help of a wooden staff. He shouted a happy greeting at Abid. They hugged and talked for a while; Abid introduced me and left. Shafi shook open the door and led me in. We climbed a creaking wooden stair and entered a neat room with a layer of cheap green distemper on its mud walls. In a corner a bedspread covered a stack of bedding; there were no wardrobes. Shafi pulled two pillows from the stack, adjusted them as cushions against the wall, and asked me to sit.

In another corner a short, plump, dark woman sat near a kerosene stove. On the wooden shelves on the wall facing her were a few cups, plates, and utensils. "She is my wife," Shafi said. I greeted her; she shook her head and muttered a greeting. She rose and pulled down a curtain between the makeshift kitchen and the drawing-room area. Shafi asked for tea, saying to his wife, "Do not add sugar. He will take as much as he likes." His eyes seemed to disappear behind the thick glasses. His cheeks were deeply hollowed, though his hair was still brown and curly. He lit a cigarette, bent toward me and said, "I was at Papa-2 for seven months."

IN 1990, AT THE AGE OF 19, he had decided to join a militant group. JKLF was the most influential and charismatic group in his part of Srinagar, and he joined its student wing. His war with India began: attacking patrols of Indian soldiers, moving with guns from one hideout to the next, and evading arrest in crackdowns. "We thought Kashmir would be free in a year or two." Instead, he was arrested by a paramilitary patrol. After an initial interrogation at a local center in Srinagar, he was sent to the Kot Balwal and Talab Tilloo jails in the southern province of the state of Jammu. Two years later he was released. Back home, he met his comrades-in-arms. "I began working for the movement again."

One day in the autumn of 1992, he was walking in central Srinagar. A local boy recognized him. "I knew him," Shafi said. "He had become a BSF informer and pointed me out to the BSF personnel. I was not carrying any weapons and was arrested that very moment." Shafi's wife called from behind the yellow curtain: "The tea is ready." He rose, brought a tray full of biscuits, two cups, and a flask. He began pouring tea but fumbled with the cups, squinting. I volunteered to help, and he let me. I put his cup next to him and he touched it as if reassuring himself of its presence. "They kept me in the local BSF camp for a week before shifting me to Papa-2." At the BSF camp, he was interrogated, beaten with fists, feet, batons, guns. They wanted information about his group; they wanted his weapons. He did not tell me whether he gave them the information. I did not ask. It is hard to ask that question if you are a Kashmiri.

Shafi was moved to Papa-2. "It was hell," he said, fumbling now to find the cigarette almost burned off in the ashtray. He was thrown into a room crowded with twenty men. The floor was bare. Smears of blood blemished the whitewashed walls. Every man had a coarse, black blanket for bedding. "We called them lice blankets," Shafi said, and laughed. Shafi and his fellow prisoners slept laid out like rows of corpses. Throughout the night men woke up shouting, cursed the lice, tried to sleep again, only to be woken by the next man battling the vermin.

Some managed to sleep, though the electric lights were never extinguished. "During the interrogation I was made to stare at very bright bulbs. Even in our room the light burnt my eyes. I craved darkness."

Darkness came. "I began losing my eyesight there. I can barely see now despite my glasses."

After his release from the prison, doctors prescribed a surgical operation to restore his sight. "Why didn't you have the surgery?" I asked.

Shafi smiled. "I cannot afford the cost."

He could not find work anywhere. In summer he sold secondhand garments on a wooden cart in Lal Chowk; in winter he followed his brother to Calcutta, hawking Kashmiri shawls door-to-door on commission. His family wanted him to get married and begin a new life. They looked for a girl for him, but nobody would marry Shafi, physically and psychologically shattered by his militant days, his prison years, his nonexistent prospects. "You would know how choosy Kashmiri girls are," he said.

His brother knew a Muslim family in a Calcutta slum. They had a squint-eyed girl whom nobody would marry. Her family was happy to marry her off to Shafi. Now she was there behind the curtain, asking whether we wanted more tea. "She is pregnant and I have to take her to Calcutta for the birth." He sounded tense.

He lived off a thousand rupees that Yasin Malik, the JKLF chief, gave him every month. "I did ask other leaders for help. I said that I am here because I spent my youth for the movement." Some separatist leaders asked him for proof of his being a militant, of his jail days. "They live in big houses and drive big cars bought from the money that came for the movement. But they are not willing to help those who destroyed their lives for the cause." His face contorted with anger; he took long, hard puffs from his cigarette. "I never went to them after that. None of the separatist leaders except Yasin had to go through what the boys endured. They cannot even imagine what being tortured is like."

Shafi drank the last gulp of tea and lit another cigarette. "They made you sit on a chair, tied you with ropes. One soldier held your neck, two others pulled your legs in different directions, and three more rolled a heavy concrete roller over your legs. They asked questions and if you didn't answer they burnt you with the cigarettes." He paused for a while and as if suddenly remembering something said, "The worst part was the psychological torture. They would make us say *Jai Hind* (Long live India) every morning and every evening. They beat you if you refused. It was very hard but everyone said it except Master Ahsan Dar." Dar was a top commander of Hizb-ul-Mujahideen. Then Shafi stopped speaking abruptly. "I cannot talk about it. It makes me crazy. I am sorry."

He said I should meet Ansar, another former militant who had been in Papa-2. Ansar would talk about the torture and what it did to people.

I MET ANSAR AT HIS BROTHER'S GROCERY SHOP near the grand mosque in downtown Srinagar. We sat in a small, poorly lit room in his house behind the roadside shop. Ansar was a robust, mustached man in a beige *shalwar kameez*. He had joined a separatist organization, People's League, in the mid-'80s and became one of the earlier members of its militant wing. One day he was visiting his parents when the BSF raided their house and arrested him. "They had information that I was here. Someone in my neighborhood was the informer." He talked about various prisons he had been in.

"And Papa-2?" I asked.

"How can I forget it? Not even stray cows would eat the food they threw at us there." He passed a plate of plum cake to me. "That place destroyed most people who were there. You do not live a normal life after that torture. It scars you forever.

"They beat us up with guns, staffs, hands. But that was nothing. They tied copper wire around your arms and gave high-voltage shocks. Every hair on your body stood up. But the worst was when they inserted the copper wire into my penis, deep into the urinary canal, and gave electric shocks. They did it with most boys. It destroyed many lives; many could not marry after that." After his release Ansar was under treatment for urinary tract infections and some other disorders he did not mention. "I was not ready to marry. But my family supported me. I agreed to marry only after I was treated for a year and a half. Thank God, now I have a daughter and run my small business."

I HAD HEARD ABOUT THE PRACTICE OF TORTURE throughout my adolescence, but only now, in my late twenties, did I understand what it meant. A few days later I called Shahid, a doctor friend at Srinagar's Sher-e-Kashmir Institute of Medical Sciences. I talked to him about Ansar. "We have had hundreds of cases here," he confirmed. "Those electric shocks led to impotence in many." Shahid, a short, jolly man, grew up in a southern Kashmiri village. On weekends he drove home and treated the villagers for a nominal fee. "I am going home on Sunday. If you come along I will introduce you to someone with this problem."

On Sunday morning I set out with Shahid to his village to meet his cousin, Hussein, who after being tortured in detention thought he was impotent and refused to marry. "The problem is that he is not ready to meet a doctor. He does not even talk to me," Shahid told me as we drove toward the south Kashmir town of Bijbehara. We passed through clusters of mud and brick houses, groves of walnut and willow trees, and vast stretches of fields.

A handpainted Red Cross sign hanging from a roadside wooden shack with his name misspelled announced Shahid's clinic. It was barely nine in the morning and a crowd of patients was already waiting for him. Hussein, his cousin, was there. We sat on an empty shop front in the sun. I offered Hussein a cigarette, which he reluctantly accepted. Instead of asking about his life, I told him about Shafi, Ansar, Papa-2, and the medical correction of torture-imposed disorders. He listened in silence, for the most part expressionless. Finally he began to talk about his experience.

He was in the first year of college when the armed militancy began in 1990. He was the eldest son of a teacher and had four siblings. One day he left home with a group of thirteen other young men. After spending three days in the northern Kashmir town of Baramulla, they boarded a truck and drove toward the town of Kupwara near the LoC. Halfway from Kupwara, a convoy of the paramilitary Border Security Force stopped them.

They were taken to a local camp. In the morning, Hussein and his groupmates were taken into tiny tin sheds lit by bright electric lamps for interrogation. "I was asked to undress, be naked. The first time I resisted, was beaten, undressed forcibly, and tied to a chair. Then they tied copper wire to my arms and gave electric shocks. I could not even scream—they stuffed my mouth with a ball of cloth. I thought I would die. They would suddenly stop, take the cloth out, and ask questions. I was in no position to answer and fainted a few times. But I was brought to my senses again and they inserted a copper wire into my penis."

Most of them broke after two days of this. "You cannot bear pain beyond a point. Everybody talks," Hussein said. "We admitted we were going for training and were shifted to jails in Srinagar." He added as an afterthought, "Maybe I should have admitted straightaway. Life could have been different."

I closed my eyes for a moment, then looked away onto the road and the patients waiting their turn at Shahid's clinic. An old man walked up to us and asked me whether I was a doctor. "No, sir. I am only the doctor's friend." The old man told me how "the situation" had given him problems with high blood pressure. Hussein and I walked down the road leading out of the village through the fields. We sat down on a parapet by the road. Hussein lit his cigarette and resumed the story. "I can't tell you about the pain one feels when they give the electric shocks. I thought I would die. At times I thought every shock lasted for a minute or two, at times it seemed an hour," he said.

After his interrogators threw him back in his cell, Hussein kept losing consciousness. "At least during the blackouts I felt no pain." He was bleeding when he urinated, his penis was swollen, and pain crawled up it like a leech. By the time he was moved to the detention center at Srinagar, an infection had set in and he saw pus and blood in his urine. There was no medical aid for weeks.

"Then a Sikh paramilitary officer asked me about my condition. I told him what happened. He was an angel; he got me some medicine, cotton, and Dettol antiseptic lotion. That helped a lot." Hussein became very emotional when speaking of this, and it made me think of what Ansar and Shafi told me about different interrogators: "Some were sadists and some were decent men." They had both remembered the first names of the "good" and "bad" interrogators, names like Ravi, Nishant, Anand, names like my friends in Delhi had.

Hussein was released from jail two years later. A year afterward he began running a very small business that dealt in carpets and shawls. His family insisted he marry; he refused. He thought he was impotent. He had not spoken about it to anyone.

One night he did not sleep until he heard the morning call to prayer. "I went to the mosque, prayed, and broke down while asking God for help. Only God knew what I had been through."

Hussein decided to talk to his brother-in-law, a school teacher, who listened patiently and suggested they meet a doctor. "For a year I went to various doctors at Anantnag district hospital. They wrote a long list of medicines but it did not help much." Shahid, his cousin, wanted to take him to the Medical Institute at Srinagar for psychiatric counseling.

Hussein was not comfortable talking to Shahid. He refused to meet any more doctors, spent his days running a small grocery and praying at the village mosque.

His family gave up until another crisis arrived—Hussein's younger brothers were getting married. In Kashmiri tradition a younger brother does not get married before the elder. Hussein's father, brother-in-law, and uncles tried to convince him again. He insisted his younger siblings go ahead with their lives. They did. Hussein plays with their kids.

We walked back to the clinic. I turned to him and said, "Hussein, you will be all right. I have spoken to some urologists and read in the most respected medical journals that your condition is curable, just like nasal congestion."

I told Hussein about Ansar's marriage and his three-year-old daughter; I told him about the corrective urological surgeries I had read about, about the drugs, about psychiatric counseling, about Prophet Muhammad saying that hopelessness is a crime. Hussein listened patiently. We entered Shahid's mud-walled, bare-floored clinic and waited until the patient he was examining left. I turned to Hussein and urged him to talk to his doctor cousin. He looked into my eyes and smiled. "I will. Thanks." We shook hands, and I walked out of the clinic.

THE MILITANCY CHANGED MANY PEOPLE. My father survived a landmine blast by militants, who had decided that his work for the Indian government was compromising. My cousin Tariq was killed in late 1992 in a raid on his hideout in a village a few miles from mine. Pervez joined the militancy after he left our boarding school and was killed. Manzoor stayed away from boasting about meeting any militants, trained as a paramedic, and worked in a hospital in a nearby town. My grandfather had a habit of arguing with everyone, both Indian soldiers and Kashmiri militants, and the family made great efforts to quiet him down. Eventually he did.

I could think of only one friend who had been in the militancy and left, and that was Asif, with whom I'd been at boarding school. Asif's father owned large, prosperous apple orchards, but also went into court sometimes and practiced law, as a hobby; as for Asif, he was a dandy. I remember envying him the female attention he received at our boarding school, and his accessories—like his Kamachi shoes, a Russian sneaker favored by militants. The militants made the war a sort of fashion runway; they wore Kamachi shoes, so schoolboys wore Kamachi shoes. Militants replaced the stones in their rings with pistol bullets, the boys replaced the stones in their rings with pistol bullets. An entire range of militaristic jewelry became fashionable. The militants modified the Sufi tradition of wearing an amulet by adding a Kalashnikov cartridge to the string.

One day in August 2004, I took a bus to Anantnag, where I boarded another bus for Asif's village further south. I wasn't sure whether he would be there; I didn't even have his phone number. The bus passed through scores of Kashmiri villages surrounded by groves of mulberry, poplar, and apple trees swaying in the wind like drunken men. Indian soldiers in bulletproof jackets, carrying Kalashnikovs and machine guns, patrolled the roads or stared from behind their bunkers. An hour later the bus stopped at a military checkpost near Asif's village. I followed the routine of raising my hands, showing my identity card, talking about coming from Srinagar to visit a family friend. The frisking, providing proof of identity, the rude questions—all were routine now, like brushing your teeth.

The soldiers let us pass; the bus moved on and stopped in the village square. I walked through the bus yard to a grocery store with a Coca-Cola billboard. It displayed a life-size picture of the Miss Universe turned Bollywood actress Aishwarya Rai. Two boys idling at the shop front volunteered to show me Asif's house. Hens and cattle competed with us for the right of passage through a maze of lanes, which brought us to the entrance of a mansion with wooden balconies jutting out from the first and second floors. One of the boys rushed inside and returned with a lean, balding man wearing a Nehru jacket. This was Asif's father.

"Is Asif around?" I asked.

"Who are you?" he said, surveying me keenly.

I introduced myself. His face relaxed and he welcomed me into the house. "I am sorry," he said. "One has to be careful." We sat in a carpeted drawing room. Asif was visiting an uncle at the other end of the village. His father sent the two boys to fetch him. "We got a phone booth for the whole village last year," he said, "but the militants thought it could be used to inform the army about their whereabouts, so they blasted the house where it was installed. The house was damaged and half the family was killed. Nobody even thought about getting another pay phone after that." His village and the adjoining village were known to have a strong military and militant presence. People obeyed one group or the other. Asif's sister brought tea. She was at the university studying literature, while Asif studied history. I asked Asif's father about his practice. "Well! I visit the court occasionally. My heart was never in law. I make my living from my apple orchards." He paused and then added wearily, "I always dreamt of politics. I wanted to contest elections, be a politician. That remains my sole ambition."

"Have you joined any political party?"

"You think I want to die?" he laughed.

"Basharat!" An eager voice came from the door. "Where have you been all these years?"

Asif was now a tall, athletic young man with cropped hair. We greeted one another and he sat down. His father went outside to his orchard so we could talk freely. I was there to ask about Asif's militant life, but I found I could not. It felt wrong to meet an old friend only so I could understand what my own life could have been—it felt selfish. But after a while Asif began to talk about it himself. He had gone back to his village after school and joined a local college. In the lap of brown barren mountains, his village was a militant stronghold. Militants paraded in the open, slinging assault rifles from their shoulders, hanging hand grenades from their belts. Indian troops stayed away most of the time. There was no television, no telephones, not even a hospital or proper municipal services. Militants stayed with the locals and ate at their houses.

Asif befriended some militant commanders. He was impressed, and their influence on him grew. He left home. At various hideouts, he learned to use an assault rifle, throw a hand grenade, blast a land mine, and plan an operation. He roamed from one village to another with his comrades-in-arms. I tried hard to picture Asif in fatigues, carrying deadly weapons or using them. He had been a militant for two years.

"What was it like?" I finally asked him.

"Scary," he said.

"My battalion treated me very well. We moved around together and were generally quite happy being the way we were. But at a personal level it hurt me when we had to move from village to village, seeking shelter and food. I felt people hosted and fed us because they were scared. I felt unwelcome, almost like an armed beggar. I had grown up in luxury and my parents bought me everything I asked them. And then I was a militant sleeping in a house whose owner was scared that the army might come there, who smiled at me and wished we would leave. I could not sleep and I missed my family."

I had an urge to ask him if he had shot anyone. I couldn't. "One day our commander told us that we had to attack an army convoy. I picked up my Kalashnikov. We were about to leave and I began shivering. I was too scared and death seemed so real. I left soon after that. My commanders were kind enough to let me go."

We left his house, walked to the bus yard, bought two Cokes from the shop with the Aishwarya Rai billboard. Asif loved Aishwarya and watched all her films. I thought she was plastic and told him so. The talk lightened the atmosphere. We were boys again. Asif said he was thinking of going to school in Delhi or some other Indian metropolis. I voted for Delhi. "It is the best Indian city for a student," I said. "You find good teachers and wonderful libraries. You must try for Delhi University and Jawaharlal Nehru University."

He agreed. "It must be fun being there."

"It can be great."

He had a mischievous smile on his face. "Tell me something?"

"What?"

"Did you go to a discotheque in Delhi? Did you dance with the girls?"

I told him some stories of my awkward and comical attempts at dancing. I told him that he would be better at it than I was. A shadow of longing flitted across his face.

I REACHED ANANTNAG AFTER SUNSET. The town was deserted, the shops closed. A few groups of commuters huddled together in the bus yard. I decided against heading for Srinagar and waited instead for a bus to my own village. An auto rickshaw stopped and the driver yelled the name of an area near my village. Soon I was knocking at the iron gate of my ancestral house. No one answered; the silence dragged on for minutes. Then my grandfather asked, "Who is it?" "It is Basharat, Baba!" The door opened. I shook hands with my grandfather and two of my cousins, who were standing behind him like bodyguards. They were unsure who might be at the door. +

Critical lives

New from *Reaktion Books*

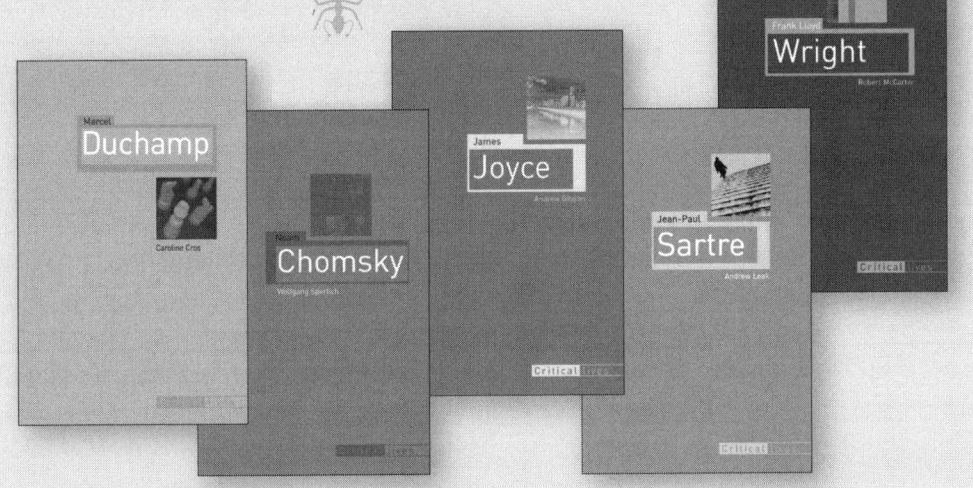

Marcel Duchamp
Caroline Cros
Paper $16.95

James Joyce
Andrew Gibson
With an Introduction by Declan Kiberd
Paper $16.95

Frank Lloyd Wright
Robert McCarter
Paper $16.95

Noam Chomsky
Wolfgang B. Sperlich
Paper $16.95

Jean-Paul Sartre
Andrew Leak
Paper $16.95

New pamphlets from PRICKLY PARADIGM PRESS

The American Game
Capitalism, Decolonization, World Domination, and Baseball
John D. Kelly
Paper $10.00

Phantom Calls
Race and the Globalization of the NBA
Grant Farred
Paper $10.00

The Turn of the Native
Eduardo Viveiros de Castro, Flávio Gordon, and **Francisco Araújo**
Paper $10.00

Distributed by **The University of Chicago Press** · www.press.uchicago.edu

ZOË MENDELSON, *BAMBIFICATION*, 2005,
PEN ON DRAFTING FILM, 11½ X 8½". COURTESY OF THE ARTIST AND GALERIE SCHLEICHER + LANGE, PARIS.

PORNUTOPIA

Nancy Bauer

CRITIQUES OF PORNOGRAPHY, though now by and large relegated to academic journals, have not changed since the 1980s, when they routinely made front-page news. The average antiporn argument still turns on the idea that there is a vast underground pornosphere, the horrifying details of which are not public knowledge. A locus classicus of this genre is the 1986 report of the Meese Commission on Pornography, which contains a bullet list of the titles of what it says are 2,325 distinct pornographic magazines. Here is a sampling from the Gs:

901. Girls Who Crave Big Cocks
902. Girls Who Eat Cum
903. Girls Who Eat Dark Meat
904. Girls Who Eat Girls
905. Girls Who Eat Hot Cum

This goes on for some fifty pages.

The members of the Meese Commission then give us a taste of the contents of the materials they have catalogued. Here, for example, is the first part of a plot summary for the book *Tying Up Rebecca*:

Chapter One introduces 13-year-old gymnast Becky Mingus and her middle-aged coach Vern Lawless—who hasn't had sex in seven years. In the locker room a 15-year-old cheerleader named Patty begins to masturbate, but mistakenly sticks her fingers in Becky's vagina. Patty then goes into the boys' locker room, discards her towel, rubs her breasts, and exposes her genitals. A boy forces Patty to her knees; Patty tongues his anus; he shoves her face in the drain; Becky masturbates; the boy performs cunnilingus; Patty performs fellatio; the boy has vaginal intercourse with Patty.

64   Nancy Bauer

Chapter Two. At home, Vern's wife wants to make their marriage better, and has bought a skimpy bra and crotchless panties from a girl in the lingerie store who had submitted to Vern's wife's uncontrollable sucking on her breasts and fingering her vagina. Lawless is aroused and masturbates when he sees his wife lying on the rug in the lingerie, but he loses his erection when he spots a picture of Becky. Vern explains his problem, and his wife says she understands and goes to the bathroom to masturbate.

Chapter Three. Becky's father, Henry, sits at home remembering a teenage encounter with a girl and masturbates. He accidentally ejaculates on Becky's face just as she comes in the room. Her face dripping with semen, Becky sees her father's erection and runs to her room crying. The next day, Louise decides to tell Henry, Becky's father, about Vern's lust for Becky. They go to a room upstairs that is equipped with leather clothing, ropes, chains, metal sheaths. Henry unbuttons her blouse, pulls up her skirt, pulls down her panties. His erect penis splits his pants. He performs cunnilingus and analingus. She performs fellatio.

Tying Up Rebecca is the only novel the report discusses in detail. One imagines that the commissioners' agenda in letting it stand as *the* example of pornographic writing was to license their condemning in the strongest terms the eroticization of, at least, adultery, pederasty, incest, and rape. But of course the plot summary itself *reenacts* this eroticization. The commissioner-author forgoes the possibility of arid description and resorts instead to conventional pornographic lingo ("tongues his anus," "uncontrollable sucking on her breasts," "dripping with semen"). And the sense that the summary was written in pornographic breathless haste is reinforced by the writer's sloppiness: the ambiguity about the recipient of the Chapter One boy's oral favors; the failure to identify "Louise" as Vern's wife; the unintuitive uses of the concepts of "mistake" and "accident."

I suppose it's conceivable that the members of the Meese Commission were too busy crusading to see that to describe a piece of porn is to produce a piece of porn—that in this subgenre of writing, at least, intentions count for nothing. There are people who enjoy accusing Andrea Dworkin, the iconic antiporn feminist, of being asleep at the same wheel. But, as implausibly extreme as her views were, Dworkin was no Meese Commissioner. She understood that readers of her 1981 book *Pornography*, which is basically one graphic *Tying Up Rebecca*–ish plot summary after the next, are at least as likely to hold their genitalia as they are their noses. Dworkin's strategy was to persuade us that the sensibilities of contemporary men—*all* men, not just habitual users of porn—are founded on pornography's eroticization of the subordination and abuse of women. Her goal in documenting instances of porn was to get us to experience the discomfort of becoming aroused by what she hoped she had convinced us is fundamentally soul-crushing, and not just for women.

What Dworkin demanded of us was a species of deep self-hatred, the kind you might live with if you weighed 300 pounds and were desperate to lose weight but just couldn't stop yourself from succumbing to the temptation to eat a pint of Ben & Jerry's. Dworkin hoped to elicit in ordinary prurient adults the kind of self-loathing our present culture hopes to elicit in pederasts. In other words, Dworkin was asking us, we who cannot just throw off our pornographic investments, to inhabit a state of shame. This demand differs from that of the moralistic Meesian, who in his bad-faith posturing would have us pretend that pornography and decent people by definition have nothing to do with each other, that only certain fringy folks get aroused by anything other than the touch of another human being (preferably, one's spouse), and that everyone but the real sickos has the wherewithal simply to swear off smut. Dworkin wanted all of us to recognize and despise the sickos within ourselves.

THIS DESIDERATUM, THAT WE HATE OURSELVES for having sexual feelings, is itself soul-crushing. And the idea that porn is the root determinant of men's sexuality, and that men's sexuality is itself invariably and dangerously misogynistic, was hyperbolic and empirically untestable. Which may be why the culture so resoundingly rejected it.

And yet there is a nub of truth in Dworkin's understanding of how porn works. The objectification of other people is arousing. Not always, not under every circumstance, not for every person in every situation. But everyone is sometimes sexually aroused by the objectification of a person or people whose humanity is, at that moment, beside the point. This experience is not unique to porn consumers: every normal adult is familiar with that twinge of desire that a stranger, real or depicted, can instantly evoke.

My fellow feminist philosophers have produced an enormous literature on what's wrong with sexual objectification. Their abiding faith in reason's ability to quash desire has resulted in a certain consensus on how to condemn these urges. The standard tactic is to define objectification as "treating a person like an object." You give an analysis of what an "object" is (something that can be owned and therefore used or transformed or destroyed), and sometimes what "treating" comes to (not just conceiving of a person as a thing, but reducing her to that status). Then you argue that people are not like objects in certain important ways (because people are autonomous, for example) and that to treat people in these ways is to violate their humanity.

There's nothing particularly controversial in this analysis. That's precisely the problem with it. No one argues that people are the same as things and so can always be treated in the same way. We don't need a philosopher's help to grasp that to the extent that pornography objectifies people, and to the extent that this objectification is dehumanizing, it's morally problematic.

No philosophical analysis of pornographic objectification will enlighten us unless it proceeds not from the outside, from the external standpoint of academic moralism, but from the inside, from a description of pornography's powers to arouse. Such a description reveals that, within the pornographic mise-en-scène, there is no space for the concept of objectification. The world as pornography depicts it is a utopia in which the conflict between reason and sexual desire is eliminated, in which to use another person solely as a means to satisfy one's own desire is the ultimate way to respect that person's humanity and even humanity in general.

In the real world, the unbridled expression of sexual desire is fundamentally incompatible with civilization, and in every culture there are harsh punishments for those whose lust gets the better of them. Most of us, the lucky ones, can discipline ourselves, more or less, not to act on our sexual urges when we don't think we should. We sublimate, harnessing our sexual vitality in the service of advancing civility and civilization.

In pornographic representation, civilization, though it sometimes gamely tries to assert itself, always ultimately surrenders to lust. But sexual desire is shown to be a gentlemanly victor: rather than destroy civilization, it repatriates it. Civilization pledges to uphold the laws of the pornutopia, in which the ordinary perils of sexual communion simply don't exist. Everyone has sex whenever the urge strikes, and civilization hums along as usual: people go to work and school, the mail gets delivered, commerce thrives. The good citizens of the porn world, inexorably ravenous, are also perfectly sexually compatible with one another. Everyone is desired by everyone he or she desires. Serendipitously, as it always turns out, to gratify yourself sexually by imposing your desires on another person is automatically to gratify that person as well.

Here, we see Kant turned on his head. Rather than encouraging us to live as though in a kingdom in which our common capacity for rationality enjoins us to regard all people, ourselves included, as ends-in-themselves, the porn world encourages us to treat ourselves and others as pure means. And what's supposed to license this vision is the idea that desire, not reason, is fundamentally the same from person to person, as though our personal idiosyncrasies were merely generic and reason could have no role to play in a true, and truly moral, sexual utopia.

In the pornutopia, autonomy takes the form of exploring and acting on your sexual desires when and in whatever way you like; to respect your own and other people's humanity, all you have to do is indulge your own sexual spontaneity. No one in the pornutopia has a reason to lose interest in or fear or get bored by sex; no one suffers in a way that can't be cured by it; no one is homeless or dispossessed or morally or spiritually abused or lost. When Daddy fucks Becky, she doesn't experience it as rape. She comes.

TWENTY YEARS AFTER THE PORN WARS RAGED at their height, the triumph of pornography is everywhere evident. Its imagery is just a couple of clicks away for anyone with an internet connection or a cable-TV remote.

According to the old battle lines, the pornographization of everyday life constitutes a victory for the proponents of free speech and a defeat for conservative moralists and radical feminists. But we are past the point, if we ever were there, at which a bipolar politics of pornography, for or against, could be of use to us. It does not help us understand the massive proliferation of porn since the mid-'80s if we insist on analyzing it in terms of free speech protections or advancements in artistic expression or, on the other side, as incitements to violence against women or a sign of moral lassitude.

We lack the words to articulate the role of pornography in our lives. What we need now is not a new politics of porn but, rather, a candid *phenomenology* of it, an honest reckoning with its powers to produce intense pleasure and to color our ordinary sense of what the world is and ought to be like. Such a reckoning will have to involve a refocusing of our attention, from the male consumers who took center stage in the porn wars to the women for whom the pornutopia provides a new standard both of beauty and of sexual fulfillment.

I have in front of me as I write a back-cover advertisement for the September 11, 2006, issue of the *New Yorker*. Actually, there are two identical back covers, twinned with a two-page front cover. The topmost front cover features a tightrope walker holding a long balancing rod, his head almost bumping into the Y in *Yorker*, against a white background; the second front cover positions the same man, in an identical position, over lower Manhattan, directly above the empty footprints of the Twin Towers. We are to recognize here the spirit of Philippe Petit, the tightrope artist who in 1974 changed the tide of negative public opinion against the expensive and aesthetically questionable World Trade Center, then still under construction, when he surreptitiously strung his wire between the buildings and, as thousands of early-morning commuters stared up in astonishment, literally danced his way across.

While the "Soaring Spirit" on the white page looks as though he is dancing on air, on cover two he seems to be in helpless free fall, not a single other soul in sight, the concrete and steel survivors of lower Manhattan standing not as monuments to human achievement but as stolid witnesses of our self-delusion. The front covers ask us to reflect on the powers and limitations of the human spirit in the making and losing of civilization. A solitary man, apparently a thoughtful man of focus and courage and joie de vivre, is attempting to maintain his balance in a life-or-death situation, one in which it is no longer clear whether a genuine civilization will be there to cradle him if he should fall.

On each of the back covers, two women are suspended against a black background. The one on the right is dressed in a very shiny red latex bodysuit covering everything but her face. Two little devil's horns spring from her head. She is heavily made-up—wet crimson lips, kohl eye shadow, penciled parentheses for eyebrows. Her mouth is open, as though in the middle of a word, maybe a roar. Facing us, she cocks one of her hips ever so slightly toward her counterpart. This woman is dressed in an impossibly tight full-length white Lycra gown, its armpits cut down to her waist, ending in a puddle of fabric. Her nipples are erect. Arching her back, she stands sideways, her rear end just a couple of inches from the devil woman's out-thrust hip, her head resting on the devil woman's shoulder, her pelvis pushing forward, and her two-foot feathery wings clasped to the devil woman's chest. The angel woman, ethereally made-up, has long, blond, wavy hair, the ends of which fall exactly at the devil woman's pubis. The devil woman's sinuous red "tail" wraps around the angel woman, so that its pointy tip aims directly at the C in the big Campari logo at the bottom of the ad. One of the angel's hands holds a bottle of Campari; the other, a rocks glass. Her eyes are shut, her lips are slightly parted, as she surrenders, not obviously without fear, to the grip of ecstasy.

The back covers ask us to pledge our allegiance to what they represent to be a much more desirable and robust world than the precarious one of the front covers. Here, there is no room even for the idea of a human spirit, no question about whether there are any souls to be found—let alone to be saved. Two female sexual archetypes feed on the pleasures of instant sexual reciprocity, pleasures that, our own helpless consumption suggests, stand to multiply magically and endlessly. We are asked to take even more pleasure in being savvy enough to get the joke—to entertain the idea, just for the fun of it, that there could possibly be an important difference between the angelic and devilish. The choice between heaven and hell turns out, in this fantasy civilization, to be a product not of any kind of reasoned struggle, moral or otherwise, but a matter of mere preference—blonde or brunette? submissive or dominant? straight or on the rocks? It doesn't matter. Everyone lives more and more happily ever after.

New Yorker front covers as a rule include a half-inch gutter running down the left margin. In this issue, the gutters of both front covers, like the backgrounds of both back covers, are black, which means that, when you lay the open magazine down to save your place, the back cover appears to creep onto the front. How is it that we manage not to see what is going on in the juxtaposition of these images, that we are able to ignore the clash between civilization and the pornutopia, as these two visions of the world compete for space in a magazine that prides itself on its sophistication and encourages us to congratulate ourselves for our own?

CONTEMPORARY PORNOGRAPHY IS noteworthy for cataloguing the incredibly huge range of things that get our blood flowing. The Meese Commission's interminable list of fetish magazines hardly makes a start on the project. Look on the internet and you will find websites devoted to people who are sexually excited by the sound of balloons popping (and those who find these people disgusting because *they* think that what's sexy about balloons is blowing them up to just *before* the popping point); instructions on how to make love with a dolphin (including an exhortation to go back to the sea the next day to reassure the dolphin that you still respect her, or him); advice on how to tie your leg up so that other people will think it's amputated and stare at you, or how to find a doctor who will actually amputate a limb or digit for you (possibilities which some amputee-obsessed people find sexy and others experience as lifesaving in roughly the way, they say, that transgendered people experience coming out).*

Part of the process of becoming civilized—of becoming a genuinely human being—is learning to keep the finer details of your sexual longing to yourself and your consenting intimates. Freud occasionally voiced the view that we are inclined to move too far in that direction: we overestimate the extent to which civilization is incompatible with sexual expression. (I am thinking here of what he says in *Civilization and Its Discontents* about the persecution of homosexuals.) Freud didn't have a T1 connection and so could not possibly have imagined just how polymorphously perverse we human beings are, but I don't think that the vast array of pornography on the web would have fazed him. It might even have pleased him, for pornography allows us to explore and even come to grips with our sexual desire in all its quirks and moral instability. It enables the discovery that the twists and turns of one's erotic longing are not sui generis, that no one is a true sexual freak. Insofar as it substitutes for the psychoanalyst's couch, it can increase our real-world sexual self-awareness.

---

* Carl Elliott, a philosopher at the University of Minnesota who a few years ago in an article in the *Atlantic Monthly* brought wide attention to the phenomenon of voluntary amputation, has raised the question of whether perversions are contagious: whether you can catch one simply from becoming aware of it. It may well be the case that certain sexual preferences are largely a function of learning what's out there. But this does not change the fact that there's a whole lot out there.

That ought to be a good thing. The Meese Commission incriminated itself when it found no room in its 1,960-page report even to wonder about what the wide diversity of interests represented in the thousands of one-off fetish magazines it rooted out in urban convenience stores and sex parlors might say about the nature of human sexuality. But it is not clear what will happen to pornography's power to enlighten us about ourselves, what the cost of it might come to be, as the everyday world gets more and more pornographized and as we accustom ourselves to the mindless enjoyment of all the twinges of arousal that ordinary culture increasingly represents as our birthright.

MORE THAN FIFTY YEARS AGO, Simone de Beauvoir observed in *The Second Sex* that, for women, the line between full personhood and complete self-objectification is whisper thin. A genuinely human being, Beauvoir argued, is one who experiences herself as both a subject and an object—and at the same time. A subject, she said, is a being who has the wherewithal to express her sense of what matters in the world, to dare to have a say in it. But part of being a subject, Beauvoir thought, is allowing yourself to be the object of other people's judgment, rational or irrational: to risk being ridiculed or condemned or ignored or, worse, to find yourself convinced that the harsh judgments of others are true—or, maybe worst of all, to be confused about these judgments, to discover that, after all, you don't know who you are.

For Beauvoir herself, the path to humanity took the form of writing about her own experience as that of a representative human being. She was daring to test whether, to invoke Emerson's famous formulation, what she knew in her own heart was true for all people. But the second half of her groundbreaking book is all about how difficult true self-expression is for women. The world sets things up so that we are wildly tempted to expose ourselves to public judgment, yes. But the vehicle of this exposure is not supposed to be self-expression. It's supposed to be self-objectification.

Women are rewarded—we are *still* rewarded—for suppressing our own nascent desires and intuitions and turning ourselves into objects that please the sensibilities of men. It's because it threatens the man-pleasing enterprise that feminism long ago hit a wall as a political movement. The very idea that we are now in some sort of postfeminist era hints at our extraordinary "separate but equal" schizophrenia: we believe that we have achieved full social parity with men, and we take this supposed achievement to license a hyperbolic reinvestment in feminine narcissism. Everywhere we turn we find images daring women of all sexual temperaments to revel in and express their fuckability, as though a woman's transforming herself into the ultimate object of desire should or could satisfy her need for other people to attend to the depth and breadth of her true self, even her true sexual self.

"Look—but don't touch." That's the incoherent rule that used to govern displays of feminine self-objectification. It enjoined women to take their pleasure in arousing desire in men and then withholding the satisfaction of this desire. Some pleasure. Some rule. But the new rule, having emerged from the pornographic subterranean and now ubiquitously shoved in our faces—"Don't just look—touch!"—has proved to be even more bizarre. It makes sense in the pornutopia, where everyone arouses everyone else's desire, and physical contact between and among human beings inevitably leads to orgasm all the way around.

Its oddness in the real world emerges in my female students' explanation for spending their weekend evenings giving unreciprocated blow jobs to drunken frat boys: they tell me they enjoy the sense of power it gives them. You doll yourself up and get some guy helplessly aroused, at which point you *could* just walk away. But you don't. Instead, you take pleasure in arousing the would-be fellatee's desire—and then *not* withholding the satisfaction of it. The source of the first phase of this pleasure is easy to identify, since it is identical to the pleasure afforded women under the old order of female narcissism. It's the pleasure of reveling in someone else's discomfort and frustration—in a word, of sadism. Women who play by the rules—that is, women who wish to survive in a man's world, rather than undertake the daunting work of attempting to transform it—have always been tempted to substitute the pleasures of sadism for the pleasures (and pains) of Beauvoirian subjectivity. But we still have the question of what pleasure there could be, as a young woman affects to walk away from her prey, in turning around and allaying the discomfort and frustration she worked so hard to produce.

I don't want to condescend to my students, and I don't want to speak for them. But I wish I could understand, at least, why they have so little interest in being serviced in return. An astonishingly large number of girls, as they have reverted to calling themselves, have told me that they feel more comfortable confronting a strange man's exposed hard-on than exposing their own, always shaven, vulvas. (We now live in a world where no part of a woman's body is too private to be subject to public standards of beauty.) Here, we are beyond the point of self-objectification. You forgo your own pleasure, be it sadistic or orgasmic, for the sake of another person's; you perhaps experience discomfort and frustration as you carry out this sacrifice; and then you find yourself not just pretending to enjoy, but actually reveling in your own self-effacement.

My students' experience in their sexual interactions with men confirms the logic of the pornutopia: to please someone else sexually is to please yourself, and there's no reason to wonder whether what's making you happy is something that you really desire, or whether you're really fulfilled at all. One wonders: could the pleasure of providing some guy with an unreciprocated blow job be the pleasure of masochism? Of martyrdom, even? Or if it is an internalization of the logic of the pornutopia, what precisely has driven it, and what sustains it in the face of the realities of real-world sexuality? I find that when I ask my students what sense they can make of their experience, they, like all of us, are at a loss for words. +

MARK SACKMANN, *EXERCISE ROOM*, 2006,
WOODCUT ON RAG PAPER, 7 X 11". COURTESY OF THE ARTIST.

THE TELEVISION DIARIES

Eli S. Evans

I'VE BEEN AT MY PARENTS' HOUSE IN MILWAUKEE for about a week now. I enjoy coming to Milwaukee to see my parents, but it's impossible, while I'm here, to lose count of the days, because nothing happens in them. I have been here for almost six days. My mother and my aunt Sue met me at the airport, my mother because she was excited to see me, my aunt Sue because she was eager for me to see—and perhaps more eager to see me react to—her recent face-lift. And I did. And she did. And it looks good. A little saggy around the jaw line, but she looks quite a few years younger, not exactly like someone you'd see on TV, but still pretty good, and although in truth I am relatively indifferent to whether or not my aunt Sue looks this good, I played up my sense of awe for a very specific reason: I want her to give me her Volvo.

Hers is a very nice Volvo, approximately three years old and with 55,000 miles on it, which is approximately 70,000 fewer miles than my car has on it, and it is not simply newer than my car but was much nicer to begin with. It has wide leather seats, and you can control the temperature separately for driver and passenger; and the seats themselves have heaters and massagers in them in case you or your passenger are feeling chilled or uncomfortable. Most important, you can control the stereo from the steering wheel. This means something to me. Whenever I think about the difference between doing poorly, economically, and doing much better economically, I always excuse the fact that I'm doing poorly economically by arguing to myself that unless you're a part of the small class of people whose money is practically infinite, the difference between those of us who are doing poorly economically and those who are doing better economically—in other words, the difference between somebody like me, a writer, a part-time college teacher, adjunct faculty, a good-for-nothing, a traveler, an occasional gourmet, and my friend Andy, for example, the same age or, actually, a year older (as I remind myself from time to time) and an up-and-coming associate at a prestigious Silicon Valley law firm—is negligible. It's not a fundamental difference, I tell myself, but simply a slight difference of scale, and I tell myself that a slight difference of scale does not warrant giving up on the things you believe in and the things you love. I tell myself: The difference between somebody like me and somebody like Andy is that somebody like me will drive a Honda or a Toyota and somebody like Andy will drive a BMW or, perhaps, a Volvo, and I tell myself that this is a negligible difference: both, or all four, are cars, and both, or all four, are charged with the primary labor of getting you from point A to point B, and all these cars do in fact do this, and in the end perhaps the BMW or the Volvo does it more smoothly, more prestigiously, and with better acceleration, but I tell myself that you only notice these differences at first. I tell myself that when you have been driving a Toyota and you suddenly get behind the wheel of a BMW, you may notice how much smoother the ride is, and how much easier it is to merge in traffic on the highway because you can accelerate so quickly, but that shortly thereafter you have adapted to these changes, you've begun to take them for granted, and now the vehicle is simply a car again, the same as any Toyota.

I tell myself that the difference between a car and a car, when you get down to it, is no difference at all, and so I will not become a lawyer in Silicon Valley; I will remain a writer in mid-city Los Angeles, the author of several unpublished novels, and work as a part-time adjunct faculty member for the regular paycheck, in order to pay the bills or, more often than that, to not come up as short as I otherwise might.

But then when I come home to Milwaukee, I often have the privilege of driving my aunt's Volvo, and I must admit that I want that privilege. I want the whole Volvo, but what I especially want—or perhaps this simply becomes my image of what it is that I want, of what is somehow at stake—are the stereo controls on the steering wheel. With them you can adjust the volume on the stereo, or even advance to another song on the CD, without even having to move your hands. Imagine: a life without wasted motion.

So I compliment my aunt's face-lift, tell her that she looks at least twenty years younger, and hope that, come the end of the summer, she decides to take pity on me and give me the car. My car, after all, is carrying around 125,000 miles. I put 25,000 on it this past year, driving twice a week from the loft in mid-city Los Angeles that I share with several roommates, to the college at which I function as adjunct professor in Orange County, and twice a month from my loft in mid-city Los Angeles to Santa Barbara, 120 miles north along the coast, where the girl, or woman, with whom I have been involved romantically lives and goes to graduate school.

My old Toyota car suffers from a weak set of brakes and peeling paint, but what really matters to me is this: about nine months ago, the key chamber on the driver's side of my car broke, which means that you can no longer put the key into the key chamber on the driver's side of the car, which in turn means that, from the outside, you can only unlock the car from the passenger door. Which means that even when I am alone—and I'm often alone—I can only unlock my car from the passenger side. What I do is walk around to the passenger side of the car, unlock the door, then walk back around to the driver's side to get into the car. It may not sound like much but it is a small humiliation, a reminder of what I am not, the comforts and prestige I do not have, the difference between one car and another, every time I have to pace around to the wrong side of my car and then march back around to the right side. Why should I have to waste my life?

WHEN I'M HOME IN MILWAUKEE I WATCH TV. I do other things, as well, of course: I play Wiffle ball and catch, and eat crackers and cheese, and make up songs for the dog, and read and reread the hundreds of *Archie* comic books that I read and reread as a child, and later as a teenager, and which are now stored in a milk crate in the basement. But mainly I watch a lot of television. Especially yesterday, when I wasn't feeling well. I don't know what it was. The day before, my father asked me to take a tree that had fallen in our backyard and chop it and saw it and clip it into small pieces that could be stuffed into brown plastic bags, and then stuff all those small pieces into those brown bags—bags that are specially marked for the disposal of yard (not household, not pet) waste, bags that can be purchased at True Value Hardware or Ace Hardware or the Home Depot—and then carry those bags to the front of the house and set them where Public Works will retrieve them some time later in the week. I did this, and later, in the stultifying Wisconsin summer humidity, I went for a run, and after that went out to dinner with my mother to an Italian restaurant in downtown Milwaukee where I had chicken parmesan and bread, the problem in a place like Milwaukee being that they give you too much chicken and no end of bread. My chicken parmesan consisted of two steroidally enormous slabs of chicken, and I also had two balloon glasses of wine, and because the waitress kept bringing more bread when I finished the bread she had already brought me, I ate far too much, and by the time I got home from dinner I was feeling very ill. At first I thought I had simply overeaten, but the sensations of having overeaten pass with digestion, and when the sensation of illness did not pass, I came to the conclusion that perhaps, chopping and sawing and clipping and bagging and dragging and then running, or jogging, in this Wisconsin summer humidity, I had become dehydrated, and so I consumed ounce upon fluid ounce of electrolyte-bearing sports drink, and a number of ounces more of unmodified water, and did it all over again, and when I still did not feel any better I was forced to conclude that something more serious might be wrong with me than dehydration. By the time I went to bed, my throat was raw and my glands were pulsating.

I woke up at 2:30 in the morning to a prank caller on my cell phone asking me how I felt about "big penises." All my muscles ached, and my throat felt as though it had been sandpapered, and my head throbbed, and my ears were ringing. My heart was beating hard with anger at the prank caller to whom, I did not realize until too late, I should have said: "I like my own big penis." I hung up and lay awake thinking, over and over, of how good that would have been if I'd said that, and did not sleep again.

At 5:30 in the morning my phone rang a second time, and this time the prank caller was threatening to "fuck me up." By now I'd had enough, and besides, the number carried a Los Angeles area code and I was in humid Wisconsin, so I knew how little I was risking.

"Let's go, baby," I said. "Tell me where you want me to meet you and I'll be there. I'll be there and I swear to God I'm going to fuck you up. I'm going to rip your face off. I'm going to break your kneecaps. Let's go."

There was an awkward pause.

"Why are you handing me this?" I heard a girl say at some distance from the telephone.

"Because," I heard a guy say—the same guy who had been making the threats, I think, but now sounding much less threatening—"I was just messing around. I don't want to get beat up."

So it was all something of a misunderstanding. The girl, who pleasantly introduced herself as Valerie, explained to me that her stupid friends had found a cell phone earlier in the evening and had been calling people all night acting stupid but that they really didn't mean anything by being stupid.

"Listen," I told her, softening. "I'm not really going to break their kneecaps, in fact I'm not feeling very well over here, to be honest with you I think I might be under the weather. So I really don't need these people calling me in the middle of the night asking me if I like big penises."

There was a pause.

"They asked you that?" she wanted to know.

Another pause.

"Because I like big penises," she said.

And, finally, after the pause that precedes inevitability:

"Do you have a big penis?"

I would like to say that at that point I hung up my phone. But I did not. Valerie and I talked to each other, about subjects other than my penis, for a number of minutes after that. And then there was still the matter of my body, which was exploding with the sensations of sickness. When I got off the phone, at nearly six in the morning, I went into my parents' room and told them what had happened and how I was feeling.

"So you got tough with the guy?" my dad wanted to know.

"In a way," I said.

He put out his hand so I could give him five.

"Now get out of here," he said. "I'm trying to get some shut-eye."

I DID EVENTUALLY FALL ASLEEP, but not until half past eight, and I slept until almost noon and then spent the remainder of the day taking my temperature and watching television on the couch in the living room. I watched the same *SportsCenter* several times over, in the constant expectation that it would somehow become new again. I turned on the ESPN Classic network and watched, in anticipation of that night's Mike Tyson fight, a number of old Mike Tyson fights. That guy really was incredible. He fought fifteen times during the first year of his professional career. He was fighting once every other week, at one point during that first year, and knocking out everybody he faced, not just knocking them out but knocking them flat, knocking them silly. I felt inspired. The old

Mike Tyson fights gave way, on ESPN Classic, to replays, in anticipation of the next night's second game of the NBA Finals, of old NBA Finals games, including Game Four of the 1984 NBA Finals between the Boston Celtics and the Los Angeles Lakers, a game I now watched in its entirety, thinking all the while of how when Robert Parish, the Celtic, was caught with a pound of marijuana he claimed it was all for personal use.

Eventually, I tired of watching old basketball games from the '80s—the short shorts and all that—but luckily the Milwaukee Brewers baseball game was coming on. I watched that as well. The Brewers came from behind to take the lead, thanks to some nifty hitting on the part of their 23-year-old prospect Ricky Weeks, but ended up losing to the Philadelphia Phillies when a former Philly and current Brewer by the last name of Bottalico gave up a three-run home run in the bottom of the seventh inning.

Nuts.

Luckily, there was another game to watch after the Brewers game, and so disappointment gave way to eagerness. But they were giving updates on the Mike Tyson fight—it was $50 to actually get that fight live—on ESPN's evening edition of *SportsCenter,* and having seen all those early Tyson fights I had become somewhat invested in this Tyson fight, and so I was having trouble deciding between the baseball game and *SportsCenter.*

My father, who had come into the living room to join me at some point, became irritated with my constant switching back and forth between channels and went to serve himself a glass of red wine.

They keep red wine in the refrigerator at my parents' house in Milwaukee.

You can't do this, I tell them. One does not keep red wine in the refrigerator.

"I know what you're getting at," my father says to me, "but we don't drink our wine at quite the same rate as you. If we don't refrigerate it, it'll go bad before we finish it."

Joined by my father, I kept my vigil in front of the set. Sick or not-so-sick—although watching TV always makes me feel a little sick all by itself—this is what I do when I am home.

o   o   o

For the last six days, I have been measuring my chances for the Volvo like a meteorologist rating the likelihood of rain. I call my lady friend in Santa Barbara with occasional bulletins.

"Twenty percent chance of Volvo," I tell her.

"Three hours ago you put it at thirty-five," she says.

I think there is a part of her that does not want me to get the Volvo, because she knows that there is a part of her that would hate me for it if I did.

I'm willing to take that chance.

I tell her: "My aunt went to the dealer and saw that they were selling one just like hers, the same mileage and everything, for twenty-one."

"Thousand?"

"That's right," I say, and think it over. If she's checking prices at the dealership, that means that she wants to give me the Volvo but isn't sure if she can afford it, but she can afford it. If she could afford a face-lift, she can afford to buy herself a new car, and if she wants to give the Volvo to me, there's a good chance that she's going to find a way to give the Volvo to me.

"Thirty-five," I say, revising my estimate, on the phone to my lady friend.

"I thought it was twenty."

She tells me that I'm putting pressure on my aunt to do something that she probably can't afford to do, and that it's not fair because now she's going to have to feel bad about not doing something that she should never have been expected to do in the first place.

This is true, but I like to think that things in my family are a little different. Around here we're free to beg and we're free to tell each other no. That way everything is out in the open. Even my lady friend has to admit that much. If my aunt gets sick of me asking for the Volvo she'll tell me that she's sick of me asking for the Volvo and that will be that, and I may or may not stop asking. If she gives me the Volvo, I'll probably run a lap around the block with my shirt off and then start wondering how I'm going to afford the gas when I get it out to Los Angeles, and if she does not give me the Volvo, I certainly won't harbor any ill will toward her for that. It all seems fair, but then perhaps it always seems fair when you're the one doing the asking.

○ ○ ○

MY AFFAIR WITH THE TELEVISION IS MUTUAL: in fact it pursues me perhaps even more doggedly than I it. In the afternoons I use my membership card for the Hollywood YMCA to gain admittance to the downtown Milwaukee YMCA, but the two are very different. In Los Angeles—and perhaps this tells you everything you need to know about that city—all the treadmills and exercise bicycles and other exercising machines face mirrors, so that as you exercise you are always looking at yourself, and yet many if not most of the people looking at themselves either are, have been, or would like to be on television; whereas at the YMCA in Milwaukee, all the exercise machines, the treadmills and bicycles and rowing machines and so forth, face television sets, so that everybody watches television as they exercise despite the fact that very few, if any, of the people exercising at the downtown Milwaukee YMCA have any interest in or realistic hope of ever actually appearing on television unless they are the perpetrators or victims of some hideous crime. You'd think it might make more sense for the YMCA in Los Angeles, television land, to install television sets in front of its exercising devices. And yet the reverse will make more sense to you once you've lived in LA.

The televisions in the downtown Milwaukee YMCA hang above the windows, and the fifth-story windows look out across Milwaukee Avenue, toward buildings that could, from the angle at which you are seeing them, just as easily find a place in downtown New York City or downtown Los Angeles. Of course the people in the downtown Milwaukee YMCA would have no place in downtown New York City, but I can tell you, although it might surprise you, that for the most part the people in the downtown Milwaukee YMCA are in far better condition than the people you will find working out in Hollywood or New York or any other place that thinks it's more attractive.

I try to run with my head down, paying attention to the seconds turning into minutes on the clock that ticks away on the treadmill's information panel. But I can't stop looking up at the televisions. To my left, just close enough that I can see it, is a TV tuned to ESPN. The others are set to various news channels. On my first day back in Milwaukee, running on a treadmill at the downtown YMCA, all these news channels were busy documenting a car chase through Los Angeles. The chase had begun, sometime around nine in the morning, in Thousand Oaks, and then proceeded south down the 405, and then east on the 10, at one point passing through mid-city, past the Arlington exit, just blocks away from my apartment. Hey, that's my exit, I thought. The chase headed east into the Inland Empire while I ran and sweated and looked out the windows toward what could be downtown New York City, and as I looked around at the pasty, unfashionable, somehow unmistakably midwestern and yet all the same extraordinarily fit people who could not be in downtown New York City, Hey, I wanted to say to them. That's my exit. On TV.

I could not even escape what the television was saying. All the TV sets in the downtown Milwaukee YMCA offer closed captioning, so that even if you don't plug a pair of headphones into the headphone portals available on every machine, you still have to know, if you are watching, what they are saying.

"I'm not sure," one of the news readers on one of these indistinguishable news channels was saying at this point. "It's been a number of years since I've been out to LA, but I have been there, my wife does have family there... but I think he's heading in the direction of Pasadena."

Of course he's heading in the direction of Pasadena, I wanted to say, but there was no one for me to say it to, everyone being plugged into their iPods or portable CD players or into the portals at every exercise machine, all of which can be adjusted to transmit the audio from any of the available television channels. Of course, I wanted to say, but he's a long way from Pasadena, and right now he's passing my exit. I exited at that exit yesterday.

But no one wanted to know, so I was stuck with it.

The car chase through Los Angeles fluctuated, even as I watched it; at times high speed, at other times low speed. Cars along the I-10, most of them well aware, from radios and the people calling on cellular phones, that a man was fleeing in a white van, of course, down the I-10, and was believed to be armed, all rather antiheroically pulled to the side of the highway when he passed, to let him through, to protect themselves, I suppose. It must be strange, I thought, to find yourself suddenly in the car chase, but I imagine as well that it must be powerful, a kind of theater of cruelty: We all enjoy the show when we're at a safe and uncrossable distance from it, but what happens when that distance is eradicated, or that boundary between inside and outside destabilized? Artaud wanted to know. Brecht wanted to know. When the car chase being broadcast on television and radio suddenly pulls up behind you, you probably know. But did these people know what they were knowing?

I ran. In place. The guy next to me was running as fast as I was. 7.6, treadmill speed. At the Hollywood YMCA, more often than not I'm the fastest runner in the room, but not so in Milwaukee. You wouldn't think so, what with this city's reputation for obesity, but Milwaukee, in addition to being one of the most obese cities in the country, is also one of the fittest. A city of contrasts...

The car chase or, in any event, the chase part of the car chase, came to an end maybe fifteen or twenty miles east of downtown Los Angeles. I couldn't stop watching. I wanted to stop watching but every time I looked up, there it was. It bothered me. It made me strangely nostalgic for Los Angeles despite the fact that I am, this summer, as I am every summer, glad to be out of there for a few months and headed to Spain. It made me nostalgic because something like this, broadcast into houses and apartments and gyms across America, makes something spectacular out of something incredibly banal: my exit. Life in Los Angeles isn't like this. There aren't car chases and helicopters and gang warfare everywhere you look. Or there are, I guess, but it's like anything else. You're not looking, not if the cameras aren't. In any event, the chase ended because the police executed a spectacular maneuver. It involved a police car clipping the back wheel of the fleeing van, thus causing the van to start to spin, as though it were slipping on ice, and at that point three or four police cars all sort of came together to pin it against the retaining wall to the far side of the highway. I ran. I tried to pay attention to other things. I increased the speed on my treadmill to 7.8 and less than a minute later the guy next to me did the same.

What was this?

I increased the speed on my treadmill to 8.0.

Match that, fatty.

He did. He wasn't fat at all. I was out of gas. I dropped back to 7.8 and dug in for another mile.

THE POLICE CARS THAT HAD PINNED the fleeing van against the retaining wall were replaced one at a time by black armored SUVs of the sort that you might see in a news report about governmental officers visiting Iraq to admire their handiwork. The only difference was that these SUVs were matte, whereas the SUVs you would see in the news report about Iraq would be glossy. So there were three or four matte black SUVs pinning this white van against a retaining wall. The suspect was inside. New reports suggested that if the suspect was armed at all, it was with a kitchen knife. Each of the SUVs was filled with special officers. None of them moved for a long time. Although initial reports suggested that the suspect may have had a hostage in the van with him, more recent reports indicated that he was likely alone with his kitchen knife.

So nobody moved. Most of another mile passed underneath me and, miraculously, despite the fact that I was exhausted, I still hadn't moved. Such is modern life, you move very fast and never go anywhere. Neither had the car chase progressed; at this point it was no longer a chase at all but rather a number of cars, which were in fact not cars but other varieties of motor vehicle, gathered together in a clump against a highway retaining wall. Then, suddenly, for reasons I could not understand, something happened. Or rather I can understand why something happened; it was because something needed to happen. The situation was inexorably pregnant, it was ten months pregnant. But why did they sit there for so long, at least ten or twelve minutes, maybe longer, doing nothing? And why was this moment, of all possible previous moments and future moments, the moment of action? It happened quickly, and, while I ran—while I struggled toward five miles and then, tricking myself, decided to go a half mile more (after all, it was only half a mile, if you only run half a mile at a time, you never have to run a whole mile)—the situation was replayed over and over again, in slow motion and then slower motion, with explanation and clarification.

This was how it went down: a "special officer" reached out of one of the matte black SUVs with a long pole, which he used to smash the rear passenger-side window of the immobilized van. Then, either that same officer or, more likely, some other officer, pitched some sort of low-power grenade—but a grenade, nonetheless—through the broken window, and it detonated, releasing a gas intended to render the subject unconscious. At that point, when the subject appeared to be unconscious, another special officer leapt out of another of the black SUVs, accompanied by a vicious dog which, from what I could see watching television images filmed from a helicopter hovering in the LA sky, appeared to be perhaps a rottweiler; that special officer yanked the driver's-side door open and fled back into his matte black SUV and the dog went to work on the unconscious body of the suspect armed perhaps with a kitchen knife. You couldn't see much of the suspect for all the smoke in the vehicle, but you could see the dog's head thrashing back and forth. The closed-caption text scrolling across the screen indicated to me that the news readers—now, on the second or third replay, reconciled to the fact that something had actually happened, and having already relegated that which had happened to the status of a foreseen event, even if, with the assistance of experts and analysts, they were only foreseeing it in retrospect—were actually complimenting the courage of the officers.

I'm thinking to myself, running in place: You know who was courageous? The suspect. Whoever he is, whatever it is that he's suspected of, that guy laid it on the line.

What happened, eventually, was that the attack dog dragged the suspect's limp body out of the vehicle and deposited it on the highway, at which point he started to attack it again, and then, finally, officers intervened to remove the dog, and then paramedics arrived with their stretcher. The scene shifted back to the newsroom where the news readers—one man and one woman—appeared shaken but also, from what I could tell, watching as I ran in place, vindicated. Once again, order had triumphed over chaos, and they had fulfilled their role in the mission of bearing witness.

WHY DO I WANT THAT VOLVO, ANYWAY? Perhaps I would like to seem well-made, attractive, and powerful, but modest and decent about it: a sort of Volvo of a human being. Yes, the Volvo would really improve my image in my own eyes. Now I would be traveling between my loft and school in a late-model Volvo, just as such a character as myself might drive on a TV show if you were meant to believe in his dignity and seriousness. If you were meant to see him as a pathetic person, a figure of fun, then you might require him to unlock his car from the passenger side, and circumnavigate the vehicle to its driver's side, whenever he wanted to make even the shortest trip.

A DAY OR TWO LATER, I was getting my teeth cleaned at the dentist. I had been tilted sharply back in the chair, the hygienist's gloved hands and rasping instruments were active in my mouth, and perched above me—I thought how it could crush me, if it fell—was a black TV. Tuned to CNN. They're everywhere: the bank, the post office, the airport. Every time you raise your eyes, there they are, and you're right in the middle of it, all of it, whatever it is. The story is always half-told, even when it's all over. (There's the commentary.) The most important part is always still to come. Unless it's sports, I don't like television. It makes me itchy, uncomfortable, stuck. The same thing happens to me when they play the bad Hollywood movies on transatlantic flights to Spain. I don't hook up the headphones, but that doesn't help. I still find myself watching. You would think that not having the audio would render the utterly familiar experience of watching some cheap, or rather, expensive Hollywood movie unfamiliar, displacing it, perhaps even converting it into something interesting. But the interesting thing is that it's not interesting. Watching a Hollywood movie without the audio is watching a Hollywood movie, except without the audio. You are not displaced or destabilized. You always know exactly where you are, exactly what's happening, exactly where it's going, and perhaps for precisely that reason you can't take your eyes away. Or, perhaps, you do take your eyes away, but because, when you go back, you will once again know exactly where you are, exactly what has happened, is happening, and is going to happen, as though you haven't been gone at all, not for a moment. Anybody who ever stayed home from school and watched TV all day knows what I'm talking about. What you watch when you stay home from school and watch television all day—either because you are sick, or because you are sick and tired of school—are, for the most part, soap operas. They're what's on from the time you wake up—late, because you haven't had to go to school—until the time your parents or siblings come home from school or work and the regular rhythms of household life resume; during the period of time in which you are out of time. You find yourself, almost immediately, deeply involved in the soap opera story, whatever program you happen to be watching, and experiencing a vague sense of panic over the possibility of improving health, or the impossibility of faking illness and thus staying out of school forever: after all, the stories are always on the brink of resolution, and you have the sense that if you miss tomorrow's episode you will never find out what happens. But eventually you miss school again, either because you're sick again or pretending to be sick again because you really are sick of the kids at school again, and you find yourself at home during that strange period of the day when home isn't home because the people who make it home and the rhythms that make it home are absent, and you find yourself, inevitably, watching the same soap operas again, and always, no matter how long it's been—a month, a year, two years of perfect, uninterrupted health—you know exactly where you are again. It's not a matter of minutes before you have found your place again within the narrative, but a matter of instants, or perhaps not even that. Instantaneously, you are right back in the middle again.

MONTHS PASS. That makes this a coda, or a postscript. I leave. I go to Spain. I return to Milwaukee. I go back to Los Angeles not by airplane, but by automobile, and then even return to Milwaukee again while the Volvo—now my Volvo: hurrah!—sits in a parking lot outside a hotel in El Segundo. The last time I was home I ran the toaster and the microwave at the same time and blew a fuse, of course. (The TV was already on.) I should have known better: the same thing happens when I run the toaster at the same time as any other powerful appliance in my own apartment, except that in my own apartment I know better, so I don't do it. When my roommates do it I lament their stupidity. I must have been assuming that my parents had stronger fuses or something. After all, they're my parents. But, alas, the fuses of Milwaukee are no stronger. The toaster and microwave blinked off. So, too, the light I had left on across the kitchen above the sink. A moment later, a human wail came from the room that used to be my bedroom but now, although it retains the appearance of my bedroom—the Nerf basketball hoop above the door, the baseball-and-glove light fixture and so forth—serves as the computer room. The computer, apparently, is on the same circuit, and so it had turned off as well.

The wail came from my mother. "No!" she wailed. "Right when I was in the middle of the internet!" +

MFA

MASTER OF FINE ARTS
with a major in
Creative Writing
and specializations in
Fiction or Poetry

In the Texas Hill Country between Austin and San Antonio

TEXAS STATE UNIVERSITY
SAN MARCOS

The rising STAR of Texas™

Texas State University-San Marcos is a member of the Texas State University System.

TEXAS STATE

The Roy F. and Joann Cole Mitte Endowed Chair In Creative Writing
2006-2007 Denis Johnson
2007-2008 Tim O'Brien

FACULTY

Cyrus Cassells, Poetry   Debra Monroe, Fiction
Dagoberto Gilb, Fiction   Tim O'Brien, Fiction
Tom Grimes, Fiction   Kathleen Peirce, Poetry
Roger Jones, Poetry   Steve Wilson, Poetry

ADJUNCT THESIS FACULTY

Lee K. Abbott • Craig Arnold • Rick Bass • Ron Carlson
• Charles D'Ambrosio • Rick DeMarinis • John Dufresne
• Carolyn Forché • James Galvin • Shelby Hearon
• Bret Anthony Johnson • Hettie Jones
• Patricia Spears Jones • Li-Young Lee • Philip Levine
• Carole Maso • Elizabeth McCracken • Heather McHugh
• Jane Mead • W.S. Merwin • David Mura
• Naomi Shihab Nye • Jayne Anne Phillips • Alberto Ríos
• Pattiann Rogers • Nicholas Samaras • David Shields
• Debra Spark • Gerald Stern • Marly Swick
• Rosmarie Waldrop • Sharon Oard Warner • Kate Wheeler
• Terry Tempest Williams • Eleanor Wilner • Mark Wunderlich

RECENT VISITING WRITERS

Charles Baxter • Aimee Bender • Junot Diaz
• Charles D'Ambrosio • Roddy Doyle • Percival Everett
• Carolyn Forche • Richard Ford • Forrest Gander
• Barry Hannah • Jane Hirshfield • Carole Maso
• W.S. Merwin • E. Annie Proulx • George Saunders
• Jean Valentine • C.D. Wright

Visit *Front Porch*, our literary journal
www.frontporchjournal.com

**$45,000 Morgan & Lou Claire Rose Fellowship
for an incoming writing student**
Additional scholarships and teaching assistantships available

Tom Grimes, MFA Director   Phone 512.245.7681
Department of English   Fax 512.245.8546
Texas State University   Home page:
601 University Drive   www.english.txstate.edu
San Marcos, TX 78666-4616   e-mail: mfinearts@txstate.edu

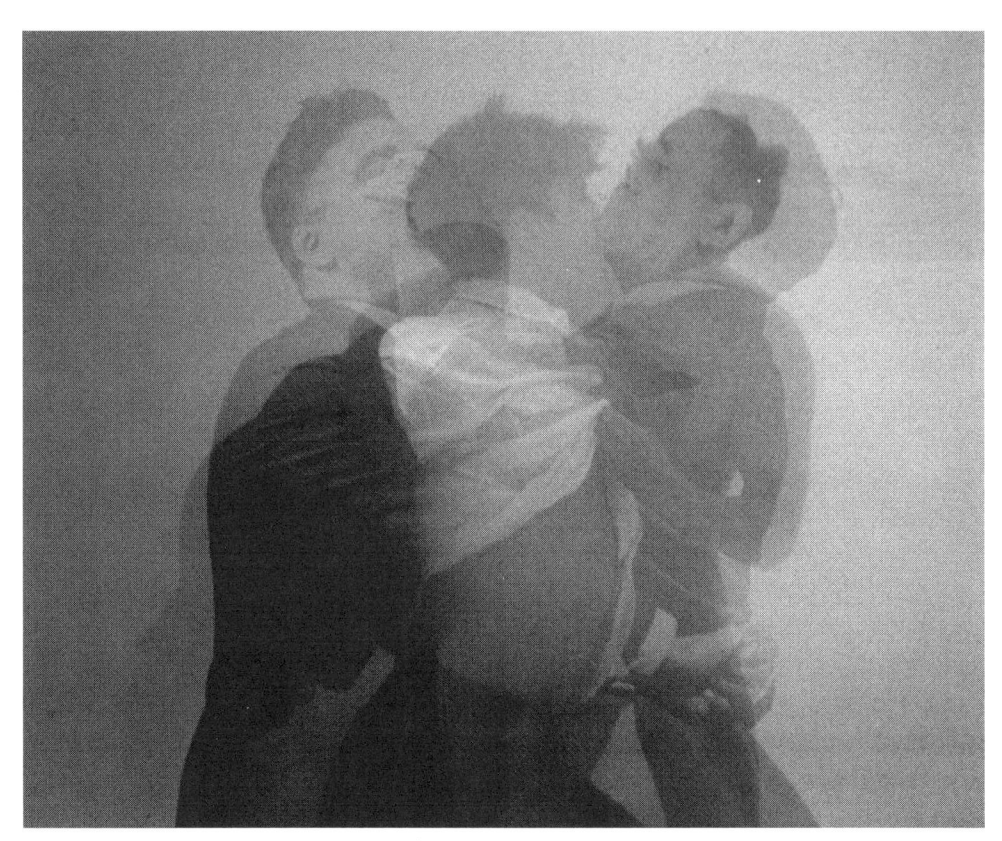

ROBERT FLYNT, UNTITLED, 1996,
CHROMOGENIC PHOTOGRAPH, 20 X 24". COURTESY OF THE ARTIST AND CLAMPART, NEW YORK.

THE MEANING OF LIFE II
ANAESTHETIC IDEOLOGY
Mark Greif

A YEAR AGO, I WROTE AN ESSAY about a modern crisis in experience. I defined experience as the habit of creating isolated moments within raw occurrence in order to save and recount them. Questing after an ill-defined happiness, you are led to substitute a list of special experiences and then to collect them to furnish your storeroom of memories: incidents of sex, drinking, travel, adventure. These experiences are limited in number, unreliable, and addictive. Their ultimate effect can be a life of permanent dissatisfaction and a compulsion to frenetic activity.*

Since then, I've felt I paid too little attention to a phenomenon which is the opposite: the desperate wish for anti-experience. The connection between the quest for experience and the wish for anti-experience isn't chronological. You don't wake up the morning after some final orgy of experience and discover that you can't stand any more. It seems to be, instead, arbitrary and eruptive. You reach points in life at which you can no longer live like other people, though you don't want to die. Experience becomes piercing, grating, intrusive. It is no longer out of reach, an occasional throb in the dark. It is no longer a prize, though it is the goal everyone else seeks. It is a scourge. All you wish for is some means to reduce the feeling.

This *anaesthetic* reaction, I begin to think, must be associated with the stimulations of another modern novelty, the total aesthetic environment. For those people to whom a need to reduce experience occurs, part of their discomfort seems to be strongly associated with aesthetic intrusions from fictional or political drama—from the television, the newscast, the newspaper, the computer headlines, or any of the other unavoidable screens of pixels or paper. "I just had to turn the TV off. I couldn't stand it anymore." This is the plea we accept, more or less, as

---

* "The Meaning of Life I: The Concept of Experience," *n+1* Number Two, Spring 2005.

we mirror the strange look on the sufferer's face with an odd look of our own. We will accept it this far and no further, because much more of the suffering comes from us—the "normal" others—who obnoxiously recount our daily lives, too, as a series of rare adventures. The anti-experiencers will want to turn the TV off; then they'll want to turn us off. There comes a point at which they will want to turn the sights and sounds of life off—if life becomes a nightmare of aestheticized, dramatized events.

The hallmark of the conversion to anti-experience is a lowered threshold for eventfulness. You perceive each outside drama as your experience, which you could not withstand if it really were yours. It leads to forms of total vulnerability, as if the individual had been peeled or deprived of barriers. I don't know what word can connect the three levels of unavoidable strong experience, broadcast and recounted and personal, except the omnipresence of *drama.*

I also don't know why the nightmare comes for some people and not others, at some times and not others. After considering it, it surprises me that this breach, the fall into painful over-experience, isn't more common. Why of a hundred seekers of experience and dwellers in the total aesthetic environment do only two, or ten, turn? Unless there are features of the aesthetic environment which are themselves also anaesthetic and that manage to regulate the experiential lives of the majority, to keep them from cracking.

Suppose you have reached that point. You no longer feel you are among those whom William James called the "healthy-minded." You can tell because you watch the healthy ones gaping laughter at violent movies or sitting calmly across from you at the table, over dinner, recounting from that day's news a sex scandal, an airplane crash, an accidental shooting. You hear from the healthy-minded the battles *they* have fought that day and the experiences they have won. You detect them questing after the things they desire, talking about them with natural spirit, nourished by hope and aggression like their natural milk. They are nature's creatures, in the full grace of modernity. The sad truth is that you still want to live in their world. It just somehow seems this world has changed to exile you.

In the last essay, I spoke of solutions to a first crisis, the endless quest for experience, in practices that redeem experience by expanding it: aestheticism and perfectionism.* The solutions to this second crisis in experience, the wish for anti-experience—both from tradition and in the present—are the *anaesthetic ideologies*. They diminish experience's reach. They "redeem" experience by weakening or abolishing it. They are, in a sense, aestheticism's and perfectionism's inverse.

Anaesthetic ideologies are methods of philosophy and practice that try to stop you from feeling. Or they help you to reduce what you feel. Or they let you keep living, when you can no longer live, by learning partially how to "die." I preserve the word *ideologies* because of the methods' potential duplicity—and also because of our perhaps justified suspicion that such undertakings are, at some level, inhuman.

THE GALLERY OF HEADS IN THE WEST, marble smooth, marble eyed, begins near the entrance with Plato and Aristotle. Plato put a megaphone to the mouth of Socrates. Thus we learned of the Forms, the permanence of Justice, and the objectivity of the Good. Aristotle held the dissecting tool to nature and the yardstick to man, systematizing all the forms of matter and the forms of life. We learned man is a political being whose good lies in the fulfillment of his potential. Plato led to Aristotle as the only alternative to himself, and the two of them together gave us Western philosophy as a line of action and actualization.

In the ancient world, though, rival traditions competed with theirs. These philosophies did not lead toward our modernity, defined by the quest for experience. They created traditions of nonstimulation, nonsusceptibility, nonexcitement, nonbecoming, nonambition; also antifeeling, *anaesthesia*. Thus at the *origins* of philosophy, thoughts were devoted to the restriction of experience. These traditions were at least as central to the concerns of the West, once upon a time, as were the lines we have received as active common sense and normalcy. They can help us at least as much today as the "Eastern philosophies" that have been for many moderns the only, marginal way to attain some distance from one-sided Western ambition.

---

* Aestheticism and perfectionism work by putting experience under the control of the active individual, teaching him to make rare experience *always* and from *anything*. Aestheticism teaches its practitioners to find rarity or beauty in any object or event; perfectionism finds moral reflections upon the observer in the same sources. They turn even banal or ugly things into objects of singular aesthetic interest or into moral examples that would encourage the constant transformation and appreciation of the self, thus exploding the *quest* for experience by putting it always at hand.

The students who followed the example of Socrates did not all join Plato's Academy. (My account of Socratic successors draws on the writings of A. A. Long, the great scholar of Hellenistic philosophy.) One of the earliest, Diogenes of Sinope, called Diogenes the Cynic, led a beggar's life, upheld the example of Socrates' insulting speech, and taught Socratic freedom from "property, fine appearance, social status," while preaching, unlike Socrates, nonallegiance to any city. Philosophy for him was the use of reason for each individual to talk himself out of the material needs that everyone else claimed, and thus to be free of the fears to which everyone else was subject. This freedom from conventional need and this freedom from fear—even when they meant a refusal of the world—came to be combined with the philosophical hedonism of Aristippus of Cyrene, one of Socrates' direct pupils. Cyrenaic hedonism said that pleasure and pain are prior to all other motivations, and *should* be, too. These views made a different founding to philosophy than the one mediated by Plato.

In moods of peaceful hopefulness, I think that Epicurus, a genius of the next Greek generation, should be our perfect philosopher now, for America. He was a hedonist, as we are today. But he would have freed us from the pain of our search for experience, our mistaking of the most valuable pleasures for the rarest and hardest to attain. He came to maturity while Aristotle was still alive, and began teaching a very different doctrine: that pleasure is the goal of life, but pleasure defined as the end and absence of pain. "For we are in need of pleasure only when we are in pain because of the absence of pleasure, and when we are not in pain, then we no longer need pleasure." The Epicurean ideal was *ataraxia*, imperturbability and mental detachment. This imperturbability couldn't be accomplished through avoidance—pain would come whether you wanted it or not—but only through the right way of thinking about all unavoidable experience.

Unsought pleasures, whatever they were—a lavish banquet, a night of erotic love—were never bad in themselves. The difficulty with most positive pleasures, however, was that "the things which produce certain pleasures bring troubles many times greater than the pleasures." Luxuries of experience involved you in uncertainties and pains—whether you would ever have them again, or whether you could sustain them. If pain is more to be avoided than positive pleasures are to be sought, it is "the freedom of the soul from disturbance" that is "the goal of a blessed life."

Everything natural is easy to obtain and whatever is groundless is hard to obtain.... Simple flavours provide a pleasure equal to that of an extravagant life-style when all pain from want is removed.... So when we say that pleasure is the goal we do not mean the pleasures of the profligate or the pleasures of consumption, as some believe, either from ignorance and disagreement or from deliberate misinterpretation, but rather the lack of pain in the body and disturbance in the soul.

"For we [Epicureans]," the founder wrote, "do everything for the sake of being neither in pain nor in terror." Epicurus, on the outskirts of Athens, began the Garden, where his friends and followers "included household servants and women on equal terms with the men," as the scholar D. S. Hutchinson has noted—arrangements inconceivable to the rest of Athenian society. There they lived in peace and tranquility. They took their pleasure from a little wine mixed with water, and if you ever wanted Epicurus to enjoy an extravagance, he said, you could send him a little pot of cheese. Friendship mattered. Friends reminded one another that true happiness was freedom from fear, that death was meaningless and pain tolerable. They sought to help one another to resist being touched by any disturbance, to win a gentle victory over strong experience.

IN MORE TEMPESTUOUS OR HARSHER MOODS, my thoughts for the hidden sufferers in America go over to the tougher anaesthetic of the late Roman Stoics. The Stoa existed in Epicurus' time as a place of conversation and teaching in Athens, like the Academy, the Garden, and Aristotle's Lyceum; but Stoicism seems to have come into its most emphatic and lasting form many generations afterward. If you want a simple program and definitive dogma, you look to Epictetus. He is a much later figure than his Greek predecessors, and much better documented. The violence of Epictetus' rhetoric can be tonic. Really, we will eradicate experience, not just learn to be happy with barley cakes and watered wine. Then we can withstand anything, the richest luxuries or the heaviest blows.

The Stoic system is not so different from Epicureanism in its methods of controlling needs. It disposes of the feeling for pleasure, however, as a root for the mind's disciplining of experience. Epictetian Stoicism tells you to divide the world into what is up to you and what is not up to you. All that is left for a person to do, then, is to master his desire and aversion—so that he will never have either desire for or aversion to anything not up to him. He must never desire what he cannot control—not honors, not events, not other people's thoughts, behavior, or reactions, not all the good experiences of his body. And he must have no mental aversion to anything that comes to him without his choice, like illness, death, or the bad experiences of his body. He can groan in illness, but he must not care about it. The fates of things are up to nature, not to you.

> In the case of everything that delights the mind, or is useful, or is loved with fond affection, remember to tell yourself what sort of thing it is, beginning with the least of things. If you are fond of a jug, say, "It is a jug that I am fond of"; then, if it is broken, you will not be disturbed. If you kiss your child, or your wife, say to yourself that it is a human being that you are kissing; and then you will not be disturbed if either of them dies.

Life, Epictetus intimates at one point, is like a tourist visit to Olympia; you go because, well, who doesn't go? But it's bound to be incredibly annoying. "Do you not suffer from the heat? Are you not short of space? Do you not have trouble washing?... Do you not get your share of shouting and uproar and other irritations?" You will shrug it all off. "What concern to me is anything that happens, when I have greatness of soul?"

The only thing the Stoic should invest *any* emotion in is his own choice, which determines that "greatness of soul." He will feel pride when he remains absolute master of his choice and of his desire and aversion. He feels displeasure when he fails temporarily to be master of himself. Stoic reason makes a man absolute master of his judgments and eradicates everything that is bad while clarifying the only thing that is truly good: the right use of choice.

It is the denial of any meaning to immediate experience, apart from the judgment one places upon it, that is truly anaesthetic—a will to control one's judgments and minimize their effects, to make experiences not matter except for the inner experience of mastering experiences. The Stoic ideal was *apatheia*, release from passion and feeling, but it freed itself from everyone else's cares precisely in order to be able carelessly to do what everyone else did. It became supermilitant, because it continued to live in the world while denying it. "Practice, then," Epictetus teaches, "from the start, to say to every harsh impression, 'You are an impression, and not at all the thing you appear to be.'"

This meant not only not giving credence to impressions, but, in a sense, never aestheticizing them, never enjoying them as more than accidental facts or conjunctures, never investing them with any aura beyond their material constitution and fate, never giving them a place in a drama to be remembered or dwelt upon emotionally. Hence the hostility of Epictetus to the tragic drama and the epic of strong feelings. What sort of person complains and lets passion and experience get the better of him, saying, "Woe is me"?

> Do you suppose I will mention to you some mean and despicable person? Does not Priam say such things [in the *Iliad*]? Does not Oedipus? . . . For what else is tragedy but a portrayal in tragic verse of the sufferings of men who have devoted their admiration to external things? . . . If one had to be taught by fictions, I, for my part, should wish for such a fiction as would enable me to live henceforth in peace of mind and free from perturbation.

Then, typically, Epictetus washes his hands of the question of drama, to return his followers to their choice: "What you on your part wish for is for you yourselves to consider."

Epicureanism and Stoicism survived, even predominated, for centuries—centuries in which Platonism and Aristotelianism had gone into relative eclipse. (These latter were revived in the first century BC.) The anaesthetic doctrines' memories now sit under a layer of dust. They are neglected by us, and their masters sit among the unrecognizables in the hundred forgotten generations between classical and modern.

IN THE LAST ESSAY, I SPOKE OF SOME SPECIFIC MEANS of collecting the most important experiences: drugs and alcohol, sex, and travel. I suggested they are unreliable by themselves and contribute to dissatisfaction with existence by creating the need always to be searching for more.

Outside the disciplines of full anaesthetic ideologies—what we can find among Epicureans and Stoics, as life philosophies—I begin to wonder if our banal searches for experience today don't often contain a shot of anaesthetic; something that allows these activities to serve the moderation of experience as well as its collection. What's more, modern solutions to the intolerability of experience have a way of flipping back and forth between *reactions* to the too-painful experience of late modern economy and *adjustments* to it as extensions of its reach.

With drugs and alcohol, the anaesthetic effect may seem just too obvious. Drowning your sorrows in drink is recognized to be the first and cheapest means of escaping experience. Whiskey continues to be a fine painkiller even if it is no longer used medicinally. You start drinking to look for fun, for experience. You end in another place. Alcohol is a means to collect experiences, and then, too, alcohol is abusive as well as abused, the cause of troubles with experience as well as a reaction to trouble with experience. If drinking fails us, which ideal is it failing—the life of fun, on a high, or the life of anaesthetization, shut off and protected?

Sometimes I find myself thinking about those high school and collegiate and postcollegiate figures, the "stoners." What were their futures? They might have had their only natural social existence, without penalties, while still in school. But it seemed a plausible existence, like that of a creature who had found the right ecological niche. This penaltyless stoner was someone who would rise in the morning and take a hit from the bong, smoke through the day, take all experience (classes, social interactions) with a hazy anaesthesia that made it not quite experience, yet not quite anything so positive as "fun"—then finish off a bowl before going to sleep, to start the next day in the same way. It seemed a life of anti-experience, different from physical addiction. No doubt there is something myopic in a nostalgia for what the stoner proved was possible, if only for a few short years. No one thinks it ends well. But there was something about his manner, wreathed in smoke, that made him seem not like an adventurer but a symbol of a bizarre but real reaction to something we can't name.

For the small group of people who insist on the legalization of marijuana, who can even become marijuana "activists," the logic of their movement has become ever more oriented to the wedge issue of medically recognizable anaesthetization, the anaesthesia of cancer patients and the terminally ill. That is because it is the only way to make marijuana legible to our world, a world of experience and not anti-experience: by the recognized evil of interior *bodily* pain rather than the wish for a life less acute, or the acknowledgement of a healthy physiology that could prefer, somehow, haze in experience to our supposed clarity.

Sex and the search for sex hold out the acquisition of experience, much praised and discussed in our culture, against the unspoken moderation of experience by sex as a reassuring and intimate repetition. We speak of an alternative only in marriage: *conjugality*, the repetition of sexual experience as an act of love, but also as a kind of interpersonal comforting. Conjugality repeats, it does not much change, and it never needs to change unless its participants decide on change, since it is not ever done with anyone else. It is not precisely anaesthetic, but anti-experience. The larger culture of experience, of course, suggests that sex, in some sense, should *always* be done with someone else, in a new way. Your spouse or helpmate must become continually somebody new, somebody unknown, to share new experiences with. Our culture has become pornographic at all levels of its narrative structure: it always seeks a further experience beyond the last one, with more reach and extremity, even where the human mind seems limited to repetition, and human habit seems to prefer it. It is probably the case even in the carnival of dating, switching of partners, anonymous intimacy, that in the act of seeking and acquiring the sheer bodily presence of another person, whoever he or she may be, there is self-reassurance and even near self-anaesthesis: what matters in the moment will be not only the recountable events but silent, forgettable, forgotten-in-the-moment acts of mutual oblivion.

There are, of course, better-organized ways of seeking some relief from experience—non-naive ways, modern ideologies. The "voluntary simplicity" movement of the last decade was a self-conscious plan for the reduction of possessions in order to unclot experience, to find out which experiences, of so many options, were really needful. Simplicity would limit the acquisitive instinct in favor of the retention of a small number of indispensable items. You would learn first to get rid of a closet of clothes, for the most useful; get rid of many friends, for fewer; stop attending to much foreign news, for news closer to home; eventually, in the "advanced" techniques, have one car instead of two, then no cars at all, a smaller house, an easier job, and a diminished but possibly more manageable or more vivid experience. The ideology was not always precisely anaesthetic; sometimes it was purifying of experience.

But wherever it did not acknowledge its own real *opposition* to experience of the dramatic kind, and could be co-opted by aesthetics of more vivid, purified and improved experience, simplicity had the capacity to flip. It could become a matter not just of fewer clothes but of more perfect, ideal clothes, even *new* clothes. It furnished the basis for its own lifestyle magazine, *Real Simple*, a glossy for those who wanted to organize and vary, to switch between simplicities, or to stylize their environments in "simpler" hues of eggshell and porcelain and light pastel—rather than to reduce objects or even learn to accept the old, ugly, and easy, which exist already and therefore might be less spiritually intrusive.

I think the organized spiritual system of the greatest anaesthetic use to the largest number of people in America today must be Buddhism. And yet this still recruits only a tiny minority of seekers. Buddhism is the genuine article, an ancient system, however complicatedly it makes its way to us for modern purposes. Contemporary "nonattachment," as it is sometimes described to me, sounds a good deal like Epicurean imperturbability and, in some formulations, Stoic apathy. The more I hear of "mindfulness," the more I hear traces of aestheticism and perfectionism, though in mindfulness they are removed at last from the limiting requirements of artistry or moral self-scrutiny and are made instead a function of permanent biological habits (breathing, attention, basic sensation) in a kind of hybrid aestheticism-imperturbability. The Buddhist would protest, justifiably, that his practices came first and should be judged on their own. (I am not a Buddhist myself and therefore a bad judge.) What is striking in the Americanization of Buddhism, however, as it appears in books and pamphlets and tapes and talks, is the mixture of different methods and aims. We may just be seeing a diversity of sects and practices, or we may be seeing the perennial Janus-faced quality of American auto-therapeutics. Something like mindfulness will be a way to moderate experience for some and to collect and intensify it for others; a way to drop out for some and to get ahead for others; a system at odds with convention for some, and an adjustment to conventional life, reducing friction, for others. We knew already that yoga could be imported to this country and, for some, retained as an interlocking series of total systems of practice, knowledge, and devotion—while it was made a form of gym exercise to slim down and improve muscle tone for others.

Then there is the promise of the New Age. It is surprising how often New Age solutions come to us from aliens: interplanetary beings, men of the fifth dimension, and oceanic tribes preserving ancient wisdom lit by the glassy filtered blues of their bubbled Atlantis. I suppose these fantasy archaisms and interstellar revelations are no different finally from our worship elsewhere of the Orient against the Occident—our idea that truth must come from our morning rather than our eve. No different, probably, from my own desire to rediscover anaesthesis in the heart of the West, among sandal-wearing Epicureans or Stoics, while I willfully reinterpret their complex doctrine. We cannot take advice from ourselves, and so we take it from men and women with very strange ways. The stranger the better, so estranged are we from our fellow citizens, who can see no problem.

Certainly, all these systems, however practiced, are better than depression—perhaps the major arena for involuntary anaesthesis in our time (with its attendant losses of pleasure, will, and caring). What is often enough said by the mildly depressed—though we suspect them of magnifying their own problems into social problems—is that their depression is a logical and reasonable response to an environment of experiences and demands that are too intrusive. From the opposite perspective, and with much more authority, the severely depressed are inclined to say that their death in life cannot be a logical or reasonable response to *anything*, for their sense of the negation of experience goes beyond what any human being could want or will as self-protection. Depression does not save the self, it tells it to die. This seems so extreme as to be outside the reach of cultural analysis, even though anaesthesis, in its many other organized forms, is often a way of learning to "die" without dying. One wants to say something about depression, still stopping short of the point at which generalization encroaches on the individual malady. If there is a cultural world shared between the rise of "experience," searched for as the only means to furnish happiness, and the steady creep of depression as a frequent, dominant affect for people who expected that their lives might be deserving of full happiness, then maybe there is also some causal connection. Maybe it is a sign that when experience has become intolerable, for whatever specific reasons, the mind and the body will *unideologically* attempt to solve what could only be solved with a practice, a system, and an ideology.

We do not live in an age of the arts. The novel, theatrical play, and piece of symphonic music don't matter very much. Art forms that seemed like the fruit of long lines of development, including opera, ballet, painting, and poetry, are now of interest to very few people.

We do, however, live in an aesthetic age, in an unprecedented era of total "design." The look and feel of things, designed once, is redesigned and redesigned again for our aesthetic satisfaction and interest. Design, which can reach the whole world, has superseded art, whose individual objects were supposed to differ from one another and hold a sphere apart from the everyday.

But the particular aesthetic manifestations that interest me here are *dramatic*. It interests me that there is no end of fictions, and facts made over in the forms of fictions. Because we class them under so many different rubrics, and media, and means of delivery, we don't recognize the sheer proliferation and seamlessness of them. I think at some level of scale or perspective, the police drama in which a criminal is shot, the hospital drama in which the doctors massage a heart back to life, the news video in which jihadists behead a hostage, and the human-interest story of a child who gets his fondest wish (a tourist trip somewhere) become the same sorts of drama. They are representations of strong experience, which, as they multiply, begin to dedifferentiate in our uptake of them, despite our names and categories and distinctions.

We often say we watch the filmed dramas of strong experience for the sake of excitement or interest. This is true for any representation *in the singular case*. The large dramas of TV and movies, presumably, reflect back on our own small dramas. I, like the ER surgeons, have urgent tasks; I, like the detectives, try to solve things. If one watched, say, a single one-hour show once a month, the depicted experience might come across as genuinely *strong* experience. If one watched (or carefully read) the news once a month, it might be a remarkably strong and probably an anguishing experience.

But since the spread of television, people have not, by and large, watched dramatic events singly, one a month or week. They've read more than one newspaper and magazine for longer than that. The newspaper itself was always a frame for diverse, incommensurable disasters. We watch and read in multiples. The media of the dissemination of dramas have not been substitutive, either; they have been additive. Not newspaper, then film, then radio, then TV, then internet, but all of the above exist today, all the time, in more places, with more common personalities and more crossover of tone, character, content, than before. The claims that fictional dramas exist to "excite," "thrill," or "entertain," like the claims that news exists to "teach," or to "let us know" or "be responsible," have become increasingly incoherent or irrelevant, modeled as they are on viewings of single, focused events. In the era of the total aesthetic environment, the individual case is not as significant as is the effect of scale. While a single drama on television may be thrilling—as it renders the strongest experiences, of life, death, blood, conflict—the aggregate of all dramas on television can hardly be said to be thrilling, since the total effect of television upon a regular viewer is above all *calming*, as any viewer-in-bulk can testify.

This is the paradox. Watching *enough* represented strong experience is associated with states of relaxation and leisure, the extreme loosening and mellowness in which we find a person deliberately "vegetating" in front of the TV—while the walls are painted with criminals' spattered blood, the muscle is pulsating between the doctors' hands, and the hostage is beheaded, and beheaded again, and again, on several competing twenty-four-hour news channels, which no longer promise "up-to-the-minute" but "up-to-the-second" coverage, and show precisely the same events. Over a lifetime, you will also see the same events and scenarios acted out with different faces, sometimes in different genres, some real and some fictional—but "excitement" will very rarely be the reason you turn on the TV.

It used to seem that the news existed as a special case. I think people would agree, at first, if I said that prime time exists for relaxation but the news exists for rigor and truth. Yet what has the news ever been if not also, in some way, calming—or why would one watch the eleven o'clock news before going to bed, as other people take sleeping pills or sip warm milk; why would one watch the six o'clock news, which is even more brutal, more "serious," while eating dinner—when we know in human life that the desire to eat and the ability to sleep are two activities that vanish with genuine disquiet?

With the rise of twenty-four-hour channels, news has become the core and most general case of the total aesthetic environment, because twenty-four-hour news does not play the old game of pretending you can choose to turn it off. Rather, it uses the conceit that there is always something "happening," an experience—though somebody else's—that you *must* also know about, and the TV is only connecting you transparently to phenomena that should be linked to you anyway. This lie is predicated on notions of virtue, citizenship, responsibility.

I say I watch the news to "know." But I don't really know anything. Certainly I can't do anything. I know that there is a war in Iraq, but I knew that already. I know that there are fires and car accidents in my state and in my country, but that, too, I knew already. With each particular piece of footage, I know nothing more than I did before. I feel something, or I don't feel something. One way I am likely to feel is virtuous and "responsible" for knowing more of these things that I can do nothing about. Surely this feeling is wrong, even contemptible. I am not sure anymore what I feel.

What is it like, to watch a human being's beheading? The first showing of the video is bad. The second, fifth, tenth, hundredth are—like one's own experiences—retained, recountable, real, and yet dreamlike. Some describe the repetition as "numbing." "Numbing" is very imprecise. I think the feeling, finally, is of something like envelopment and even satisfaction at having endured the worst without quite caring or being tormented. It is the paradoxically calm satisfaction of having been enveloped in a weak or placid "real" that another person endured as the worst experience imaginable, in his personal frenzy, fear, and desperation, which we view from outside as the simple occurrence of a death.

The old philosophies of aesthetics were based on the experience of a single drama, going back to Aristotle's pity and fear in the witnessing of just one tragedy. Tragedies were presented in small clusters on a special festival day at a rare time of the year. We do not now encounter dramas on designated days of the year. The old aesthetics increasingly slip away when it is not one, or a few, doctors' dramas we watch once a year, but 5,000 episodes of 100 dramas over the course of a lifetime, amid 10,000 other renderings of dramas of equally strong experience; not one representation of a beheading but the same one run 100 times, followed by 1,000 other atrocities themselves rerun. The scale of drama can become a training in how *not* to relate the strong emotions of representations back to your own experience, not so that they unnerve or paralyze you, while you still learn to fashion your own experiences in the narrative manner and style of dramatic representations.

Then, too, with the change of scale, more of our strictly personal experiences are likely to be experienced *simultaneously* with outer dramas, whether "fiction" or "news." The screens continue to proliferate. Televisions play silently with closed captions in the restaurants where I go to dinner. (I remember they used to be only in bars.) They play with sound in the waiting rooms for visitors to the hospital; they play in the waiting rooms for emergency patients. One played in the garage where I had a flat tire repaired, where I saw the drama of a Florida man shot by air marshals. A wide-screen played by the men's changing rooms at Macy's. Flat-screens are on the machines at the gym and on the elevators in office buildings. Airport terminals are full of televised news, and it follows you to the screens on the backs of the seats on planes. Screens are promised on the subway, where the public rationale will be that they will only show news (to justify the remaining minutes of paid advertising)—the drama of the necessary news, which so mendaciously justifies all other drama. A few offices may have TVs on the work floor, where they are redundant, since the drama comes through on the work space itself, the screen of the computer. When I read my email on Yahoo, it is accompanied by headlines of distant events, fifty-six killed, a hundred killed; video clips from movies; ads for the dating sites that will find me a new mate and reconstruct my own life as drama.

Happiness has wound up in an ideology of the need for experiences. Very well. This is our "health" and our quest. But is this happiness-by-experience itself then regulated and moderated by the constant chatter of strong represented experiences, whose effect is not, finally, to stimulate strong experience in their viewers, but to make up some hybrid of temporary relaxation and persistent desire? Does the total aesthetic environment, that is, become anaesthetic as well as aesthetic? We know its advertisements channel desire toward particular products—and don't much mind. That's just advertising. Its dramas also create and channel desire. Suppose those dramas were capable of a paradoxical, anaesthetic attenuation or deferral of all this desire, to the point where desire could be mobilized ceaselessly without pain to the viewer and without personality destruction. This would forestall the conversion to anti-experience—never causing the full and radical crisis that might occur to an unhabituated and unanaesthetized individual, facing all of these dramas and horrors and strong renderings and commercial demands and new needs, as single instances, for the first and only time.

I want to think this is partly right; then the system, and its perilousness, make sense. The trouble then would be that for some people the drama-induced anaesthetic might *wear off.* Their form of experiential illness would represent a breakthrough, in other words, of aesthetic events to their original, singular effects—so that they disturb the person who is supposed to be protected, soothed, and regulated, as if he were now encountering each instance *singly*, at full strength.

If individuals in our society are afflicted suddenly with the inability to take represented experiences in a ceaseless flow, but instead undergo each and every event as if it were happening to *them*—as if fiction were real, and the real (the news networks' medical horrors, beheadings, thousands of deaths) *doubly* real, because publicly attested to and simultaneously experienced as somehow one's own—then no wonder they withdraw. If they feel every outside representation, from however far away it comes, as if it belonged to the context of their private lives and individual drama, then no wonder they tremble. And they may in part have been *asked* to feel things that way—by a system of representations that doesn't truly believe, or wish, that anyone *will*.

("If one had to be taught by fictions," said Epictetus, "I, for my part, should wish for such a fiction as would enable me to live henceforth in peace of mind and free from perturbation. What you on your part wish for is for you yourselves to consider.")

I see: Severed heads. The Extra Value Meal. Kohl-gray eyelids. A holiday sale at Kohl's. Red seeping between the fingers of the gloved hand that presses the wound. "Doctor, can you save him?" "We'll do our best." The dining room of the newly renovated house, done in red. Often a bold color is the best. The kids are grateful for their playroom. The bad guy falls down, shot. The detectives get shot. The new Lexus is now available for lease. On CNN, with a downed helicopter in the background, a peaceful field of reeds waves in the foreground. One after another the reeds are bent, broken, by boot treads advancing with the camera. The cameraman, as savior, locates the surviving American airman. He shoots him dead. It was a terrorist video. They run it again. Scenes from ads: sales, roads, ordinary calm shopping, daily life. Tarpaulined bodies in the street. The blue of the sky advertises the new car's color. Whatever you could suffer will have been recorded in the suffering of someone else. Red Lobster holds a shrimp festival. Clorox gets out blood. Advil stops pain fast. Some of us are going to need something stronger.

I DON'T KNOW WHY ANYONE CRACKS, and the reasons, each time, will be different, deep, and personal. The aesthetic presentations, which seem to be everywhere, as dramas, playing out the strongest experiences—which others can receive in a manner relaxed or blasé—become intolerable. If there was indeed something formerly anaesthetic about this ceaseless flow of strong sensations, then it has just worn off, worn off for oneself *alone* as it often seems, and it is terrifying. The baffled sufferer can't understand what has happened to him.

So he tries to recover the anaesthetic. He may try first the double-dealing strategies, those that add experience in some modalities and preserve you from it in others: alcohol, sex, or another kind of plunge. There are the horrible depressions, ambiguous and painful. There is medicine. There are organized practices and systems, from Buddhism through the many traditions of the East, from Epicureanism and Stoicism back to the origins of the West. Each stands ready to be retrofitted for today. There is organized religion, I forgot to mention. There is staying in your house and never coming out.

There is also the dream of an alternate aesthetic, of a world in which aestheticized experience worked only on things that were *ordinary*, local, small, repetitive, and recalcitrant, on things that really did happen to most of us in the everyday. This would imply a challenge to drama as we know it. Would it be too much to ask for books in which there is no conflict and no disaster but mere daily occurrences, strung together by the calm being who notices them; television shows on which people sit around silently noticing one another, watch sunsets, type, chat, cook meals without teaching the viewer how, and go about their business in the dull but reassuring knowledge that nothing is going to be very different than the day before? Could there be repetition in a state of grace? Could there be "aesthetic" representation, for those for whom the worldly anaesthetic had worn off, while the systematic ideologies seemed too inhuman and restrictive? Could people live a life in the garden, in our world with its many technologies?

What would remain would not be drama, or "experience," but life. Perhaps there is a way back to life, in people's tentative steps in the interstices of this world, if they cannot live on its grid. Circling life from the cluttered outside, one asks its meaning again and again. How to get back to it: by aestheticizing everything, as before, to explode the questing aesthetic? By anaesthetic efforts, as imagined in this essay, to cut down experiences to neutral occurrences incapable of being made over as drama? Meaning starts to seem a perverse thing to ask for, when what we are really asking is what life is when it is not already made over in forms of quest or deferral. Could *this* life be reached—unmediated? Would there be anything there when we found it? +

ECHO EGGEBRECHT, UNTITLED, 2006,
PENCIL ON PAPER, 7 X 8". COURTESY OF THE ARTIST AND NICOLE KLAGSBRUN GALLERY.

THE NEAR-SON

Rebecca Curtis

I KILLED A NEAR-SON TODAY. Naturally I did not tell my lover about it. But when I was at the clinic his ex-girlfriend was there and she recognized me, and when that snitch got home she called my lover on the phone and told him what I'd done. She probably snuck it in as if she didn't mean to let it slip. "Oh I saw Mona today at the clinic," she would have said. "You knew she was there, right? We chatted a bit..." and so forth. We hadn't even chatted a bit.

She walked out of the clinic as I walked in. She was wearing a silver sheath and looked glamorous. In the exit she paused and I did too because she'd blocked my way. She took her sunglasses off and bobbed her chin at me. I guessed she had an idea who I was but wasn't sure, and I knew I should not bob back. But part of me thought: Maybe it means, We're friends. I bobbed back. Her lip curled. She stepped aside and I said, Thanks! and went in and got it done.

When I got home I was thinking, Scot-free, scot-free! I tried to walk normally even though it hurt. My lover was lying down on the couch with a compress on his head. The TV was on the sports channel, but he wasn't watching TV.

How was the mall? he said. But he said it in a dull, sarcastic voice, like he was dead.

I should have known then, but I didn't.

The mall was great! I said. I held up some pretend shopping bags, as if I'd almost bought a million things. Pretty expensive though, I said.

My lover looked at me with his narrow blue eyes, the ones that first convinced me we should really have sex.

My near-son died today, he said. I felt a tingle when you did it.

I knew I was in trouble then. So I hung my head to show I wanted to be forgiven. Even though he was making the tingle up. He got the tingle from his friends, because they all had stories about the tingles they'd felt when their near-sons were dead. Also, ever since his friends had found out they had even one near-son, they'd decided they each had a few dozen. To find out their real number, they multiplied each girlfriend they'd had by four, five, or six. The number came from a formula that involved a woman's height-to-weight ratio, how much money her parents made, and the width of her hips. My lover's friends liked to get together and drink French roast and reminisce, as in, "I almost met my near-son today." They were all great friends. According to them, the way you met your near-son was, you felt the tingle and knew his spirit was close. Or if you were sensitive, you might see him full-blown, about 17 or 18 and about to wave before he vaporized—the only way to know it was him, besides being sensitive, was that he looked like you knew he would, which was a lot like yourself in your prime. The other way to see him was to see a real guy who resembled him, in which case you might confuse the guy for a spirit and say, "Hey near-son, wanna toss a few back?" and the guy would say, "Go screw."

I don't know why you did it, my lover said, or how you could. He adjusted the compress on his head.

I don't know either, I said.

But I had reasons. For one thing, I knew a son would cry all day. For another, I was low on cash. I worked hard as a waitress to support my lover and myself. My lover was an out-of-work fiscal analyst. But what he wanted to analyze, I wasn't sure, and neither was he. The economy was pretty bad. Sometimes my lover spent whole days sitting with his friends, also out-of-work analysts, eating potato chips and drinking beer and discussing how in these dark times no one appreciated analysts. Mostly I didn't care though because his eyes were so blue and he made me forget myself in bed. I forgot myself a lot. But I made enough money to pay the taxes and buy us a lot of ham and bread. I think we both felt if we waited long enough, things would turn good. Everyone we knew felt that way. As in former times, people were waiting for a king to be born. It was said he would be a near-son who'd slip past the forceps, come out alive, and swim for a week in the vat. On the eighth day a nurse would find him. She'd marvel at his perfect toes and powerful legs, then stick him in her purse and bring him home. At home she'd feed him clam chowder and he'd grow strong. By age 4 he'd grow a faint mustache. By 6 he'd start to do little miracles, like turn plain toast into garlic bread. The nurse, who was poor and had once been slutty, would think greedy thoughts at night. Soon she'd ask the boy to do better miracles, like help her and her friends get bigger apartments, and the boy would reprimand her, then explain that he couldn't do real miracles until he became a man and dealt with his mother. After that, he'd say, his work would start. No one was sure what his work was, but everyone agreed that once he started it, the economy would be great. I thought this story was silly. But everyone talked about it all the time and when they did we felt rich, even if we were eating ham and bread.

Now my lover was not looking at me. He'd put the compress back over his head. That afternoon we had to go to a wedding. I was supposed to buy the present. I was supposed to get it at the mall. But obviously I had not. The wedding was for his best friend.

One sec, I said, as if he were still paying attention to me. Then I got dressed in my red silk frock.

Ready! I said. I thought if I was in a good mood he'd get in one too. Let's go get the present, I said.

Do you really think I feel like going to a wedding? he said. But he followed me out to the car.

We went to the mall, and at the mall we went to Whitman's, our favorite store. It had nice silverware and a very fancy line of coffeemakers and dishes, and it was where his best friend had registered. My lover was his best friend's best man, and he'd practiced his toast all week, so he wanted to buy an expensive gift. We walked up to the registron. She wore her black hair in a tight black bun and a shiny black dress that was tight everywhere except at the ankles, where it poofed out into an umbrella skirt. We told her what party we were with and she looked up the list.

We want to buy something expensive, my lover said. It's for my best friend. He took my wallet out of my purse.

I knew it was practically empty so I hummed a song about how key chains make pretty good gifts.

The registron lifted her glasses. They have signed on for the titanium pepper mill, she said. It is yet unbought. Will that do?

My lover must have looked skeptical, because she said, It prepares fresh pepper at a verbal command, with a choice from among five grades: very coarse, medium coarse, coarse, not coarse, and regular. It was designed in France. It is yet unbought. Will it do?

Oh yes, my lover said.

It is $500, the registron said, and her eyes turned from brown to black.

No problem, my lover said.

He opened my wallet. He found a five-dollar bill and a ten.

He looked at me. Then he looked at the wallet. Where's the money? he said.

What money? I said.

This morning you had $500, he said.

I smiled a silly smile. But he did not smile back. I turned to the registron. Do you have anything cheaper? I said.

Then my lover started to cry. He'd realized where the money went.

The registron's eyes teared over with pity. What's wrong? she said.

I opened my mouth but didn't speak. I hoped he wouldn't tell her what I'd done.

Nothing, he said.

I sighed in relief. He was going to be discreet.

My near-son died today, he said.

I'm so sorry, the registron said. Her name was Alberta. It said so on her tag. You have Alberta's sympathy, she said. Was he many weeks?

I could see my lover mentally counting. At least twelve, he said.

Terrible, Alberta said. What a loss.

He might have had toes, my lover said.

No toes, I said.

I couldn't help that. I knew I shouldn't have said it. I should have let him grieve. But the thing looked more like cheese than a near-son and I was getting defensive. Plus he'd lied about the twelve weeks. It was more like six or seven.

Toes or no toes, my lover said. He was still my near-son to me.

Who did it? Alberta said. If I may ask.

I looked around the store. I'll just look around the store, I said.

She did it, my lover said.

Oh, no, Alberta said. She looked at me. I'm sorry to hear that.

Yeah well, I said. Me too. Because it hurt like a motherfucker, I'll tell you that.

I was trying to be funny but no one laughed.

How can you say that? my lover said angrily. You're walking and talking. Think about how it hurt him!

I made a point of checking my watch. It was 2:48. The wedding was at three. I wanted us to get there and to have a good time. I felt bad about the near-son myself. If it had grown up it might have been cute. But as I said, we were broke, and I don't like kids. Usually my lover and I got along well. I loved him. When he became unemployed, I told him I'd support him as long as he needed and that if an analyst was really what he was meant to be, he shouldn't feel pressured to do other work, like wash dishes at a restaurant or paint government tenement houses. And I was keeping that promise. My lover was an analyst and nothing else.

I turned to Alberta. What's your cheapest thing? I said.

The key chain was $14.99 and we couldn't afford the silver-sky gift wrap, but I thought it looked nice in the blue tissue paper that Alberta gave us for free.

My lover perked up on the way to the wedding. He even practiced his speech, and every time he read it I clapped. We arrived late, but we saw my lover's best friend and his best friend's fiancée make their vows, and we watched all the parents and relatives cry, and then my lover started crying too and I thought, Oh no, now he'll blab it to everyone, but he stopped when everyone else stopped, so I figured it was normal wedding crying.

At the dinner I was starving, because I'd been told not to eat for two days before the operation. I put three salmon steaks and two partridges on my plate.

Control yourself, my lover said. So I put one of the partridges on his plate for me to eat later. The place where they had the dinner was the banquet hall of an old church. There were tall stained-glass windows and walls made of huge limestone blocks. The food was delicious, especially the partridges, and even though my lover said he couldn't eat, I hoped it was because he was nervous about his speech. I held his hand under the table, and for a while he let me. Then he shook it off. We were sitting with some people I didn't know. I'd been hoping he'd introduce me, but he didn't. I said something about it and he shrugged. Then he pointed to two people far across the room and said, That's Bobby. That's Joe.

They didn't look up so I said, Now I know, and ate my fish.

When the forks hit the glasses, my lover stood up.

He walked to the podium, which stood atop a granite platform at the front of the room. Everyone stopped talking. My lover adjusted the microphone. He brushed a hand through his hair. He grinned in the way that showed his teeth and meant he was out of sorts. Benny, he said. That was the groom's name. Benny, how long have we been friends?

There was silence.

I don't know, Benny said.

There was silence again.

Well, a long time, my lover said. And all that time we've been friends.

Benny smiled.

This is a good wedding, my lover said. People nodded. My lover said, To your happiness! and everyone drank, and then he said, Many happy returns! and we all drank again. My lover wiped sweat off his nose with a finger.

I've known Benny since I was 12, he said. We had a group of friends. We were very close. Benny was the first to grab a boob.

People laughed. But I was worried because none of this was part of his speech.

Benny, my lover said. Remember when we were teenagers, and we went hiking in the national park, and you pooped on the sacred Indian monuments?

My lover waited, but nobody laughed.

Right then the drugs they'd given me at the clinic wore off. I felt a sharp pain like forks poking my insides. I crossed my legs but it didn't stop. So I made my face normal and under the table I held my hand over my crotch. When I looked back at my lover, he was frowning at me.

Actually, he said. This is not my speech. I've been extemporizing. I had a speech. But I can't give it because something sad happened today.

What happened? Benny said.

My lover's blue eyes narrowed. The thing that happened is sad, he said. If I tell you it'll dampen your wedding.

I was thinking: Crap. Also: Ow. I shoved my fist into my crotch.

Tell me, Benny said. Tell us all.

My lover glanced at me. It's all right, he said. Let's have the next speech.

We want to hear, Benny said. Throughout the audience were murmurs of agreement.

The forks poked my crotch hard and without thinking I opened my mouth. NEXT SPEECH, I said.

I was sorry as soon as I said it. I looked around like "Who said it?" so someone else might think they had. But people glanced in my direction.

My lover's chin lifted. I had a near-son today, he said.

On a wedding day, someone said.

Yes, my lover said. Then he pointed at me. She did it, he said. All around the room were large circular wooden tables and each one was full of people and all the people at each table glared at me.

My lover leaned toward Benny.

Pssssst, he said.

People leaned forward to listen.

Benny, my lover said. I wanted to get a good gift. But I had to get you a key chain because she spent the gift money.

Benny frowned. I have a key chain.

I know, my lover said. She spent the money.

Oh, Benny said.

My lover adjusted his tie. Actually, he said, in a happier voice, addressing the crowd, I do have a speech, a totally different one I made up at eleven-oh-five today when I felt the tingle.

My lover looked up. He had nothing in his hands. He must have memorized it. I was impressed because he's not good at memorization. He held his head high and said:

Benny. You are married today. Congratulations. But you should also congratulate me. I had a near-son today.

A few people clapped.

He weighed a pound, my lover said. He was blond, like all the Mintch men. His age was fourteen weeks.

Six weeks, I said quietly. Half an ounce. Looked like cheese. But no one heard.

Eighteen weeks, my lover said, making it up as he went. The surgeons said that, remarkably, he sang a song as he died. If he lived, he would have been a jazz musician. You like jazz music yourself, Benny.

Benny nodded.

What do you say to the death of a musician? my lover said.

I love jazz, Benny said.

Yes I know, my lover said. But what do you say to a death?

There was silence. Someone said, Boo hiss. Then a lot of other people said it, Boo hiss. The guests at my table pushed their chairs back. I wanted to say, "Why are you standing up?" but I didn't. A minute later the guests at the tables near mine got up and walked off too. The ones who couldn't find seats leaned against the limestone walls.

What do we do, Benny? my lover said. What do we do about this?

At that point I knew that kiss he'd given me when I'd eaten the second partridge was a real trick kiss. I'd heard about other times like this and none of them were good. But I knew the thing to do was not to seem afraid. I'd heard from the other waitresses at the restaurant that you had a chance of getting forgiven if you pretended to be sorry. I stood up and faced the crowd.

I cleared my throat. What can I do? I said. How can I make it up?

You can't, my lover said. It's too late.

Maybe it's not, I said. I'll go check!

But the exit was far away. And it was a door that led to another room, not to the outside, and some people were standing in front of it.

I felt desperate then and said the first thing that came to my head. I guess that I made a mistake, I said. However, I think you should know that in this case, the near-son was very small. It only weighed half an ounce. And even though it was precious to me, it didn't know the alphabet.

No one laughed.

It was smaller than a tonsil, I said.

Boo hiss, someone said. Boo hiss.

And furthermore, I said, a bit mad now, this bit about the tingle is bullstuff. Nothing happened at eleven-oh-five. That is just way off.

I thought you'd say that, my lover said. In fact I knew you would. Because I made that part up, about eleven-oh-five, as a test. So let me guess. Was it one-fifteen?

No, I said.

I didn't think so, he said. Because I didn't feel a tingle right then. Was it noon?

No, I said.

He paused. Ow! he said. Ow! He grabbed his own neck and squeezed it, then punched himself in the gut. He was acting out what he thought his near-son must have felt. Ow, ow! he said. Does it look like it hurts?

No one spoke. Then several people said, Yes.

Because you know what I really felt, my lover said, addressing the crowd, was a slow steady tingle all day. And do you know why?

Why? everyone said.

Because, my lover said, today was the day that my near-son was dead!

Everyone cheered then, and I knew that my speech had not been good enough.

You assassinate an assassin, my lover said. And you punch a bully. But what do you do when a near-son is dead?

Quickly I prepared a speech in my head. I knew that whatever I said had to be full of pathos and had to convince everyone in the room that as a person I had many facets. I thought of my good qualities. There weren't many. Several times in the last month, I had helped an old lady cross the street. But it was the same old lady, she lived nearby. As for my interests, I liked walking through the woods, reading books in the bathtub, and having sex. But everybody liked those things. I knew there must be something momentous about me. But I couldn't think of what it was. So I decided to make something up.

I see auras, I said.

No one paid any attention. All the people who had been seated in the red room and the green room of the church were now in our room, the blue one, and they'd gathered along the walls.

I looked at my lover. I love you, I said.

My lover glanced at me. I love you too, he said. Then he looked back at Benny.

I ask you as a friend, my lover said. As my best friend and a handsome guy. What do we do about this?

The crowd moved forward.

I stretched to my full height, five-three.

I'm not sorry, I said.

They were almost to me so I got up on my chair. I'm a waitress, I said. I serve mostly dinners. Sometimes I do breakfast buffet. For the last three years I paid my lover's rent. I pay the gas bill and sometimes I take him to movies. I do it because he's an analyst, and if I'm not around then who will support him?

Hands yanked my dress.

There's no such thing as a near-son, I said. It's just a story. Please don't touch me. But that was all I got to say. +

UNITED FLIGHT 93 RECORDER, GOVERNMENT EXHIBIT P200066 01-455-A IN THE TRIAL OF ZACHARIAS MOUSSAOUI. GETTY IMAGES.

TORTURE AND THE KNOWN UNKNOWNS

Keith Gessen

IN THE IMMEDIATE AFTERMATH of the September 11 attacks, one insistent strain of commentary focused on the way in which Western societies had created, by their technological innovations and their open, democratic procedures, the ideal conditions for highly motivated individuals intent on destroying them. It was an old Marxist idea—that any political-economic system will necessarily sow the seeds of its demise. The terrorists used the fantastic technologies developed in the West, the satellite and cell phones, the internet, and finally the airplanes, and turned them against their inventors. "It was the system itself," wrote Baudrillard, "which created the objective conditions for this brutal retaliation." More ominously—because no one was about to start rolling back cell phone and internet and airplane use in the West—it was said that they took advantage of our open borders, our freedom of movement, of how nice we were. "They relied upon everything from the vastness of the internet to the openness of our society," FBI director Robert Mueller told Congress. They plotted for years and we knew nothing about it.

It was a compelling irony, and partly true. But what also began to emerge, as the newspapers and commissioners launched their analyses of the failure of the CIA and FBI and NSA to share information properly—and what has emerged more recently in book upon book upon book—was just how stupendously well the surveillance and information-gathering technologies of our system had in fact worked. We knew a huge amount; it seemed all we did was know. Over the years, the NSA had intercepted thousands of relevant emails and phone conversations; in Yemen, the FBI had fruitfully interrogated several key figures in the bombing of the USS *Cole*; in Kuala Lumpur, in January 2000, the CIA had asked local intelligence agents to monitor a major al Qaeda "summit"—and within days received photos, reports, and even digital traces from the computers the summiteers used at internet cafés in the city. In the first days after the attacks, there seemed to be some question, in the media, as to who was responsible. In fact, as soon as the CIA saw the flight manifests, at around 11 AM on September 11, they recognized two al Qaeda operatives, Khalid al-Midhar and Nawaf al-Hazmi: they had even known that these two were in the country. That this incredible amount of precise information was not properly shared, that it was not acted on in a timely fashion, that it was misinterpreted along the way: all this is true. But the amount of it, much of it collected with the technology that was supposedly our undoing, was—as Richard Clarke said upon seeing the first images sent back from Afghanistan by an unmanned Predator drone back in September 2000—truly astonishing.

There was a gap, but it was not technological. The problem was "humint," in intelligence-community parlance—human intelligence. The CIA had no "assets" in the al Qaeda camps (no humint on the ground); when a Western intelligence agency did manage to infiltrate al Qaeda, they did not know what to do with the information (no humint at home base). And finally, this most of all, we couldn't quite understand, on a human level, why someone would want to blow us up (no emotional humint, so to speak). The failures compounded one another. It's been speculated, for example, that the reason the CIA failed to alert the FBI to the fact that two known al Qaeda operatives had entered the country was that they were hoping to "turn" them; so the initial failure to infiltrate al Qaeda led to the catastrophic failure to keep an eye on al-Midhar and al-Hazmi. The intelligence community would not begin grasping the truth about al Qaeda—it would not make the leap, as FBI agent Dan Coleman put it, "from information to knowledge"—until it had camps of its own, not for training but for torture, and until it began interrogating people, and one person in particular, in brightly illuminated rooms.

THAT PERSON, KHALID SHAIKH MOHAMMED, grew up in a prosperous middle-class family in Kuwait, then attended college in the US, at North Carolina A&T State, where he received a degree in engineering. He spent his time there with other Muslim students; they mostly gathered in one another's rooms and discussed the problems of the Arab world. Otherwise KSM (as he is known in the literature) was quiet and unremarkable. When it emerged, not long after September 11, that he was the mastermind and organizer of the entire plot, his old physics professor expressed to the Associated Press the befuddlement of physics professors everywhere when their students begin to blow things up.

Other facts were known about KSM before he was arrested. He was not a devout Muslim, for example. When he lived in Manila while hatching an earlier plot, he was a frequent client of the strip clubs and even courted a pretty dentist that he'd met. He was vain and vainglorious: his initial plan for the 9/11 hijackings was to capture ten planes and crash nine of them into strategic targets. The tenth would be hijacked by KSM himself, who would land it, "release the women and children," and then make a televised statement to the world. We knew also that while equally senior al Qaeda members had gone into hiding—and only bin Laden himself had more cause to go into hiding than KSM—KSM had remained in the big Pakistani cities, had remained operational. He knew that if he didn't move around much or use the phone, he'd be safe. But he moved around and used the phone. He even invited an Al Jazeera reporter to his house in Karachi. The reporter later indicated its location to his bosses in the government of Qatar, who promptly told the CIA.

Perhaps KSM wanted to be caught. Perhaps for a man who's spent time in the States, the mere admiration of the Muslim world is not enough. In this he was different from his boss, bin Laden. The offense given bin Laden was feudal and local in nature: the Saudi government and its friends in the West would not bend to his princely will. The offense against KSM was modern, globalized: like Dostoevsky's young men in big cities, he had been ignored.* The one direct statement of KSM's that has reached the outside world in the past three years was introduced as part of exhibit 941 in the trial of Zacharias Moussaoui. In it, KSM, at pains to distinguish his modus operandi from that of his enemy, brags that al Qaeda had performed its operations with a minimum of paperwork—something, KSM claims, "the Western mind cannot understand."

But we can keep things off the books, his interrogators might have replied. This interrogation, for example: Which books, in your opinion, is it on?

---

* In a similar vein, statements of al Qaeda fighters who survived the devastating aerial bombardment of their positions by US forces in Afghanistan in the fall of 2001 have repeatedly expressed outrage at the refusal of American troops to *face* them.

○ ○ ○

THE ARREST OF KSM IN KARACHI was officially announced in March 2003. It took place in the middle of the night, producing a now-iconic photograph of a portly, unshaven man in a shirt that lay off the neck in all directions, revealing a very hairy chest and back and shoulders, his chin thrust out and scowling at the camera. The FBI had taken to calling him the "Forrest Gump of international terrorism," for his habit of showing up at some point in every major operation they encountered. But this was not a sweet lucky half-wit staring from the photo. This was Bluto Blutarsky.

KSM was interrogated by the CIA for three long years. Very few people knew where, exactly. It was speculated that KSM was in one of the secret CIA prisons in Jordan, or Romania, or Thailand. Others said he was on an American warship, far out at sea, a ship so secure that any vessel that got within five miles of it would be obliterated, no questions asked. Still others said he was simply in a holding cell on one of the enormous bases our military constructs in sympathetic countries like Germany, Japan, and Afghanistan. When trying to get access to KSM for the purposes of their investigation, the two former Congressmen who headed up the 9/11 Commission were told that President Bush himself did not know where KSM was.

In the meantime, his name would pop up in reports from the front lines. He was invoked whenever the Bush White House sought to justify its position on the Geneva Conventions, KSM being, in the words of journalist Ron Suskind, "the theoretical justification for all the administration's legal maneuvering on the question of torture." In late 2001, when the first detainees began coming in from the invasion/dragnet of Afghanistan, a CIA agent told the *Wall Street Journal* that the time had come to play a little "smacky-face" with the other side. No one doubted that KSM would get the smacky-face treatment. A list of interrogation techniques approved by the government began to be spoken of; it was later confirmed by ABC News. Compared to the interminable lists of discrete torture practices documented by the various commissions investigating Abu Ghraib, this one turned out to be touchingly brief:

1. Attention grab
2. Attention slap (to the face)
3. Belly slap
4. Long-time standing (sleep deprivation)

    5. Cold cell

    6. Waterboarding

In 2004, the *New York Times* matter-of-factly stated that KSM was being deprived of sleep, subjected to cold temperatures, and waterboarded—as per the list.

It could have been worse. KSM could have been handed over to the Egyptians (for the past ten years, our largest prisoner-trading partner), where he would have received electrical shocks to the genitals; they'd have hung him from his limbs and kept him in a cell with filthy water up to his knees. Had we given KSM to the Moroccans, as we gave Binyam Mohammed to the Moroccans, they might have covered his entire body, including his penis, in tiny little cuts from a razor—cuts that were very painful but shallow, leaving no scars. Uzbekistan, an emerging player in the international torture-exchange circuit, is said to be partial to the partial boiling of a hand or an arm. This is not even to mention the regimes of the past, with their own idiosyncratic interests and proclivities, to which we might have sent KSM in a time machine. The Iraqis, under the Baath, enjoyed seeing what kind of changes they could wreak on a body before it died—so, for example, they cut off ears. The Germans during the Second World War were also famously experimental in their tortures, though primarily they hung people by their arms, until their arms popped out of their sockets—this is what they did to the philosopher Jean Amery.

But KSM had not been sent to any of these places. He was in American custody, though not exactly in America, and our torture was mild and pleasant by comparison (except when it wasn't). In a long *Atlantic* essay on the "dark art of interrogation," from late 2003, the investigative/imaginative journalist Mark Bowden described the look on KSM's face in the photograph taken on the night of his arrest: "He had woken up into a nightmare." The very no-placeness of KSM's imprisonment soon emerged as a key component of this nightmare. Egypt, Morocco, Uzbekistan—these were actual places, with foods and cultures and a climate. But KSM wasn't there. "In this place," Orwell wrote of the interrogation center in *1984*, "you could not feel anything, except pain and the foreknowledge of pain." That's where KSM was.

His value as an interrogatee has been hotly debated. The Bush Administration claimed he was talking, but Bush has repeatedly and cynically lied about the value of intelligence extracted from captives. Others nonetheless confirmed it. "He's singing like a bird," a European intelligence official boasted to the *Times* in early 2004. In the *9/11 Report*, issued in mid-2004, KSM talks and talks; in fact, despite the inability of the *Report*'s authors ever to meet, hear, or even read a transcript of KSM's interrogations (they received interrogation summaries), they felt comfortable enough with his testimony that in the main text and especially in the footnotes they humanized him to a considerable degree with the use of semi-emotive verbs of attribution. "KSM notes," we are told, "KSM claims," "KSM adds," "KSM also contends," "KSM maintains." On the other hand, Ron Suskind reported that KSM received the harshest treatment possible in his first sessions with CIA interrogators but refused to give up anything. (The interrogators became so desperate that they threatened to harm KSM's little children, who were also in custody; KSM did not care. "They will be with Allah in a better place," he said.) According to this account, KSM's subsequent disclosures about the "planes operation" were proffered in a spirit of collegiality, one spymaster to another.

Finally, with the increased public scrutiny and with any further intelligence value exhausted, KSM was transferred to Guantánamo Bay in September 2006. The next month, *Time* magazine reported what FBI forensics experts had been asserting since shortly after KSM's arrest: that he was the man who had severed from its body the head of *Wall Street Journal* reporter Daniel Pearl, then held it up, by its hair, before the camera.

So WE KNEW EVERYTHING ABOUT KSM, and also we knew nothing. We knew him as a social type, and we knew him as a psychological type, and we could identify his hand on three seconds of video posted on the internet. But we didn't know what it was like to *be* him, to face down the West with the lone purpose of wreaking havoc on it. (Bin Laden might be said to have an ideology; KSM has only his professionalism.) Yet by the time we sent him to Camp Delta, the successor to Camp X-Ray, an accidental Defense Department name that accidentally suggested that it was created to look inside the brains of individuals, KSM's brain had already yielded all that it was going to yield.

We had run into a classic epistemological problem. At the beginning of the war on terror, some intellectuals argued that the events should become a catalyst for a national ideological mobilization—"the fight is for democracy." Instead the war, which began with a failure of intelligence, immediately turned into an enormous mission for the gathering of knowledge. Book after book has promised to help Americans "know the enemy," the better presumably to spot him in our midst. Academics produce monographs about Islam, or Iraq, and these are then literally issued to the occupying army. (They sit and read them in their armored Stryker vehicles.) How it must have pained Edward Said, originator of the idea that Western study of Eastern cultures is a form of domination, to see, toward the end of his life, that his long-time nemesis Bernard Lewis was turning into a national celebrity. Or perhaps it gave him a dark pleasure, to have his theories so neatly confirmed. Professor Lewis of Princeton was not being invited to the White House, after all, because the people there entertained a speculative curiosity about the East.

We were going to *know* the enemy. And then? Well, and then—we were going to kill him. The trouble for the producers of this knowledge is that narrative demands sympathy and identification. The *9/11 Report* made KSM sound like a lovable eccentric—not least of all by giving him a cute triple initial, as this essay has also done. (It also created a dramatic story, almost despite itself, from the relationship between United Flight 93 pilot-hijacker Ziad Jarrah and his long-time girlfriend, Aysel Senguen.) Suskind's *The One Percent Doctrine*, which is devastating on the Bush Administration and takes a strong anti-CIA position on the question of torture, nonetheless evinces a great affection for CIA director George Tenet. Lawrence Wright, whose *The Looming Tower: Al-Qaeda and the Road to 9/11* is the best journalistic account of the rise of al Qaeda and the American intelligence officers who tried to stop it, really likes the FBI's John O'Neill, the Saudi Prince Turki al-Faisal, and, eventually, bin Laden himself. Only Peter Bergen, the dean of bin Laden studies in the anglophone world, manages to avoid the pitfall of narrative, and this in an oral history. Throughout his fascinating *The Osama bin Laden I Know*, Bergen expresses frustration with the clumsiness of American attempts to physically capture bin Laden: the failure to keep watch over Al Jazeera headquarters was foolish, while the refusal to hunt down bin Laden at Tora Bora was downright suspicious. In the afterword to the paperback edition, Bergen goes further, speculating as to bin Laden's hideout (in the so-called tribal areas of northwest Pakistan, near Kashmir, but also near enough to modern facilities that he can make his propaganda videos) and even proffering a guess as to where bin Laden's *wives* may be hiding. "And then, of course," Bergen continues,

> bin Laden may make a mistake that reveals his location. In that case American Predator drones, which are armed with Hellfire missiles and can provide real-time video of their targets, have proved successful in killing several al Qaeda leaders both in Pakistan and Yemen.

This is taking the knowledge mobilization to its logical endpoint, and with the perfect weapon, at that: initially a magic surveillance device, the Predator was armed with its now famous Hellfire missiles after September 11.

And yet even this—a scholar advocating the assassination of the subject of his research—cannot be said to implicate the knowledge-mobilization in a murderous orientalism. (Hannah Arendt, too, for all her mockery of the Israeli trial of Adolf Eichmann, endorsed his execution.) Because one thing we've learned from this presidential administration is that power will use knowledge just as it pleases; this has been the peculiar theoretical contribution of the twin epistemologists of the Bush White House, Dick Cheney and Donald Rumsfeld.

Cheney is the key. Suskind's *One Percent Doctrine* is named for a concept articulated by Cheney very soon after September 11: "If there is a one percent chance that [something might happen]," he told a meeting of the national security apparatus, "we need to treat it as a certainty in terms of our response." Taken literally—and how else were his employees to take it?—Cheney's doctrine is bold and startling. He sees that, despite its vast electronic surveillance machinery, the US has no human means to turn the information reliably into knowledge; in fact there is no means at all with which to create the knowledge that we seek. So Cheney obliterates the difference. Under the one percent doctrine, all information is already knowledge—even bad information. And let God sort them out.

Cheney's counterpart was Rumsfeld; really they were like a comedy duo. Where Cheney had his one percent doctrine of ironclad epistemological certainty, Rumsfeld had a kind of politics of epistemological despair. "There are the known knowns," he famously said, "and the known unknowns. But there are also the unknown unknowns." Later on, in a private memo: "We lack metrics to know whether we're winning the war on terror." This last has been roundly mocked—"An exponential increase in the number of terrorist attacks seems to be one relevant metric," writes Bergen—and yet on the face of it it's perfectly reasonable. We might not lack metrics in general, but the old metrics (Rumsfeld had a restless old man's hatred of old things) were out of date. The comment was disturbing, however, as an expression of what might be called Rumsfeld's 99 percent doctrine. Cheney would immediately act on antiterrorist intelligence that had a one percent chance of being true; Rumsfeld would fail to act on information that seemed about 99 percent true. These remain the essential doctrines of the Bush Administration even post-Rumsfeld, because they've been proved so wonderfully effective in an age of a prostrate media. Cheney told us that we were in grave danger (true enough) and the danger was being interdicted at every turn (impossible), while Rumsfeld kept telling us we were winning the war. It worked so long as people kept believing them. Then, just before the Congressional elections, it stopped working; Rumsfeld was fired. By that point, the damage was done. We were catastrophically stranded in Iraq. And then, as if to mock all the people who claimed that Rumsfeld's greatest crime was not sending in enough troops, George Bush announced that what America really needed was a larger military.

TRADITIONALLY, COUNTRIES FACED with a knowledge crisis (brought about by rapid social or ideological dislocations) have turned to their novelists. Our own writers have tried to be helpful, too. John Updike wrote a book called *Terrorist*, about a Muslim boy in New Jersey who joins a terrorist group and sets out to perform a suicide operation; Martin Amis, faced with the first footnote of the *9/11 Report*, which admitted that it could discover no reason why Mohamed Atta drove up to Maine from Boston on the eve of the attacks only to fly back to Boston the next morning, wrote a story to explain it.

Yet, for better and worse, the authors were so interested in their perennial concerns that they hardly noticed the terrorists. Amis's Atta is constipated, a kind of below-the-belt objective correlative for his psychic condition—just as Amis's Stalin is a mental case and Amis's working-class characters all have sexual issues (indeed, that may be why they're working-class). Meanwhile Updike's teenage terrorist, Ahmad, turns out to be a remarkable observer—a savant, really—of small visual, tactile, and even olfactory details. He is supposed to blow up a truck, and himself, during the rush hour commute from New Jersey into Manhattan, but "the pattern of the wall tiles and of the exhaust-darkened tiles of the ceiling—countless receding repetitions of squares like giant graph paper rolled into a third dimension—explodes outward in Ahmad's mind's eye in the gigantic fiat of Creation"—and that's just the Holland Tunnel! He refuses to blow himself up. How can he, when the world—the world of Updike, anyway—is so filled with imagery and language and the names of things? Updike's terrorist never had a chance.

In a similar way, the American writer doesn't stand a chance. The deeply offensive conspiracy theories about the September 11 planes—that they were shot down by missiles, that they *were* missiles, that Jews were emailed about the missiles in advance—emerge in large part from a kind of vanity: *I* will tell you what really happened. But they must also be related, and the vanity itself related, to the awesome apparatus of knowledge formation that immediately kicked into gear after the attacks and has not ceased churning for a moment since. It is a classic divergence between people's political power (which has remained constant or decreased) and their social power, expressed in this case in their immediate, unfettered access (through the near perfection of online search and retrieval technologies) to information in quantities previously imagined only by science fiction. Philip Roth once said the American writer's imagination was embarrassed by the mad fertile inventiveness of American reality. The more accurate statement for our own time is that the American writer is embarrassed by the myriad ways in which knowledge can be harvested.

So far, the most shocking, moving, and in their way literary texts that have emerged from the enormous post-9/11 knowledge project—Bergen's remarkable interviews with people who fought alongside bin Laden in Afghanistan; the ideologically confused and yet compelling jihadi pronouncements; the bizarre and revealing statements of American military men—have been closer in their formal characteristics to modernist literature than the novels of our contemporaries, which have mostly lost interest in modernism. Jason Burke, for example, in his very good early journalistic-academic book, *Al Qaeda*, transcribed an interview with a young jihadi in Iraqi Kurdistan who had been sent by his masters to blow up the local office run by the leftist PUK:

> I went to Abu Bakr al-Tauhidi and spent three days with him. He spoke to me about ishtishad and faith and jihad and my duty. On the third day after morning prayer I went into a car to Said Sadiq again and went to the same house and I

slept until lunchtime and ate and then waited until *Ushr* prayer and then put on my [explosives] jacket and went with my host to the bus stop. It was just after five PM but I had no watch. I was calm and not at all nervous. I was thinking about paradise. He paid one dinar to the driver and I got on the bus that went through the bazaar and I got down just before the PUK office and walked up to it with the switch in my pocket and my hand on it. I walked up to the peshmerga at the door and gave him the name of a man who I thought would be inside and said I had come to see him and he said what is that underneath your shirt and he spoke with the accent of my home town and I said nothing and he asked again and I said 'It's TNT,' and then they arrested me.

This is incredible. Burke had spent considerable time in Kurdistan, so it's possible he was not using an interpreter; still, the decision to make the failed suicide bomber sound like Quentin Compson was his. Thus the stylistic innovations of modernism, which tried to record in print the way the mind processed language, survive in a secondary art, journalism, just as they still survive in movies.

The most terrible text of all to emerge from September 11—the transcript of the cockpit recorder from United Flight 93—did not pass through any hands, but was captured by a little box that survived a crash into a Pennsylvania field at a speed of almost 600 miles an hour. For several years, the FBI refused to release the transcript: it was horrible, they said, and there was no need for it to be in the public domain. The *9/11 Report* summarized the recording briefly, but the full transcript was not made available until April 2006, during the Moussaoui trial. At that point it was published in the *New York Times*.

The transcript does not tell the full story of the flight, but it does capture three crucial moments: the pilot-hijacker Ziad Jarrah's initial announcement to the passengers that the plane has been hijacked; the final moments of the flight, as the passengers attempt to break down the cockpit door and the hijackers decide to crash the plane; and the murder of a flight attendant, Deborah Welsh.

There is almost nothing, reading it, that is not shocking, but one of the strangest aspects of the published transcript is its resemblance, on the page, to a work of modernist theater. Until the last century, theater had been based on the convention that, though mimetic in the sense that it looked like real life, it would allow people to speak their minds in a way they could never do in real life, in dramatic situations such as rarely actually happened. A certain kind of modernist playwright (Beckett, O'Neill, Pinter) stripped theater of this convention of fine speech in order to depict the latent violence of human interactions without it. This is the shock of the transcript: the sudden pressure put on words in a situation of life and death.

The transcript begins with a misunderstanding: Jarrah tries to tell the passengers that the flight has been hijacked (in an ordinary way, with a bomb), but accidentally tells this instead to ground control in Cleveland.

09:31:57	Ladies and Gentlemen: Here the captain, please sit down keep remaining seating. We have a bomb on board. So sit.
09:32:09	Er, uh... Calling Cleveland Center... You're unreadable. Say again slowly.

Jarrah never attempts to communicate with Cleveland—he has no reason to, as he intends to crash into the Capitol building. At this point the hijackers—Saeed al-Ghamdi, Ahmad al-Haznawi, Ahmed al-Nami, and Jarrah—have locked themselves into the cockpit. They have stabbed the pilots with knives and box-cutters. Deborah Welsh is trapped inside with them, and now she is heard on the recorder pleading for her life as one of the so-called "muscle hijackers," either al-Ghamdi, al-Haznawi, or al-Nami, none of whom knew English at all well, all of whom were from poor areas of Saudi Arabia, tries to tell her to sit down.

09:34:27	Please, please, please...
09:34:28	Down.
09:34:29	Please, please, don't hurt me...
09:34:30	Down. No more.
09:34:31	Oh God.
09:34:32	Down, down, down.
09:34:33	Sit down.
09:34:34	Shut up.
09:34:42	No more.

As the tape continues, several conversations are happening at once. One of the hijackers is threatening Welsh; Jarrah is consulting with one of the others about the controls (in Arabic, marked by italics); and occasionally Cleveland still pipes in. Finally, the hijacker negotiating with the flight attendant slits her throat and announces to the others that he's done so.

09:35:15	Sit down, sit down, sit down.
09:35:17	Down.
09:35:18	*What's this?*
09:35:19	Sit down. Sit down. You know, sit down.
09:35:24	No, no, no.
09:35:30	Down, down, down, down.
09:35:32	Are you talking to me?
09:35:33	No, no, no. [Unintelligible.]
09:35:35	*Down in the airport.*
09:35:39	Down, down.
09:35:40	I don't want to die.
09:35:41	No, no. Down, down.
09:35:42	I don't want to die. I don't want to die.
09:35:44	No, no. Down, down, down, down, down, down.
09:35:47	No, no, please.
09:35:57	No.
09:37:06	That's it. Go back.
09:37:06	That's it. Sit down.
09:37:36	*Everything is fine. I finished.*
09:38:36	Yes.

Jarrah, the commotion behind him stilled, gets back on the plane's public address system and speaks again to the passengers.

09:39:11	Ah. Here's the captain; I would like to tell you all to remain seated. We have a bomb aboard, and we are going back to the airport, and we have our demands. So, please remain quiet.

If you had read the *9/11 Report* before the transcript, you'd have thought of Jarrah as the most complex and recalcitrant of the hijackers because of his relationship with Aysel Senguen, who became his girlfriend while both were students in Germany. Their romance became more rather than less intimate as the operation approached; the *Report* speaks of the "hundreds of emails" they exchanged during his year in the States, and it even comes to seem—when Senguen visits Jarrah in Florida and even attends a class at flight school—like he might just call the whole thing off, for love. The recent film, *United 93*, takes a similar view of Jarrah.

The transcript here reveals something different about Ziad Jarrah. After Welsh is murdered not five feet from where he sits at the controls, his English improves.

THE HISTORY OF SEPTEMBER 11 is a history of technology. The telephone was central: In the years before September 11, one of the most valuable sources of information available to the American intelligence services was the phone number of Abu al-Zubaydah, a key al Qaeda operations manager. The trail of his phone calls, which the counterterrorism unit displayed on a map of the globe, created a diagram of the al Qaeda network, at least geographically. Bin Laden himself stayed off the phone, sensing (especially after the Russian and Israeli militaries began using cell phones to kill people) that the West had scored a dialectical reversal in the technology wars, turning the terrorists' increasing reliance on advanced technology against them. He now communicates exclusively through human messengers.

The history of the history of 9/11, the historiography, is also a history of technology: of what it can and cannot do. Much of the reconstruction of what occurred on September 11 was a reconstruction of phone calls—by the passengers on the flights, by the people trapped on the upper floors of the World Trade towers, or by those on the phone when the planes hit. In the *9/11 Report*, we learn that the standard time given for the crash of Flight 93 is not uncontroversial; but the report confirms it with authority. "The 10:03:11 impact time," it writes,

> is supported by previous National Transportation Safety Board analysis and by evidence from the Commission staff's analysis of radar, the flight data recorder, infrared satellite data, and air traffic control transmission.

These technologies can fix the precise time of the crash to the second; they are awesome. But—and this is the point—they are not enough. They will never be enough. Because the Global War on Terror is a war of total information mobilization. When you go through security now at an airport, you watch as the guards gaze at your things through the X-ray machine with a kind of lazy curiosity. They cannot help you, and involuntarily you start monitoring your own fellow passengers. You profile them by race first; but also by the looks on their faces (the shoe bomber Richard Reid was said to have been extremely agitated at his flight gate). Really the only way to know for sure is to keep an eye on your suspects once the flight begins; the trouble is that anyone seeking to storm the cockpit will buy his ticket for first class.

So really the only way to know for sure is to *get it out of them*, one way or the other. Students of torture have sometimes distinguished between two types: "informational" torture, which resorts to violence because it is seeking actual operational intelligence, and "terroristic" torture, which seeks only to demonstrate its total physical and moral domination of the victim. The literary theorist Elaine Scarry, among others, has argued that torture is always and only terroristic, that information gathered under torture has long been acknowledged to be useless. She even cites an interesting study that found that countries engaged in torture routinely overburden their intelligence services to the point of paralysis because of all the false confessions and leads generated by torture. Something very much like this happened when an early high-level al Qaeda captive, Ibn Shaikh al-Libi, was handed over to the Egyptians for interrogation and quickly fabricated information about an al Qaeda–Saddam Hussein connection.

In the current situation, informational and terroristic torture have simply fused. Khalid Shaikh Mohammed cut off the head of Daniel Pearl, a very good journalist for the very good news section of a newspaper whose editorials are written by global-warming deniers and hard-power imperialists, because—as I learned from Mary Habeck's *Knowing Thy Enemy* and Shmuel Bar's *Warrant for TERROR*—the Koran can be read as suggesting that the enemy be killed in as gruesome a manner as possible, specifically by beheading. Thus KSM not only beheaded Daniel Pearl, but made an extremely well-produced video—not for nothing was he made chief of al Qaeda's media operations in 2000—of the killing, and circulated it on the internet. Then we Americans got to KSM, and started finding things out. Our ability to do so was both useful—we learned how 9/11 was planned, start to finish—and also a demonstration of our ability to do so. The distinction between terroristic and information-gathering torture collapses, in other words: We torture people to get information out of them, and then we furnish this information as proof of our power.

And if you look at the gruesome evidence about the war on terror that occasionally bubbles up into the light of day, you see how our government has fought it as a war of information asymmetry; as a war in which to terrorize someone is exactly to deprive him of information. As I finish writing, in early December 2006, the *New York Times* has just published photos of the confinement of José Padilla, an American citizen who traveled to the camps in Afghanistan in the late '90s and met with KSM about a plot, according to KSM, to set off a nuclear device in an American city. KSM suggested a more modest plan, to rent an apartment, fill it up with gas, and light a fuse. Padilla agreed but was arrested at Chicago's O'Hare Airport in mid-2002. Though an American citizen, he was immediately declared an "enemy combatant" and stripped of all rights. He was placed in the brig of a South Carolina naval base and his interrogation began. "Our interest is not in trying him and punishing him," said Donald Rumsfeld at the time. "Our interest is in finding out what he knows."

The photos that surfaced last week are awful. They show Padilla being removed from his cell so that he can visit the dentist. In the first photo, we see Padilla's legs appear through a slit, whereupon they are manacled; light floods out of the cell into the hallway. In the next photo his hands appear; manacles are placed upon them as well. Two photos follow in which the three guards, wearing full riot gear, including helmets with visors, so that Padilla cannot even see their faces, open the door to let Padilla out. In the next photo the prisoner's face is finally visible—and Padilla, it turns out, is not bloodied, his eyes have not been gouged out, his fingernails have not been pulled from his fingers. But this man—likely deranged to begin with, who once wanted to set off a nuclear device in a large American city—has been subjected to a regime of total sensory deprivation. As his interrogators demand to know everything about him, he knows nothing, sees nothing, hears nothing of them. In the photo, he leans slightly forward, humbly offering his head; the guard facing Padilla holds some contraption in his hands, to which he is going to subject Padilla. In the last photo, we learn that it is simply a pair of earmuffs. They have also placed blacked-out goggles over his eyes.

In the article accompanying the photos, a psychiatrist who examined Padilla at the request of his attorneys explained that after three years of sensory deprivation, of a total information deficit, Padilla has lost his mind. +

100 books: $5 each

Special Sale: Select any 100 Books from the Dalkey Archive catalog for $5 each

STEIN - MATHEWS - SHKLOVSKY - HIGGINS - CELA
DUCORNET - GASS - ELKIN - GREEN - LOEWINSOHN - WOOLF
CÉLINE - QUIN - MOSLEY - CREELEY - BARNES - O'BRIEN
BARTH - REED - ROUBAUD - YOUNG - COOVER - WHITE
SORRENTINO - HUXLEY - DAITCH - MOTTE - MARKSON

for more information and details about
free shipping or additional free books, visit:

www.dalkeyarchive.com

Dalkey Archive Press

EMILY RYAN LERNER, UNTITLED, 2007,
PEN AND INK ON PAPER, 5 X 7". COURTESY OF THE ARTIST.

THE ARGONAUT FOLLY

Joshua Glenn

> I set out to commemorate the heroes of old who sailed the good ship *Argo*...
> in quest of the Golden Fleece. Muses, inspire my lay.

THE GENTLEMAN'S NAME IS GORGON!

ONCE UPON A TIME, according to Apollonius of Rhodes (and before him Homer, Hesiod, Pindar, and countless forgotten mythopoets), a Greek prince named Jason was sent to parts unknown on a mission impossible: to fetch a magical golden ram's fleece. Jason commissioned a fifty-oared galley, the *Argo*, and manned it with the noblest heroes of the era: mighty Heracles; the bard Orpheus, whose voice enchanted nature itself; bronco-busting Castor and his immortal brother, the boxer Polydeuces; Zetes and Calaïs, the winged sons of the North Wind; as well as the seer Idmon, the sign-reader Mopsus, fleet-footed Euphemus, eagle-eyed Lynceus, shape-shifting Periclymenus, even Aethalides the mnemonist. After adventures on one perilous island after another, and having safely navigated the Clashing Rocks guarding the entrance to the Black Sea, the surviving Argonauts arrived at Colchis (Georgia), acquired the fleece with the aid of the witch Medea, and made their way back home.

That is what we learn from the D'Aulaires' and Edith Hamilton's books of mythology. But a wised-up reading of the *Argonautica* of Apollonius suggests that Jason's crew of ultratalented specialists was less a ship of heroes than a ship of fools. Or rather: a ship of heroes is always already a ship of fools.

Take Jason, for example. Except when under the influence of Medea's pharmaceuticals, he's more of a dandy and a cocksman than a warrior; and for someone generally considered an inspiring leader, he spends an inordinate amount of time "obsessed by fears and intolerable anxiety," as he puts it in the *Argonautica*, and lamenting that all is lost. As for the rest of the crew, they are not only a fiercely competitive but a violently quarrelsome lot. Prone to fits of drunken rage, after which those close to him often turn up dead, Heracles is accidentally marooned by the helmsman, Tiphys; when Telamon accuses Tiphys of doing this on purpose, a cynical reader can't help but agree with Telamon. And it's not a little suspicious that overweening Idas, having threatened Jason's loyal supporter Idmon, should be one of the only witnesses when Idmon is slain by a boar. Later, Idas will off Castor in a dispute over cattle, and Polydeuces will snuff Idas's brother, Lynceus; later still, Heracles will massacre Zetes and Calaïs. To be an Argonaut, then, is to be a member of an outfit that is, to say the least, agonistic.

But in what sense can the Argonauts be called foolish? They are fools for the same reason they are heroes: because each one of them is superior to ordinary mortals in a specialized fashion. When they're in their rightful element—council, banquet table, or boudoir, in Jason's case; in Heracles', the battlefield—there's no stopping them. But in every other circumstance, the Argonauts are, as Apollonius frequently notes, *amechanos*: without resource. Jason is all talk, no action; Heracles is all brawn, no brain. When Tiphys dies (after a mysterious illness that, frankly, warrants investigation), Jason collapses on the beach, lamenting, "We are doomed to grow old here, inglorious and obscure"; and when Heracles breaks his oar, he sits speechless and glaring: "He was not used to idle hands." It proves only too easy for these intrepid birds of passage to become as helpless as Baudelaire's albatross, whose enormous wings make him monarch of the air but a cripple on earth. No wonder Heracles grumbles about how they seem more like exiled criminals than heroes: to be an Argonaut is to be simultaneously a superior type and a misfit, a loser, an outlaw.

It first occurred to me to read the golden-fleece myth against the grain half a dozen years ago, around the time that *Hermenaut*—an independent journal whose title was not uninfluenced by Greek myth, and which I'd spent the 1990s editing and publishing—was foundering. A journal published without the sponsorship of a foundation or university, and also without the benefit of a trust fund or a sugar daddy, is a ship plowing uncharted waters without compass or anchor: each issue is an uncharted island harboring exotic dangers and delights, while the twin hazards of distribution and ad sales typically appear as daunting as the Clashing Rocks. The editors of such journals can only console themselves that their masthead and contributor's list will one day be regarded as rosters of genius. But in decades past, certain writers, thinkers, and artists have taken off on even more ambitious flights of fancy. For these dreamers, merely collaborating with admired peers isn't enough. Like the Argonauts, they want nothing less than to live and strive together each and every day.

I call this dangerous, alluring fantasy the Argonaut Folly.

AMONG US HIDE . . . THE INHUMANS!

I MYSELF FELL PREY TO THE ARGONAUT FOLLY IN 1989, while taking time off from college. I was 21 and living in the still mostly ungentrified Boston neighborhood where I'd grown up, on the Roxbury border of Jamaica Plain. The elevated train along Washington Street had recently come down, revealing to my eyes, as though for the first time, the disused former Franklin Brewery. I dreamed of moving into the building along with the most visionary young men and women of my acquaintance. Living and working in our massive brick habitat—which would (I fantasized) encompass apartments, offices, and studio spaces; a public restaurant and a private nightclub; a collective library of books, journals, and records; and eventually a school and rooftop playground for our children—we would form a freewheeling, democratic research seminar whose findings would change... everything.

I couldn't afford to do anything of the sort, so I went to grad school. In 1992, however, shortly before abandoning a master's program in sociology at Boston University, I launched *Hermenaut* as a photocopied zine. My coeditor Scott Hamrah and I published a new issue whenever I'd saved up enough money from one of my many jobs. In the late 1990s, I went to work for an internet start-up that was acquired by a publicly traded company, at which point I cashed in my options (less than $100,000, but a fortune to me), borrowed more from writer friends and family members, and rented a tiny office in the former Haffenreffer Brewery, right down the street from the Franklin building. Then, after a couple of heady years, the journal and I went bankrupt. Unable to afford a house in my own rapidly gentrifying neighborhood, I moved with my pregnant wife, our toddler son, and a heavy load of unsold magazines and credit card debt to West Roxbury. This sleepy Boston neighborhood's one claim to fame, I was soon reminded, is Brook Farm, New England's first secular utopian community, which failed after transforming itself into a "phalanx" modeled on the anarchistic theories of Charles Fourier. I could relate.

In 1841, Brook Farm cofounder George Ripley announced that the object of the colony was "to guarantee the highest mental freedom, by providing all with labor, adapted to their tastes and talents, and securing to them the fruits of their industry... and thus to prepare a society of liberal, intelligent, and cultivated persons [leading] a more simple and wholesome life, than can be led amidst the pressure of our competitive institutions." After failing in '47, Brook Farm would be remembered as little more than a bucolic retreat for abolitionists, Transcendentalists, and other zealous Bostonians. But here in the 21st century, when all good leftists warn that utopian schemes lead to oppression and mass murder, its reputation has been getting worse: a 2004 revisionist history of the experiment was subtitled *The Dark Side of Utopia*. The author of that book took his cue in part from Ripley's friend Ralph Waldo Emerson, who declined an offer to join the colony. Writing in the *Dial* in 1841, Emerson criticized Fourierism for regarding man as a mutable thing to be "ripened or retarded" at the will of the system: What utopians overlooked, said the arch-individualist, was the "faculty of Life, which spawns and scorns system-makers."

Although Brook Farm had its downside, its failure became a retrospective success—it spawned American literature's first account of the Argonaut Folly: Nathaniel Hawthorne's 1852 novel *The Blithedale Romance*, read today as a disguised treatise on the failings of thoroughgoing social reform. In '41, the 37-year-old Hawthorne was casting about for a place where he would have the leisure and energy to concentrate on his writing. Invited to join Brook Farm, he quit his position in the Boston customhouse and became one of the colony's founding members. A few months later, he moved out. Scholars have tended to describe the fictional colony of Blithedale as a dystopia, and Hawthorne as a proto-anti-utopian like Huxley, Orwell, or Zamyatin. Certainly, Coverdale, the semiautobiographical narrator of *Blithedale*, reflects ruefully on "our exploded scheme for beginning the life of Paradise anew." But between the lines of Hawthorne's novel we discover what Fredric Jameson calls "anti-anti-utopianism": an effort to free the imagination from the paralyzing spell of the quotidian without falling into the error of totalitarianism.

"On the whole, it was a society such as has seldom met together; nor, perhaps, could it reasonably be expected to hold together long," Hawthorne has Coverdale say. "Persons of marked individuality—crooked sticks, as some of us might be called—are not exactly the easiest to bind up into a fagot." One feels compelled to remind readers about the etymology of the term *fascism*, and to suggest that Coverdale's apparently negative comment about Blithedale's failings can be read in another, kinder light. Don't these crooked sticks, these Emersonian individualists, have anything at all in common? Just one thing, according to Coverdale: Each of them possesses sufficient lucidity to discern what has been called the invisible prison of everyday life under capitalism. "We had left the rusty iron frame-work of society behind us," exults Coverdale. "We had broken through many hindrances that are powerful enough to keep most people on the weary tread-mill of the established system, even while they feel its irksomeness almost as intolerable as we did." Not utopians, then, but cranks and slackers: these are Hawthorne's heroes, his West Roxbury Argonauts.

Unanimity of purpose was never enforced at Brook Farm, as even the new revisionist history admits; nor was it at fictional Blithedale. (Hawthorne quit his labors at Brook Farm not because he was an individualist rebelling against repressive groupthink, but because he soon discovered, as he has Coverdale put it, that "intellectual activity is incompatible with any large amount of bodily exercise.") In fact, Hawthorne's Blithedale fails because the colony's founding members cannot finally agree on the point of the experiment: Hollingsworth is entirely consumed with his own philanthropic theory; Zenobia, a character based in part on Hawthorne's friend Margaret Fuller, wants to promote women's rights; Coverdale is an aesthete and intellectual. "Our bond, it seems to me," the narrator muses, "was not affirmative, but negative. We had individually found one thing or another to quarrel with in our past life, and were pretty well agreed as to the inexpediency of lumbering along with the old system any further. As to what should be substituted, there was much less unanimity."

Again, we ought to read negativity as an affirmation. An agonistic, dissensual community whose members reject any kind of overarching ideology may be a lousy model for (what we usually think of as) a utopian social order. But for precisely that reason, it's the only kind of intentional community that Hawthorne could have joined. In his preface to *Blithedale*, the novel's author goes out of his way to salute "the most romantic episode of his own life." The very next year, Hawthorne published a rewritten myth in *Tanglewood Tales*: "The Golden Fleece."

THOSE WHO WOULD DESTROY US!

IN 1878, A QUARTER-CENTURY LATER, Friedrich Nietzsche published *Human, All Too Human*, a collection of aphorisms with the subtitle *A Book for Free Spirits*. Harking back to a fantasy he'd entertained when, as a stripling academic, he'd proposed to friends a "new Greek Academy" in which a revitalized Western culture might be forged, throughout *Human, All Too Human* the 33-year-old Nietzsche reaches out to superior types disgusted by "the ochlocratic nature of superficial minds and superficial culture," and to those "free spirits" able to overcome within themselves their "origin, environment… [and] class." It's like a *New York Review of Books* personal ad. Nietzsche implored "oligarchs of the spirit" to overcome "all spatial and political separation," by living and working together somewhere in Europe.

Like Hawthorne's Coverdale, Nietzsche admiringly describes his Argonauts as jailbreak artists, outsiders, crooked sticks. He suggests that "the prisoner's wits, which he uses to seek means to free himself by employing each little advantage in the most calculated and exhaustive way, can teach us the tools nature sometimes uses to produce… the perfect free spirit." In *Daybreak*, Nietzsche characterizes his proposed "company of thinkers" as intrepid sailors traversing the void, as voyageurs whose ship may end up "wrecked against infinity," and as "aeronauts of the spirit": birds of passage on an island enjoying "a precarious minute of knowing and divining, amid joyful beating of wings and chirping with one another." Impatiently waiting for these nomadic aeronauts and Argonauts to get in touch, he writes of them, "Is it too much to ask that they should *give a sign* to one another?"

Alas, Nietzsche's ads went unanswered, except by Paul Rée and Lou Salomé, who first proposed to him a nonsexual yet "trinitarian" workshop and living arrangement, then ran away without him. And Nietzsche, like Hawthorne, was too skeptical about human nature to go in for utopia; in fact, he was explicitly opposed to socialist utopianism. In his later works, from *Thus Spoke Zarathustra* onward, he would outline an antiegalitarian utopia organized for the benefit of a caste of *Übermenschen*, as he now called them, whose sole concern would be the cultivation of their own excellence; the rest of humankind would be put to work.

Ayn Rand, who had studied Nietzsche closely in postrevolutionary Petrograd, attempted to imagine an Argonaut Folly in this more totalitarian vein in the 1957 novel *Atlas Shrugged*. The pro-capitalist potboiler is set partly in Galt's Gulch, a fictional Colorado valley into which "the men of ability, the men of the mind," no longer willing to sacrifice their talents to their mediocre contemporaries, have secretly withdrawn. Life imitates art: neoconservative ideologues have, in recent decades, espoused a Nietzschean, Rand-inspired revolt of elites as an antidote to leveling democracy. Paul Wolfowitz, Richard Perle, and William Kristol, among others, club together in think tanks and one tight-knit group named after the Roman god of weapon-making, Vulcan. So are these Argonaut Follies, too? I would disqualify them. Bush's foreign policy advisers more resemble Jason's scheming uncle, who cynically sends the Argonauts off on a quest he believes to be impossible. They do not want to break free of the established system. They wish to run the jail.

BEWARE, THE HIDDEN LAND!

WE ARRIVE NOW AT THE INTELLECTUAL CRISIS around World War I, when one modernist, anarchist, or otherwise interesting person after another lost confidence in the theories of social progress that had prevailed since the Enlightenment. "How can one get rid of everything that smacks of journalism, worms, everything nice and right, blinkered, moralistic, Europeanized, enervated?" Hugo Ball demanded in 1916. The answer, many—or not that many—Europeans claimed, was: Argonaut Folly.

In the winter of 1914, D. H. Lawrence worked out the objectives, aims, and laws for communal life in some place far from England, perhaps an island. He named the imagined colony Rananim, and according to the recent Lawrence biography, the word became for him a cherished "fiction about living with a few friends in a better way than conventional society permitted." Lawrence—seriously? half-seriously?—urged the most talented writers of his acquaintance (E. M. Forster, Bertrand Russell, a young Aldous Huxley) and England's best young aristocrats to make this daydream a reality, but nothing ever came of it. Nor of the Forte Circle, an international network of radical pacifist intellectuals and artists—including the German anarchist Gustav Landauer, the Viennese philosopher Martin Buber, the Russian-born painter Wassily Kandinsky, the French writer Romain Rolland, and the American novelist Upton

Sinclair—who toyed with the quasi-mystical notion that a community devoted to intellectual and artistic activity might halt the progress of Europe toward war. (In 1906, Sinclair had plowed the proceeds from *The Jungle* into Helicon Hall, a New Jersey commune where eighty intellectuals and artists lived until it burned down the following year.)

The Cabaret Voltaire, however, is a different story—an actual voyage, not just a ship's manifest. The Dadaists were not exactly a movement in the usual sense of a bunch of artists committed to a particular aesthetic; they were a freewheeling band of exiles. Located in neutral Zurich during the war, the Cabaret Voltaire, named by German founders Hugo Ball and Emmy Hennings, became a gathering point not only for freethinking émigrés like Hans Arp (Alsace), Francis Picabia (France), and Tristan Tzara (Romania), but pacifists, draft dodgers, revolutionaries, and iconoclasts of all kinds. Forget for now Dada's reconceptualization of artistic practice as intervention, its pioneering of montage and the readymade: Dada's first achievement, it's been said, lies in its invention of a transnational community of misfits. To gaze upon the thrilling 1920 collage *Dada Triumphs*, in which Raoul Hausmann imagines a war room for Dadaists bent on world domination, is to catch a glimpse of the finest anti-utopian utopianism of its time, the absurdist optimism of the Argonauts on their impossible voyage.

Out of Dada came Breton's 1924 "Manifesto of Surrealism." Breton was concerned with the invisible prison of daily life, whose discourse had become "common sense." Who can escape this prison and embark on adventures? Perhaps the insane, because their imagination "induces them not to pay attention to certain rules." In that ship-of-fools vein, he adds, "Christopher Columbus should have set out to discover America with a boatload of madmen." Breton then describes just such a vessel of foolish Argonauts: "For today I think of a *castle*, half of which is not necessarily in ruins; this castle belongs to me, I picture it in a rustic setting, not far from Paris," he writes. "A few of my friends are living here as permanent guests: There is Louis Aragon leaving; he only has time enough to say hello; Philippe Soupault gets up with the stars, and Paul Éluard, our great Éluard, has not yet come home. There are Robert Desnos and Roger Vitrac out on the grounds poring over an ancient edict on dueling... there is T. Fraenkel waving to us from his captive balloon," and so forth. Sadly, in a 1929 "Preface for a Reprint of the Manifesto," we find Breton describing his vision as "something that, no matter how bravely it *may have been*, can no longer be. There is nothing I can do about it except to blame myself…"

And yet, Surrealism's failure also led to another success of a kind. Picking up some of Breton's castaways, like Desnos, Michel Leiris, and André Masson, Georges Bataille developed his nutty antifascist journals and organizations—*Acéphale*, Contre-attaque, and the College of Sociology—as an intellectual resistance to Fascism's appropriation of ancient Greek concepts of the state, the sacred, friendship, and hospitality.

Meanwhile, in America, the anarchistic Dwight Macdonald, who had split with Philip Rahv and *Partisan Review* in the early '40s, and who'd launched his own journal, *Politics*, in '44, never joined the antiutopian party. Neither did novelist and *Politics* cofounder Mary McCarthy, whose 1949 novella *The Oasis* is one more example of the American tradition of discovering an Argonaut Folly in the failure of a utopian project. *The Oasis* retells the story of Macdonald's breakup with Rahv (or so it seems to me) as a fable about Utopia, a colony established at a disused Vermont hotel by intellectuals in retreat from wartime New York. Here, the "purists," led by Macdougal Macdermott (Macdonald) quarrel endlessly over first principles with the "realists," chastened leftists led by Will Taub (Rahv). Like Hawthorne's Coverdale (who first praises Blithedale's mission, "showing mankind the example of a life governed by other than the false and cruel principles on which human society has all along been based," then rejects it), McCarthy has Katy Norell, a semiautobiographical character, conclude that every utopian colony that "treats itself as a kind of factory or business for the manufacture and export of morality" is destined to fail. Still, though Norell abandons her naïve utopianism, she does not abandon the colony. In the end, she turns her attention to imagining a "new pattern," neither wholly purist nor wholly realist.

THE COMING OF GALACTUS!

IN 1952, REINHOLD NIEBUHR SPOKE for the chastened ex-socialist writers and editors of *Partisan Review* when he rejected the widespread utopianism of the '30s as "an adolescent embarrassment." How could any program of radical social transformation be taken seriously after the Holocaust and the Moscow trials? But Niebuhr's developmentalist analogy is misleading. After all, the blueprints for proto-totalitarian utopias have always been drawn by grown-ups intent on containing the anti-authoritarian energy of youth. In the first decades of the cold war, American adolescents responded to the agonistic Argonaut Folly—in the form of cinematic motorcycle clubs, or street gangs—more than to collaborative utopian schemes. And it was primarily in adolescent fantasy genres that the dream of a noncoercive group of flawed but heroic individuals survived.

In 1961, comic-book editor and writer Stan Lee collaborated with the talented artist Jack Kirby to invent a superhero team that would compete with *The Justice League of America*, a popular but dull series about uncomplicated superheroes who got along together just fine. In *The Fantastic Four*, Lee (who in his 1974 book *Origins of Marvel Comics* describes himself as a "vociferous reader" of mythology) gave the world a team of violently quarrelsome heroes whose godlike abilities render them misfits, losers, and outsiders among their fellow humans. The Argonauts were still among us, tucked into our backpacks.

In '63, Lee and Kirby launched *The X-Men*, a comic about teenage mutants who'd been ostracized from their hometowns, and who lived together in a mansion in the suburbs of New York. Myth was mined again: the ill-tempered Beast is Hercules, the Angel is a winged son of the North Wind, Professor X is a seer, and then there's Cyclops. That same year, Lee and Kirby created *The Avengers*, a comic about a Justice League–type group of heroes whose number included Thor, whom Lee had earlier borrowed from Norse mythology, and the Hercules-like Hulk; their headquarters was a mansion on New York's Upper East Side. In '65, Lee and Kirby's Inhumans made their debut in issue 44 of *Fantastic Four*: Black Bolt, Crystal, Karnak, and two others straight out of Greek myth, Medusa and Gorgon, were a peripatetic team of superpowered mutants, exiled from their secret homeland in the Himalayas.

As the 1960s gave way to the era now known as the Sixties, Lee and Kirby's contemporary mythos played a crucial role: shortly after the debut of *The X-Men*, 28-year-old Ken Kesey moved to a rural property outside of San Francisco and invited a multitalented, contentious group, later known as the Merry Pranksters, along. In a semiautobiographical screenplay that Kesey wrote in '66, he had the Kesey-based character refer to the other Pranksters as his "X-Men": these were Argonauts on acid.

Comic books weren't the only type of adolescent pop culture production to produce Argonaut Follies. In their movies, from *Help!* (1965)

to *Magical Mystery Tour* (1967) to *Yellow Submarine* (1968), the Beatles portrayed themselves as roommates whose deep-seated differences were a source of creative, productive tension. And like Lee and Kirby's comics, the Beatles' productions also played a key role in the invention of the Sixties. In 1967, according to Abbie Hoffman's autobiography, inspiration for the Yippies was found on the cover of *Sgt. Pepper's Lonely Hearts Club Band*. Check it out: the album's illustration asks us to imagine a transhistorical Argonaut Folly in which the Beatles rub elbows with Edgar Allan Poe, Oscar Wilde, and Lenny Bruce.

And yet where are we now? Everything today encourages us to see the dark side, the folly, the impossibility, not just of utopia but of an anti-utopian heterotopia where we'd have a project in common besides selling our commodified labor, intellectual or otherwise. Everything encourages us to think we face a choice between detached houses in a row, where we cook our dinners in private, or else the gulag. But there can be—can't there?—community without tyranny. Sure, the company of other misfits would make you feel bad sometimes; but it also feels bad to have nothing to look forward to but marriage, work, and TV. Maybe the Argonaut Folly would always be a failure. But then atomized private life under the sign of the market is doomed to failure too, if we think of happiness, excitement, joy, or surprise. You've got to pick your failures—and I'd like to fail in good company instead of all on my own.

So permit me a lonelyhearts ad of my own: I seek talented individuals—like the Blithedale colonists, who'd "gone through such an experience as to disgust them with ordinary pursuits but who were not yet so old, nor had suffered so deeply, as to lose their faith in the better time to come"—who are neither so mature as to be anti-utopian nor so adolescent as to be naïvely utopian. Write to me in care of this magazine. I don't know what we'll do, once we've found one another. But is it too much to ask that you should get in touch? +

The Jack Kerouac School of Disembodied Poetics
SUMMER WRITING PROGRAM
Weekly workshops running June 18 - July 15
Boulder, Colorado

Faculty include: Anne Waldman, Sonia Sanchez, Jerome Rothenberg, Shelley Jackson, Clark Coolidge, Bernadette Mayer, Samuel R. Delany, Brian Evenson, Laird Hunt, Bill Berkson, Ken Mikolowski, Rebecca Brown, Peter Gizzi, Marjorie Welish, Carla Harryman, Leslie Scalapino, Wang Ping, Jennifer Moxley, Daisy Zamora, Myung mi Kim, Sesshu Foster, Camille Roy and others.

2007

for a full list of our faculty please visit our website at
WWW.NAROPA.EDU/SWP

Keeping the world safe for poetry since 1974

The Jack Kerouac School Celebrates 50 Years of

On the Road
Saturday June 30th
Sunday July 1st
2007
With David Amram, Hettie Jones, and other guests TBA

Credit and noncredit programs available
Poetry • Fiction • Translation • Letterpress

To find out more information or to receive a catalog call
Naropa UNIVERSITY **303.245.4600**

photo & ad design by HRHegnauer@hotmail.com

REVIEWS

WOMAN, THE NEW SOCIAL PROBLEM

Maureen Dowd. *Are Men Necessary? When Sexes Collide.* Putnam. November 2005.
Caitlin Flanagan. *To Hell with All That: Loving and Loathing Our Inner Housewife.* Little, Brown & Company. April 2006.
Linda R. Hirshman. *Get to Work: A Manifesto for Women of the World.* Viking. June 2006.
Laura Kipnis. *Against Love: A Polemic.* Pantheon. August 2003.

A SPATE OF RECENT BOOKS AND ARTICLES and counter-articles and letters about the articles has declared that American women are in crisis. They've been dropping out of prestigious jobs and taking on all the housework; the accomplished ones can't get a date; and then there are the kids, those black holes of endless need. The authors accuse women of abandoning their children for work, abandoning public life for their children, acting too feminine or too feminist, confusing their sexuality with pornography, and generally failing to make their lives run smoothly. Woven through these concerns, too, has been a distinct thread of anxiety about what academic social science is pleased to call "affective life," which most people call love.

This persistent litany made me wonder what other anxieties lay behind the malaise attributed to women (and somehow never to men, who apparently live without conflict, or kids). Gender seems to leave an awful lot unexplained. All these books by successful, educated professional women harp on "transformations" in mating, child rearing, and women's role in the workplace, at a time when a radically changing labor market threatens the security of everyone—not just women.

MAUREEN DOWD'S *Are Men Necessary* expanded a *New York Times* column into a full-blown cartoon (minus pictures) of straight women's romantic travails. The book's vignettes—culled largely from coworkers, friends, and of course Dowd's own life—recite pure cliché: If your date buys you dinner, do you pay him back with sex? Isn't going dutch confusing? Even when Dowd describes the new age of Googling prospective dates and indulging in wanton collegiate hookups, the past is on her mind. Her mother's copy of *How to Catch and Hold a Man* may have morphed into chick lit, but the old rules still hold. Dowd's popularity suggests that we are loath to relinquish them.

The best-known parts of her complaint come down to an insistence that attraction and courtship thrive on the substantial social differences between the genders. A successful woman cannot be happy with a less successful man, nor a successful man happy with a more successful woman. It couldn't be otherwise, we're told, because Dowd's mind is under control from elsewhere—from somewhere in her DNA: "Evolution is still lagging behind equality. So females are still programmed to look for older men with resources while males are still programmed to look for younger women with adoring gazes." Women's subordinate status, in other words, is the motor of love. But Dowd reassures us that women's achievements need not spoil their love lives—as long as they downplay their wits and résumés and indulge men's need for soothing deference. Feminism opened up opportunities for women to flourish, and flourish they should—but only at work. Over dinner, they'll get better results with feminine incapacity. Dowd lodges a book-length brief, masked as a complaint, about how a smart woman won't get her romantic due until she learns to play dumb.

DOWD'S DATING MANUAL is a panegyric to the past; Caitlin Flanagan's domestic chronicle, To Hell with All That, is an epic of sanctimonious self-congratulation. Like Phyllis Schlafly, the self-described "anti-feminist" Flanagan makes a career out of insisting on the irreplaceable importance of full-time mothering. Stay-at-home mothers, she writes, "ensure that their kids get the very best of them." Flanagan's own children get the best of both their mother and a nanny. Once in a while, she'll feel the old Schlaflian moral fervor, as when she admonishes women to pay into their nannies' FICA taxes. Otherwise, her tone is flippant—as if to prevent us from noticing how serious she is when she treats her atypical prosperity as universal.

Like Dowd, Flanagan is comfortable with categorical gender differences from an earlier era. All women, she says, share a natural homemaking expertise and high standards of cleanliness (Flanagan employs a housekeeper, too), and are attuned like sensitive radar equipment to children's needs. Men, though, had best stay in the office making more money. Even when they can be coaxed into housework, they're hard-pressed to approach womanly precision, and they're incapable of giving their kids a mother's intuitive care.

Flanagan's book, for those who take it seriously, is supposed to reopen the schism between mothers who work in the formal labor market (particularly those elites rich enough to do so for satisfaction as well as income) and those who work as full-time caregivers. This is an old fight that, once people start swinging, manages to produce a doubly bad result: alternately idealizing and denigrating caring labor, then doing the same to professional achievement. Each option's effects on the children's well-being are parsed in degrees so minute they may require a new unit of measure.

The absurdity of the debate is that it's basically about rich people. Perhaps the "opting-out" option says only this about our current moment of feminism: that a well-off, professional woman (a product of earlier feminisms) possesses a culturally approved script for exiting work—she can simply declare that she's dedicating her energies to an upscale, artisanal version of unpaid child rearing. Poorer women are far less likely to have this option—and if they do, they can't tell their story in the same self-serving way. When it comes to the freedom to choose whether to work for a living or not, gender is hardly the most important variable. Middle-class women and middle-class men have much more in common with each other, in this regard, than middle-class women and poor women.

THE CAVEAT IS THAT as long as women are the primary bearers of the burden of child care, being a woman will have a profoundly detrimental effect on your access to work and pay. Linda Hirshman has this hazard in mind as she lectures young women in her *American Prospect* essay "Homeward Bound." Incited by tales of an "opt-out revolution"—massed columns of women leaving work for child rearing—Hirshman denounces stay-at-home moms for letting down the sex by reducing the number of women in influential, high-status jobs. Such a claim requires substantial supporting data, which Hirshman collected by flipping through the Sunday *Times*—her argument rests on an analysis of women wealthy (and vain) enough to have their weddings featured in the Styles section.

Hirshman addresses college-bound women, assuming, for some reason, that they consider love the arena of their greatest ambition. She argues that they should instead be looking out for their financial security, majoring in a practical subject that will lead to a well-paid occupational niche. Career ambition should guide the search for a spouse, too. A useful husband will be older and already secure; otherwise he should be low-status enough to defer to your career imperatives. (This latter good husband sounds a lot like the "good wife" of the past.) Finally, a woman should never jeopardize her ability to compete at work by having more than one child. So Hirshman, on her way to reorganizing the world via women's role in the workplace, accepts the androcentric models according to which professional life is still organized. Her program, as a feminist, is to encourage individual women to bring their lives into closer adherence to that model: in other words, to be more "like men." So much for collective action: progress will only come if it's every man for herself.

A few months after Hirshman's essay appeared, the economist Claudia Goldin published an op-ed in the *Times* describing her study of 10,000 women college graduates, the majority of whom neither left their careers after having children nor forwent childbearing for work.

THEN THERE'S LAURA KIPNIS, video artist, academic, and newly minted polemicist. Polemic, like all forms of demolition, is an irresistible spectacle. Less so, admittedly, when the target no longer exists. Kipnis's jeremiad *Against Love* is waged against domestic monogamy of *longue durée*—what Kipnis calls "coupledom," as though it were a despotic kingdom and she the leader of a populist uprising. To be half of a couple is to be harrowed by surveillance ("You're home late") and drained by mundane demands ("You don't want to eat dinner now?"). Your inner life is flushed like prey from protective cover to sustain the ideal of intimacy. Then there's the rote quality of the sex you'll rarely have. In these circumstances, cheating constitutes a rebellion and even a critique of the organization of love. Defiance restores our self-sovereignty.

If Dowd's concerns seem about eighty years old in one tradition, going back to the earliest days of the "new woman," Kipnis's distaste is about eighty years old in the rival line. It reminds me of nothing so much as the debates of Ursula, Gudrun, Crich, and above all Birkin, D. H. Lawrence's mouthpiece, in *Women in Love*: "Marriage is a *pis aller*. . . . It's a sort of tacit hunting in couples: the world all in couples, each couple in its own little house, watching its own little interests, and stewing in its own little privacy—it's the most repulsive thing on earth." Lawrence's heated tone reflected the power of the inflexible constraints of his times. Kipnis attacks the routinized "prison" of monogamy as though she, too, wrote nearly a century ago. She seems not to notice that the bars of Lawrence's cage have long been sawed through, and that romantic commitment is now eminently revocable. You just break up or separate or get divorced. To speculate about the future of a romance is to acknowledge (even if only to oneself) that it has slender odds of permanence. When insecurity is endemic, it seems pointless to celebrate the "transformative" riskiness of cheating. What does it mean to cheat when you can just as easily move on?

It's when Kipnis tries to imply a link between contemporary social arrangements of love and arrangements of work that we see what she's really getting at. Kipnis claims that we're alienated from our work because it, like marriage, is routinized in the style of Henry Ford's production system. She tells us that the miserable drudgery of monogamy aids employers because it acclimates workers to the miserable drudgery of work. Cheating, Kipnis glibly suggests, questions the necessity of monogamy—might not the critique spill over into the workday?

This is exactly backward. You don't need to have read much political economy to know that the contemporary postindustrial service economy's dominant model of flexible specialization relies on quick changes, not predictability. Companies keep up by

---

THE ECONOMICS OF ATTENTION
Style and Substance in the Age of Information
Richard A. Lanham
"Richard Lanham is the single most interesting and persuasive interpreter of the cultural transformations now tumbling into shape in the wake of the revolutions in information technology and mass media. *The Economics of Attention* offers characteristically astute interpretations of the history of the last ten years—a history that Lanham more or less accurately prophesized."—James ODonnell, author of *Avatars of the Word: From Papyrus to Cyberspace*
Cloth $29.00

The University of Chicago Press   www.press.uchicago.edu

modifying their goods and services, and shuffling or shedding workers accordingly. Routines at work, in many cases, are likely to be fleeting.

For workers, this means that more jobs, at all levels of pay, require them continuously to work on themselves. Free agents—a euphemism for people with no guarantees—must never stop learning. Indeed, what you've already learned becomes outdated, a liability to be forgotten—employers would prefer a blank slate. Never forget that you are a salable commodity: CEO of brand *You*!

In our private lives, the transformation is just as profound. Our default serial monogamy, our noncommitment and obsession with self-refashioning—these resemble nothing so much as casualized employment. Economic and romantic life converge, in a register of profound insecurity defined by constant movement—in and out of capital markets, jobs, relationships. The increasing contingency of work creates a labor force of insecurely employed "consultants," freelancers, and part-time salesclerks, and something similar could be said about the romantic market. As long as a relationship (between boss and employee, between spouses) conforms to the utilitarian ideal of mutual benefit, the relationship will continue. If not, nothing much prevents it from ending. You'll find someone who will make better use of what you bring to the table, says your former lover, or the head of HR, as you pack your things.

THESE AUTHORS COUNSEL changes in individual behavior. Dowd and Flanagan, tongue-in-cheek or not, encourage women to retreat into "womanly" roles. Hirshman and Kipnis encourage masculinist individualism. Neither strategy seems likely to ease the tension between the demands of contemporary work and love, or to address the persistent gender inequality that cripples women's material security.

Though written exclusively by rich women, the women-in-crisis books nonetheless reveal a genuine panic about the ever heightening tensions between private life and the work demands of contemporary capitalism. Women are a logical surrogate for these concerns, because of the persistence of a sexual division of labor that assigns them primary responsibility for child care. Jobs simply weren't designed to mesh with what sociologist Arlie Hochschild calls a "second shift" at home. The more prestigious professions (and, really, any job with the chance of promotion) lean especially hard on young workers, who are supposed to build reputations, not families. In this context, caring for children becomes a flashpoint that reveals the impasse between the demands of work and private life.

So while the behavior of women—at home, at work, at dinner—is not the genuine issue, it is feminism that offers the best solution. For feminism's most important unfinished work lies precisely here: in a redefinition of our attitude toward care and care workers, and in securing for them social recognition and material support—full rights of social citizenship, in academic feminist parlance.

Debates about "opting out" reflect an unresolved ambivalence about the value of care. The second-wave feminist movement tended to reject the domestic in favor of public life. Housework was rote drudgery, and when did kids ever make for stimulating intellectual company? Pay some other, poorer woman and get a life. More recent feminists, though, have argued for a revaluation of care as an essential contribution to the social good. A combination of paid work and caregiving already characterizes many women's lives—pro-care groups like the Women's Committee of One Hundred aim to secure state support to make this mix the norm for men and women. The key point of this program is that care workers (part- or full-time, parents or nannies) themselves should be supported: with good wages, health care, and paid time off, funded by the state with tax revenue. It may sound impossibly ambitious, but what are our other options? Not Dowdism, not Flanaganism. Not, surely, the Bush administration's marriage-promotion programs.

Care of others hampers self-development—at least, development of the kind employers require. Care is long-term, it strives to create security, and it requires personal sacrifice. Thus caring labor marks the most visible point of strain between private life and the lability required to prevent free agency from turning into free fall. As long as women continue to bear primary responsibility for child care, they are at a disadvantage in playing by a flexible economy's rules. But giving and receiving care is universal. Everyone is a potential candidate for major care; and all romantic relationships, even childless ones, eventually require it. Your partner gets laid off, you become chronically ill. Care complicates moving on: you might be through with someone, but what if they can't choose to be through with their need of you?

The *pis aller* these days isn't about gender or love at all: it's about staying loose and agile—i.e., employable, desirable—enough to withstand the next round of change, whether romantic or professional. Intimacy may be an impediment to the economic necessity to make ourselves the center of our own lives; love often seems like it may only prove a period of mutual hobbling. In a bid for control and security, we deploy an absurd logic that forces us to compare the value of incommensurable goods: Do we trade love for success? Children for ambition? Care of others for our responsibility to ourselves? There's no reason love should be the hook on which to hang the meaning of our lives; but, these days, wanting or having it at all provokes anxiety. Under such circumstances, who wouldn't look askance at love? What's it going to cost, after all? Can we possibly afford it?

—*Meghan Falvey*

FLYING CARS: AN UPDATE

Urban Aeronautics. *X-Hawk.* Forthcoming.
Moller. *M400 Skycar.* Forthcoming.
LaBiche Aerospace. *FSC-1TM.* Forthcoming.
Terrafugia. *Transition.* Forthcoming.

HERE WE ARE HALF A DECADE INTO THE 21ST century and still no flying cars.

We know there are powerful interests to overcome—gravity, for one thing, and all those people making money on our baroque transport system. The Portland Cement Association, not to mention the Mob, rake it in pouring ribbons of concrete. The automakers who killed the electric car probably wouldn't mind sparing a bullet for a car that flies, while Boeing, Airbus, and the airlines are unlikely to give up their investment in the self-propelled cargo units euphemistically known as passenger planes.

But history, technology, and the earth itself are on the side of the flying car. The highway systems of the world are up to a century old, as is the basic architecture of person driving car on rubber wheels over hard-surfaced road. The technology for driverless or robot cars, able to keep their distance from others and play nice on the roads, already exists, but the historical and regulatory baggage of the land car won't let it happen.

Meanwhile our whole approach to air travel has become Kafkaesque. Massive taxation supports major airports while only government largesse—in the form of everything from indemnification to outright cash—keeps the passenger jets in the air. And these jets are the only thing worse for the environment than driving a car, putting out 50 percent more carbon dioxide per passenger and leaving earth-warming contrails besides. Of course the airliner is also the weapon of choice for today's discerning terrorist, owing to its great mass and highly explosive nature.

Twenty-first-century vehicles need a 21st-century system engineered properly to assign risk and distribute benefits. Plans are already afoot at such serious places as the FAA and NASA to develop a fully automated airborne road network called HITS, the Highway in the Sky, designed to make flying much easier and more accessible. Flying cars will be kept safely apart and guided to their destinations using Global Positioning satellites and onboard inertial and navigational sensors. The driver could follow a virtual roadway on a digital display, but really the car could make do quite nicely without the driver. Flying cars would travel at 1000-foot intervals, from 8,000 to 18,000 feet, each "lane" accommodating a given speed. Perhaps even a special lane for necking. The system would necessitate a smartly designed cockpit with computer screens in place of the cold war–era dials now common. It is precisely the kind of complete system that the current highway arrangement can't produce because of its historical baggage.

FLYING CARS COME IN TWO TYPES. Vertical takeoff and landing (VTOL) cars were originally to be adaptations of the helicopter. But the high-speed rotors on helicopters are too likely to slice someone's head off, given day to day use, and anyway your average chopper is just too delicate and complex to be used daily. So while the helicopter will always remain ideal for reporting on land-car traffic jams, spiriting victims of land-car crashes to the hospital, and filming land-car thieves for sensationalist television broadcasts, it will never become the Chevrolet of the future.

In the past decade, two other VTOL designs have begun to look feasible. They are perfect foils: one from an Israeli company with a sober business plan and links to heavy hitters in the aerospace industry and military, the other a West Coast company headed by Paul Moller, whose other interests include a company that sells "life extension" almond butter.

Urban Aeronautics, based in Tel Aviv, has been developing a concept first explored by the US military in the 1950s. And the design for their X-Hawk is only modestly more inspiring than a Merkava tank—it's similar to a 1960 De Soto but not so pretty. Usually shown in banana yellow, the X-Hawk is essentially two eight-foot fans set horizontally with the payload on a flat sled in between. You can literally step from the 25th-floor into your X-Hawk, just don't look down. Initial plans are for rescue and combat operations in close urban environments, and the company has already made a sale to an Israeli hospital. They predict the X-Hawk will enter the personnel vehicle market within twenty years.

If the world wants a flying penis car, on the other hand, Paul Moller's M400 Skycar is it. Colored bordello red, the Skycar has seating for two in a fuselage that owes a good deal to the Jaguar XKE. Unlike the Jag, however, it will lift off vertically and cruise at 275 miles an hour using four fans powered by a total of eight Wankle engines. Of course, it will cost you, and for the moment, while it awaits approval from the FAA, the

Skycar can be seen in Los Angeles hanging, motor running, from a crane.

THE CONVERTIBLE FLYING CAR is an easier (if less exciting) solution than the VTOL, as evidenced by the fact that several have made it into the air, the first in 1921. In its most basic form, the convertible is little more than an airplane with folding wings and a means to shift power from the propeller to a set of drive wheels.

The LaBiche Aerospace FSC-1TM will convert from a car to a plane at the touch of a button and be easy to fly. The plan is to sell it as a kit-car for $175,000, but for that you get a 180-mile-an-hour Corvette that seats up to five and flies. Unlike most convertibles, this one looks like a sports car, rather than an airplane, when it's on the road. It has wings that fold and then sweep in underneath the car body, a tail configuration that folds into a rear spoiler, and a small wing that folds into the hood. The little wing in front is known as a canard-wing, though precisely how these complex folding mechanisms will operate, and how their weight will be held aloft, remains to be seen. Perhaps they have the other meaning of canard in mind.

In the race for the first viable convertible, though, I'd put my money on the boy genius from MIT, Carl Dietrich. He's obviously smart because he named his company in Latin: *Terrafugia* ("escape from land"). His car, the Transition, looks more likely than the others to become a reality because it has the basic architecture of a small plane, modified to work on the road. The wings fold up neat as a sea gull's at the push of a button. When extended, the wings make for quite a blind spot, and door dings might cause serious aerodynamic problems. But there's a lot less origami going on than in the LaBiche, and the simplest solution is usually the best.

With any of these convertibles, if you start at Penn Station, you can have it airborne by Times Square (about six blocks, or 1,500 feet), assuming you make all the lights. In the near term, convertible planes will rely on the existing infrastructure for general aviation—the thousands of small airports dotting the landscape. As for the flight itself, the Transition cruises at 120 mph, and gets 30 miles per gallon in the air, 40 on the highway. Best of all in my book, it's the size of a '57 Buick and sports honest-to-goodness functional tailfins.

Will either flying car configuration save the planet from global warming? Will flying cars save on oil? In the short term, certainly not. In the short term, anthropogenic climate change is here. All we can do now is lop a little off peak greenhouse gas levels and apologize to our children.

But a flying car enthusiast should be in it for the long term. Early adopters may get their cars in a decade or two, just as wealthy gents toyed with the land car in the first decade of its existence. But any change, even a simple one like improving the average fuel economy of the world vehicle fleet, will take a generation at least. The flying car, by contrast, is the perfect jujitsu move: it uses the momentum built up over a century of ever greater mobility to break the stranglehold. You'll get even more mobility with your flying car, but you'll also get a second chance to decide how mobility should fit into daily life. The land car and road were young once, impressionable, educable. Today they are mature and set in their ways, having been shaped by a century of use. A system of mobility based on the flying car, on the other hand, is young indeed—still a twinkle in the eye. The trick will be raising it well, making it suitable for this new century and beyond. In this age of limits, perhaps we will fly much less than we ever drove, perhaps jet travel will become a thing of the past, or perhaps we will find a way to power our flight that is not so environmentally harmful. Whatever the future holds, the flying car at least gives us a chance to shape it anew.

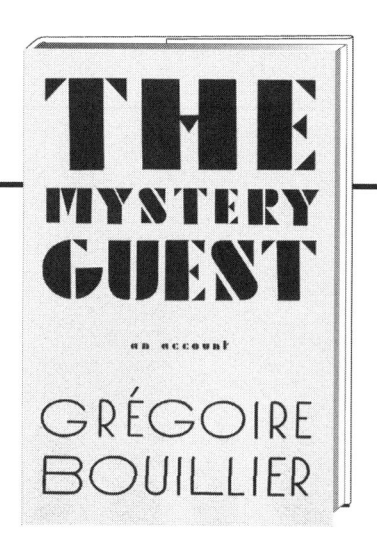

ALL RIGHT, YOU SAY, OK, but where is my Jetsons car? That thing can stop on a dime, drop the children off while hovering silently above the schoolyard, and then when George arrives at Spacely Sprockets for work it folds into a briefcase, no parking space required. The only noise it makes is a pleasant bubbling whoosh.

The careful observer will notice that *The Jetsons* is a cartoon. Still, let's look at the technology. Three forces shape the universe: the electromagnetic force, the strong force, and gravity. In the 19th century, scientists uncovered the secrets of the electromagnetic force and learned to manipulate it. In the 20th century, we unlocked the atom and ka-boom. If the present trend continues, we should be able to ferret out the secrets of gravity in this, the 21st century. To the discovery of the electron and the relationship between mass and energy ($E=mc^2$), high school textbooks will one day add the discovery of the graviton, the mechanism by which the earth keeps us down. Although not yet discovered in the strictest sense, physicists have already predicted its existence. As the theory of relativity shows, you cannot discover anything until you know what you are looking for. The Jetsons' cars clearly operate by manipulating gravitons—a simple matter a century from now.

MOST IMPORTANT OF ALL, flying cars will rid us of the roads themselves.

Once upon a time, the road was a multifunctional social space: when not being used for transport, it served as a marketplace or recreation site. In those days, say the high Middle Ages, transportation mostly meant walking; the system was so efficient that there was no such thing as traffic congestion.

Today roads are for transport only; using them casually for some other purpose can be deadly. The trouble is, everyone wants to use the roads at once. At certain times in certain places, they are filled beyond capacity. At other times, which is most of the time, roads don't have a single vehicle on them. So there they sit, day and night, wasting space, making heat islands out of cities and interrupting the natural flow of rainwater into the ground. Landscape ecologist Richard Forman at Harvard estimates that the ecological effects of one road can extend an average of 300 meters on either side of it and slice up an entire ecosystem. By this calculus, roads affect a third of the land in the continental US. Roadkill isn't just what's for dinner anymore; it's symbolic of the massive harm roads do merely by being roads.

Added to the fixed environmental cost is the ongoing environmental cost associated with land-car use. Tanker spills are the big newsmakers in water pollution, but more toxins reach our waters drop by drop out of that loose oil plug or the radiator you meant to have fixed. Rubber tires don't grow on trees anymore: they too are made of oil. Did you ever wonder where your tire tread goes after it leaves your tire? Rain sloughs all that oil into the storm drains and ultimately into the oceans.

Soon this will be over; soon we will fly. Will the roads become obsolete overnight? Certainly not; we'll always need a place to ride our bicycles. But the massive motorways will be the first to atrophy, and eventually the third of the nation used up by land cars can be reallocated to living.

IT MAY BE HARD to imagine a world of flying cars, involving as it does a wholesale reworking of transportation and land-use patterns. But the automobile once reshaped the world in revolutionary ways, and nothing lasts forever.

—Daniel Albert

FICTION CHRONICLE

Nell Freudenberger. *The Dissident.* Ecco. September 2006.
Heidi Julavits. *The Uses of Enchantment.* Doubleday. October 2006.
Elizabeth Merrick, ed. *This Is Not Chick Lit.* Random House. August 2006.
Marisha Pessl. *Special Topics in Calamity Physics.* Viking. August 2006.

ELIZABETH MERRICK EDITED *THIS IS NOT Chick Lit*, she explains in her introduction, to save female readers from our worst impulses. Left to our own devices at the local Barnes & Noble, it seems, we stumble to the bestseller table and buy the first pink paperback we pick up with our manicured fingers. How can we not? "After the millennium," Merrick writes, "it became nearly impossible to enter a bookstore without tripping over a pile of pink books covered with truncated legs, shoes, or handbags." Like the candy machine prominently placed in a middle school cafeteria, the chick-lit publicity apparatus plays to cravings young women can't resist. "Cotton-candy entertainment," as Merrick calls it, is OK for dessert (she herself reads *Us Weekly* on the treadmill); the trouble is, many women have it for breakfast, lunch, and dinner. A steady diet of chick lit "numbs our senses"; "shuts down our consciousness"; and "beat[s] us over the head with clichés that promote a narrow worldview."

Instead of chick lit, Merrick would like us to read its diametric opposite: not chick lit, formerly known as fiction written by women. Aimee Bender, Holiday Reinhorn, and Binnie Kirshenbaum boldly present the romantic woes of women who aren't obsessed with Mr. Right; Judy Budnitz, Samantha Hunt, and Mary Gordon take on subjects as challenging as Joan of Arc, the Unabomber, and a woman who likes hanging around the public library. Francine Prose and Cristina Henriquez defiantly assume male voices in stories that have little do with women's experiences. Henriquez's protagonist lovingly recalls his ex-girlfriend, but mostly what he remembers are her bangs, her wrists, and "her navy blue knee-highs pulled up past her knees like a tramp." Whatever it is, it's not chick lit.

Given Merrick's strenuous exertions, it seems worth considering this strange new genre. Not chick lit, she insists, "employs carefully crafted language to expand our reality"; "increases our awareness of other perspectives and paths"; "grants us access to countless new cultures, places, and inner lives." Some of these stories are even good. Others, less so. Curtis Sittenfeld, author of the 2005 surprise bestseller *Prep*, contributes a story about a racist, obsessive-compulsive woman who wreaks havoc at a women's shelter. "Hulking and monstrous," alone and afraid to be touched, the narrator volunteers at the shelter because she seems to believe she can save the kids from their slatternly mothers. When a new volunteer ("bumpy and greasy") threatens her status as favorite surrogate mom, she suggests she has no choice but to strangle the woman. She's a second-wave feminist, overfed and run amok. What our heroine really needs, we're made to understand, is a boyfriend, like her roommate's, who will toast her Eggo waffles.

The protagonists of Merrick's collection are certainly not chick-lit material (they don't do lunch, they're not shoe fetishists, and their sex lives aren't especially fantastic), but neither are they the young women we recognize or admire. Merrick seems strangely unprepared to acknowledge the existence of women like herself—the intellectually alive, productive female actor in the world is hardly to be found in *This Is Not Chick Lit*. In place of the middle-class suburbanite's fantasy of wealthy young urban singles, we get the young and urbane woman writer's caricature of what used to be called female hysteria. Are the articulate, prolific writers we turn to for visions of life beyond girlhood able only to imagine a string of revived Ophelias?

THIS YEAR'S MOST NOTABLE girl protagonists don't grow up, they go crazy. Recent literary fiction by and about young women seems to rest on a peculiar premise: that young adulthood is only, and always, compelling when aggressively perverse. So the heroine of Heidi Julavits's third novel revisits her stardom at the center of a rape controversy; Marisha Pessl's aptly named Blue discovers she's been abandoned by two abusive parent figures, notes signs of depression, and gleefully writes a book about it. Both of these girls turn the resources of middle-class upbringings and native intelligence toward shaping themselves not into women but specimens, equipped only for examination.

In Pessl's *Special Topics in Calamity Physics*, Blue van Meer is a bright high school student with a political science professor for a father. Her mother is long dead, and now other people around her keep dying, too. Which is lucky for Blue, because she wants to be a writer, and catastrophe (she explains) is the only thing worth writing about: "All worthwhile tales possess some element of violence." And, "without the disturbing incident in this chapter, I'd never have taken on the task of writing this story. I'd have nothing to write." Blue's opportunism might be read as lampooning the culture of victimization, in which all kinds of private disasters are worth enduring, inducing, or exaggerating in pursuit of a book deal—except that Pessl seems not to be in on the joke. Here is Blue recalling how she found the body of her favorite teacher, "hung three feet above the ground by an orange electrical extension cord":

> Her tongue—bloated, the cherry pink of a kitchen sponge—slumped from her mouth. Her eyes looked like acorns, or dull pennies, or two black buttons off an overcoat kids might stick into the face of a snowman, and they saw nothing. . . . And her shoelaces—an entire treatise could be written on those shoelaces—they were crimson, symmetrical, tied in perfect double knots.

This appears to be satire (on the self-absorption of teenagers) or maybe an acid trip, but in fact it's neither. It's the substitution of "precocious" style for the feelings and perspective of a teenage girl confronted by her first corpse. Thus the frantic garrulity, the colors and curlicues. Unable to trust the plot's theatrics—a parade of nightmarish high schools, paternal abuses, and fat men pushed into swimming pools—to stand on their own, Pessl renders them unnervingly cheerful through "vivid" description. A girl named Blue, conceivably, might notice the color of the extension cord from which her teacher hangs, and even her cherry pink tongue. But the three similes for the dead woman's eyes, presented à la carte, are a little much. As for the treatise on shoelaces, if such a thing exists, Pessl probably wrote it—but only if the laces were crimson, and attached to a corpse.

www.texttile.net

*publication design
illustration
website design
packaging*

Design for forward-thinking organizations

It seems important that Blue never falls in love, except with her father, her (female) teacher, and her own self-indulgent hysteria. She also never reads a book her father hasn't recommended. Rather than the recognizable and also more elusive flashpoints of sexual experience and intellectual maturity, we have a morbidly self-stimulating anxiety of influence. Blue is too old to be properly precocious, but Pessl seems to think she can stunt and beat her into a heroine.

HEIDI JULAVITS'S *Uses of Enchantment* is a more complicated case. A more mature writer than Pessl, Julavits doesn't take her teenage heroine's perspective as her own. Instead, she assigns her characters the task of ferreting out that perspective—the same task she assigns herself. The rapt analysis of Mary Veal (a virgin, and a piece of meat) is not only the subject of the book but the exclusive interest of every adult allowed a speaking part. It's a convenient tactic and not necessarily a hopeless one. The trouble is that Julavits confuses writing a fascinating novel with creating an object of fascination.

Teenaged Mary, we learn over the course of the novel, was abducted one day from lacrosse practice by a demoralized out-of-work prosecutor from her WASPy town. She returned a month later, having been sexually abused. Or not. Both Julavits and Mary coyly refuse to say what happened, and through this coyness the author turns Mary from a girl into material. The adults around her become a chorus, desperately asking her where she's been and what she did, all for the purpose of deciding whether she's a victim or a deviant.

None of Mary's investigators is equipped to figure her out; none is able to serve, even provisionally, as the reader-surrogate that detective fiction, even the postmodern, post-post-Freudian kind, cannot do without. The therapist assigned to her case wears ski pants to the office, agrees to let her call him "Beaton," and isn't even certified. The laid-off prosecutor who supposedly kidnapped her is a hapless type who accidentally killed a pedestrian and lives in craven fear of his ex-wife. Chapters titled "What Might Have Happened" suggest that Mary hopped unbidden into his car, and was able to stay because he was too frightened not to play along with her Humbert Humbert fantasies. It's only by comparison to these halfhearted, halfheartedly constructed creatures that Mary appears radiantly compelling. Take away the girl and you're left with a sloppy satire; remove her interrogators and Mary becomes nothing at all.

At points, as Mary pursues her more extreme lines of provocation, the book's dialogue feels both spontaneous and sharply devious. The therapist, entranced, suggests a game of role reversal. "Are you cured?" asks Mary. "Put your clothes on, Mary," says the therapist, for Mary has put on his coat over her bra, and now says: "That's Doctor to you." It's possible to believe, for pages at a time, that even a serious adult could live in thrall to the heroine's voice.

But there are no serious adults in this book. It's more like a group of people in an amphitheater, each of whom shines a flashlight on a teenage girl, who raises her own torch above her head and pours more light onto herself. Julavits deliberately obscures her heroine's sexual history; sex, in the world of not chick lit, is always, like writing, a game, a deception—What Might Have Happened. The novel suggests a connection between the power of Mary's virginity and the power of her narrative imagination: each gives her sway over other people, but only so long as she keeps it to herself while pretending to give it away. It's a game that's fun for a while but bound to end badly—once Mary has sex, or admits to it, she won't interest us anymore.

There's no continuity between the adolescent Mary and the adult Mary, no way to carry what's distinct about youth into maturity. The book turns mean in the present-day sections, which follow an adult Mary who's returned home for her mother's funeral. Mary's own life has become impossibly gray and flat, and the third-person narrator savages everyone else in sight, in part to preserve her by comparison. When two women are described as "Country Club vipers," we know instantly what we're going to get: a dull satire of wealthy women who are dreaded and dreadful, way too tan, and have "perfected the charade of appearing to observe their surroundings when in fact they [are] critiquing the room through the corners of their mouths." Mary's sisters, similarly, are each introduced by a single attribute, "Regina's prickliness and Gaby's lumpish disinterest," and nothing either says or does will complicate these depictions. Their dead mother, we're told, was an anorexic alcoholic, a toxic woman who survived on white wine and pickles. A distasteful female acquaintance with capped teeth is described as either a former hockey goalie or (without even a hint of empathy) a victim of domestic abuse. Where once there was role play, coyness, even a kind of joking—now, with the grown-up Mary, there is nastiness, disguised as social criticism.

NELL FREUDENBERGER'S *The Dissident* is not primarily about female adolescents—which, in some ways, makes it an ideal lesson in how they ought to be treated. The book's primary concerns are a visiting Chinese artist named Yuan Zhao (the dissident of the title); the Traverses, the wealthy Los Angeles clan that hosts him; and the ways they anxiously deceive each other and themselves.

The Traverses' daughter Olivia and her girls' school peers exist tangentially among adults and their concerns. These teenagers exhibit a complex ambivalence toward the postadolescent world of parents and teachers and potential lovers, sometimes courting and sometimes deflecting its attentions.

Freudenberger has an unashamed fixation on how her characters dress themselves up in the morning. Olivia's mother, Cece, notes how her son's girlfriend, from a rougher part of town, wears her sexuality on her nonexistent sleeves, whereas her daughter's friends, with their loose shirts and boudoir lingerie, "showed off their bodies, but in covert ways." These are girls who call attention to the straitjackets of their starched uniform blouses not by tearing them off but by wearing black lace contraptions underneath. It's a small and gratifying measure of how the author gives adolescents credit for subtlety and also makes plain the complicity between deviance and the rules that inspire it.

The Dissident turns out to be about performance as much as perception: about the stunning diversity of its everyday manifestations and the way the mundane is needed to produce the exceptional. Clothes are by no means beside the point. The rebellious June, one of Olivia's classmates, also receives rapt attention for her studied subversion of the school's dress code:

> She was wearing the same uniform as the other girls, and also she was not. She was wearing the lavender dress . . . but underneath it she had put on a pair of wine-colored corduroy pants, which were splattered with paint, an addition that had the effect of making the dress ridiculous; or rather, since the dress was already ridiculous, making a comment about its ridiculousness. . . . There was something strange about her shoes as well: it took a moment . . . to see that she had painted the stamped leather band on each shoe white, and rest of the upper black. The inversion was jarring, if you were used to the ordinary model.

The inversion, in short, isn't possible without the overwhelming presence of the mundane—which, as personified by Olivia, does not appear irredeemable either. June's misbehavior, which escalates in a series of increasingly spectacular performance-art pieces, is neither thoroughly self-involved nor catastrophically self-destructive. (June does not get raped, murdered, or abducted; she goes to art school.) Rather, her aesthetic vision grows naturally out of a world of well-intentioned, mostly harmless regulations, to which Freudenberger devotes as much attention as she does to June's brief explosions of brilliance.

---

bellecitypop!

Spring 2007, New Releases:

Zookeeper
Alex Dupree and the Trapdoor Band
The Sad Accordions
Ye Gods

Devoted to the wanton proliferation of quality rock and roll, Belle City Pop is a company based in Brooklyn, NY.

www.bellecitypop.com

Much of *The Dissident*'s plot hangs on questions of artistry and fraud; June turns out to be a real artist, but the distinction is not absolute and is finally almost irrelevant. Each of Freudenberger's characters has the capacity to act originally or conventionally, to become artist or counterfeiter, depending on the circumstances. Freudenberger provides a world against which her characters—adolescents and everyone else—can test themselves without making or breaking the novel, which is confident enough to include them all.

—*Carla Blumenkranz*

OUR CONTRIBUTORS

Daniel Albert is the curator of transport at the London Museum of Science. He writes about cars for *n+1*.

Nancy Bauer is associate professor of philosophy at Tufts University and the author of *Simone de Beauvoir, Philosophy and Feminism*.

Imraan Coovadia is the author of *The Wedding* and *Green-Eyed Thieves*.

Rebecca Curtis's book *Twenty Grand: And Other Tales of Love and Money* will be published this summer by Harper Perennial.

Echo Eggebrecht is an artist living in New York. She is represented by Nicole Klagsbrun Gallery. Her illustrations previously appeared alongside the Fiction Chronicle in *n+1* Number Four.

Eli S. Evans is a writer living in Los Angeles.

Meghan Falvey is a graduate student in sociology. She lives in Brooklyn.

Joshua Glenn is a Boston-based writer and editor, currently at the *Boston Globe*. He used to publish the zine and journal *Hermenaut*.

Emily Ryan Lerner is a graphic artist and writer living in Brooklyn.

Basharat Peer is a journalist and memoirist now living in New York City.

Mark Sackmann is an elementary school music teacher and an artist in New York. This is his second original woodcut for *n+1*.

Gemma Sieff is an assistant editor at *Harper's* magazine.

n+1 would also like to thank our interns: Geoff Aung, Katie Fowley, Rebecca Green, Leon Neyfakh, Marc Tracy, Annie Wyman, and Molly Young.

CALEB CRAIN, *ATLANTIC CENTER, BROOKLYN*, 2007,
BLACK AND WHITE DIGITAL PHOTOGRAPH, 5 X 7". COURTESY OF THE ARTIST.

LETTERS

SYMPOSIUM ON AMERICAN WRITING

Dear Editors,

I read with interest your symposium in Issue Four on current American writing, and greatly enjoyed most of the pieces. Elif Batuman's piece "Short Story & Novel," however . . . it is hard to know where to begin. For one thing, judging the current state of American short fiction based on *Best American Short Stories* 2004 and 2005 alone is like judging the current state of American film based solely on the Golden Globes. I myself have complained about the stories selected (or not selected) for *BASS*, an annual bellyache somewhat Lactaid-ed by my inclusion in 2005's volume. (I subscribe to Kingsley Amis's view that prizes and the like are all bullshit unless you win one.) What *BASS* represents, if anything, is merely the peculiarities and peccadilloes of each year's guest editor, and, if you read through these guest editors' invariably hedged and apologetic introductions, all avoid any claims that these are the best stories of the year. Michael Chabon, last year's editor, is no exception. Batuman, with her fatuous claim of reading two whole years of *Best American Short Stories* in "the name of science," sneakily places these stories upon an exalted pedestal that only the most droolingly credulous would accept. Ms. Batuman's pedestal, not surprisingly, quickly becomes a cucking stool.

My story "Death Defier" catches a tomato or two. First, she claims that, in "acknowledgment of the times," it takes place in the Middle East. My story takes place in Afghanistan, which is in Central Asia. Central Asia and the Middle East are at least as different from each other as the short story is from the novel. She then claims—using my story as an example—that "the first sentences" of so many *Best American* selections, afflicted with their "barrage of names," are "specific to the point of arbitrariness." My first sentence reads thus: "Graves had been sick for three days when, on a long, straight highway between Mazar and Kunduz, a dark blue truck coming toward them shed its rear wheel in a spray of orange-yellow sparks." "Would Pushkin," she writes, "have managed to inspire anybody at all had he written: 'The night before Countess Maria Ivanovna left for Baden-Baden, a drunken coachman crashed the Mirskys' troika into the Pronskys' dacha'? He would not."

Batuman has some ideas about the story—namely, that a story "can only accommodate a very specific content: basically, absences." As for the "in-your-face in medias res" of my story and others, with their "maze of names, subordinate clauses, and minor collisions," well, gosh: the masters (she cites Chekhov, Updike, and Munro) would never do such a thing. This sounds like critical snake oil to me, and nothing destroys one's trust in a critic more quickly

lucien

Restaurant/Bar   14 First Avenue, New York, NY 10009

please hold me the forgotten way
R.N.

Pink Pony
176 Ludlow St., New York, NY

than a sweeping categorical statement that dovetails with the critic's ignorance:

> In the summer of 1979, I walked into the kitchen of my friend Sunny's house near Uxbridge, Ontario, and saw a man standing at the counter, making himself a ketchup sandwich.
> —*Alice Munro, "Nettles"*

> A not quite slight earthquake—5.4 on the Richter scale—afflicted Morrison's area early one morning: at 6:07, it said later over the news.
> —*John Updike, "Slippage"*

> This was six or seven years ago, when I was living in one of the districts of T----- province, on the estate of the landowner Belokurov, a young man who got up very early, went about in a vest, drank beer in the evenings, and kept complaining to me that he met with no sympathy anywhere or from anyone.
> —*Anton Chekhov, "The House with the Mezzanine: An Artist's Story"*

Of course, I am stacking my deck, just as Batuman stacked hers, with one difference: I am aware that this is three-card Monte, and representative of nothing more than how three writers chose to begin a story—a surprising, organic, supple form as variable as the human mind itself.

Here is John Updike himself, in his introduction to *Best American Short Stories 1984*: "I want stories to startle or engage me within the first few sentences, and in their middle to widen or deepen or sharpen my knowledge of human activity, and to end by giving me a sensation of completed statement." Nothing like that can ever have truly "exhausted the conditions for its existence," unless the critic herself is dead to its pleasures, and reads as an accountant of the meaningless: where it was published, by whom, and how many proper names it uses. "Guilt," she writes, with a sagacity matched impressively by its mistakenness, "leads to the idea that all writing is self-indulgence. . . . Dear young writers, write with dignity, not in guilt. How you write is how you will be read." As for her dignity suggestion: Thank you? As for her terminal sentence: You don't say.

—*Tom Bissell*

Dear Editors,

The title of the opening feature, "The Intellectual Situation," proclaims your writers "intellectuals." They've paid big money to gain that word and won't give it up! They embrace that designation, that difference, and as long as they do they marginalize themselves. About the larger society and how to reach it they remain clueless.

An image pops into my head of one of those hybrid French museums in which the contemporary is planted hopefully amid the walls of classicism. A large plexiglass box hangs suspended from the ceiling. Inside the box, holding wineglasses, stand today's literary caretakers. The conversation is filled with standard academic jargon: "derive" this and "derive" that; derived specificity derived from the arbitrariness derived from the inutility of "an inverted vitalist." (Throw in some "genetic mysticism" and a few "imprimaturs" while you're at it.)

The buzz among the people suspended in the box is at a polite murmur. Look! James Wood and Jonathan Franzen, our culture's (supposed) Best Critic and Best Novelist, "mutual almost-admirers," are locked in debate—almost. Museum patrons struggle to listen, expecting to hear words of energy and wit, of sharp-edged conflict or spar-

ORTHOGRAPHY VARIEGATION

BECAUSE READING IS NOT A ONESIZEFITSALL EXPERIENCE

NOITAGEIRAV YHPARGOHTRO

ingFourfoldPrivationalExperience
PhantasmaticProjectionPrecipitat
all reading is a
THE SP (PPPFP(4P)E) PRINCIPLE:

T
H
E

S
P
E
L
L
I
N
G
R
E
F
O
R
M

M
O
V
E
M
E
N
T

R
E
N
A
I
S
S
A
N
C
E

E
N
S
E
M
B
L
E

THE BOOK OCTAGON IDEA

▶ START

32 TIMES 3
SEVEN NOTE ELECTRIC ORGAN SYMPHONY VIDEOTAPE SOUNDTRACK
2 PAGES PE

(THE HAMMOND PIPER AT ABOUT FIVE HUNDRED AND FIFTY-FIVE STEPS CLOSER TO THE GARDEN STATE THAN AND ELEVEN DAYS BEFORE THE GATES OF JEANNE-CLAUDE AND CHRISTO)

R SECOND M
TWO-HOUR CONTINUOUS RECORDING • 100% IMPROVISED • 100% UNEDITED • WITH A "NAME THAT TUNE" ASPECT
E D I A I N F O

kling wisdom, finding instead the dullest such exchange, from two big names, ever.

Doubleday editor Gerald Howard bemoans the conglomerates (of which he's part). He's "gloomy-hopeful" someone will find a way out of their plexiglass trap. He never asks, "Does anyone have a hammer?"

Meanwhile, outside the museum runs a stream, fed by underground springs, representing the life force of authentic culture.

—*King Wenclas*
Underground Literary Alliance

Dear Editors,

There is a category of financial support for writing that Keith Gessen seems to have overlooked in his essay on "Money"—that of living off the earnings of one's spouse. Ralph Ellison discussed this at length in his foreword to *Invisible Man*, in which a neighborhood woman accuses him of being a "sweetback." I am such a sweetback, although my being a stay-at-home dad would seem to counter the notion that I do nothing in exchange for my wife's support. In any case, there have been legions of housewife writers who were neither embedded in the academy, independently wealthy, working in journalism, nor waiting tables in order to support their writing.

—*Greg Partch*

Dear Editors,

I was enjoying Benjamin Kunkel's incisive essay "Novel." But then he takes a moment to imagine what novels people will be reading in the year 2050. If the "Intellectual Situation" ["Global Warming"] is any guide, we surely will not be reading novels in the year 2050. We will be busy building igloos and fighting off our friends, and free time will be very different.

—*Chip Mitchell*

IN EXTREMIS

Dear Editors,

Andrew Ellner ["First, Do No Harm"] is an observant, compassionate, intelligent house officer, and already a good writer. I have no doubt that he'll be a wonderful doctor. But one gets the sense that he hopes his teachers will show him a moral direction. My experience over the past forty years is that they won't. Not because they don't wish to do what is best for their patients in extreme illnesses, but because they are themselves constrained, frightened, and confused.

I recently received a patient transferred from a hospital some distance away, rushed with his family to my care for treatment of a lung cancer metastatic to the brain. He was comatose, but his wife and family were led to expect that I would operate on him immediately and save him. I spent an hour explaining that, while such treatment was possible, the end result would be that he'd wake to a severe neurological disability in order that he could live another six months—painfully and dependently preparing again to die. The family understood the folly of that idea, took him home, and enrolled him in hospice care. He died peacefully after a few days, never having awakened, never having suffered, and never having seen the inside of an ICU.

The lesson is, of course, to keep people *out* of the ICU.

The major task Ellner and his generation face will be to keep life-and-death decisions out of the courts, and out of religious politics. Because I myself grow older now, I pray they will be successful.

—*Richard Rapport, M.D.*

Only the finest writers, each and every month

Few projects have made me as proud and given me as much pleasure as writing for **ETIQUETA NEGRA**. I'm eagerly anticipating the day when it will be available on other continents, in other languages, as a living example of the creativity of our America.
—Jon Lee Anderson. Journalist, THE NEW YORKER Staff Writer, USA.

I love **ETIQUETA NEGRA**. There aren't many magazines in the world that have this adventure, sophistication, humor and energy. I am really proud of being associated with it in any way, and I love seeing my stories in it.
—Susan Orlean. Journalist, THE NEW YORKER Staff Writer, USA.

ETIQUETA NEGRA operates on an incredibly high artistic level, and I greatly admire the effort that goes into its editorial process.
—Ryszard Kapuscinski. Journalist, Author of THE SHADOW OF THE SUN, Poland.

www.etiquetanegra.com.pe
made in peru

FREE LOVE (I)

Dear Editors,

There's a bunch of us here in Minneapolis who are reading your work, though not as many who are paying for it. Love,

—*John C.*

FREE LOVE (II)

Dear Editors,

Thank you for Mark Greif's incisive essay, "Afternoon of the Sex Children." The first solution he suggests is to extinguish the worship of youth in our culture. This daunting task seems well worth trying, only how? I hope Greif pursues this.

His second proffered solution, to trivialize sex altogether, is his antidote to our culture's elevation of sex to something of unsurpassed importance. Greif muses that Aldous Huxley warned us about a future world where sex would be arranged as casually as a coffee date. He passes over the word *warn*, and reflects that this is "an impossibly beautiful idyll." What is missing here is an understanding that sex is intrinsically intimate. Perhaps it is more so for women due to the fact that it is an internal experience. Even if sex is drained of emotional intimacy, it is far from a coffee date. To deny that is to distort reality.

—*Lynn Schneider*

FREE ADVICE

Dear Editors,

Greetings from Chicago . . . Moments ago I found *n+1* on the web—I had heard of its existence, but hadn't found it in any bookshop in the city. Distribution in a world as large as this is key. Your work has to be in people's faces—like that single black hair the razor always misses under your nose.

(Don't fret. I know this has the makings of one of those letters—you know the kind.)

Twenty-seven months ago, a friend and I had an idea to launch an underground pamphlet. It was to be called *Scattershot*, which referred to the method of distribution. Instead of going the usual route and asking indie bookstores and comics shops and cafés and hookah lounges and record stores to carry a stack of copies at the door—we decided to drop copies of *Scattershot* in the toilet. Not in the toilet bowl. But on top of the porcelain. Our hit list was random.

Looking back, this idea couldn't have been more appropriate. The toilet was where *Scattershot* belonged. Despite a decent, handprinted layout, the writing sucked. Where we succeeded, though, was distribution. A note on the inside cover asked that you read the pamphlet with clean hands and not take it with you after you flushed.

I don't want to end this without talking about silence and noise. You yell out and no one responds. We had an email address . . . We never heard a single word. Looking back, it didn't make much sense that anyone would write us unless they carried their laptop to the bathroom. Still, the resounding silence made us bitter. (We never published again.)

I think differently of *n+1*. At a minimum, it belongs in a clean facility.

—*A*

TOWERLESS BROOKLYN

Dear Editors,

A comparison of the two pieces ["Building Miss Brooklyn" and "A Sporting Chance": see the Web Archive at nplusonemag.com] you ran on the Atlantic Yards development

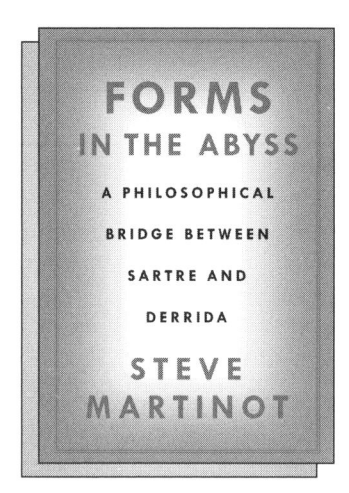

FORMS IN THE ABYSS
A Philosophical Bridge between Sartre and Derrida
STEVE MARTINOT
"The project of transcoding Sartrean language into the Derridean coordinates, and vice-versa, is an unseasonable one whose reward lies in the defamiliarization of both. Martinot's minute, technical readings avoid all facile ideological generalizations and send us back to the original texts with new eyes."—**Fredric Jameson**
$59.50 HARDCOVER

LABOR OF FIRE
The Ontology of Labor between Economy and Culture
BRUNO GULLÌ
"My sense is that Gullì's work (along with that of a few other young scholars) will renew once again the Marxist tradition. This will not be a scientific Marxism or a humanist Marxism or a structuralist Marxism. It is rather a very philosophical approach to Marx that is nonetheless centered on the concept of labor and its power of social transformation."—**Michael Hardt**, Duke University
Labor in Crisis Series, edited by Stanley Aronowitz
$24.95

TROUBLED PASTS
News and the Collective Memory of Social Unrest
JILL A. EDY
"This fact-studded book unveils the mysteries surrounding the construction of collective memories about major social crises in the United States. Edy analyzes the 1965 Watts riots and the tumultuous 1968 Chicago Democratic National Convention to reveal how journalists and political elites weave the scattered facts reported initially into meaningful narratives.... Edy's lessons can help us avoid the many pitfalls that so often produce dysfunctional collective memories."—**Doris A. Graber**
$22.95

WELFARE DISCIPLINE
Discourse, Governance, and Globalization
SANFORD F. SCHRAM
"This is a stylish and elegant book whose numerous fresh insights into the politics of welfare retrenchment represent a significant contribution to the existing literature. Persuasive, powerful, and provocative..."—**Colin Hay**, University of Birmingham, UK
$21.95

At Bookstores or Call: 800-621-2736
www.temple.edu/tempress

TEMPLE UNIVERSITY PRESS

highlights some curious divisions between the writers. Nikil Saval focuses his attention on questions concerning political coalitions, rhetoric, city zoning policies, and housing. Jonathan Liu, by contrast, focuses his discussion on architecture, sports, and the image of "history."

These discussions converge on a key figure: Robert Moses. Saval acknowledges the (usually overlooked) fact that Moses provided New York City with an astounding quantity, much of it centrally located, of public housing units. The presence of these facilities has all but guaranteed that New York will never gentrify as thoroughly as, say, central Paris or London. This acknowledgement attends Saval's support for "liberal projects [that help] the poor and displaced" of New York. All this Saval is able to do without advocating the full, problematic scope of Moses's entire building program, which was in many respects anti-poor.

By contrast, Liu's understanding of Moses stems from a more familiar narrative, in which Moses is held up as responsible for ugly "cookie cutter" constructions all over the city and for massive highway-building programs that destroyed neighborhoods. A (surely not permanent) political rejection, in the United States, of the sorts of "liberal projects" that Saval endorses for American cities has bolstered this narrative. Yet an inspection of conditions on the ground reveals that such a story is in many ways quite contrived. For instance, many of Moses's constructions—Lincoln Center, the terraces in Riverside Park, the Verrazano Bridge—are, to say the least, unique. Moreover, as Saval suggests, highways and other major government building programs are not alone to blame for the postwar destruction of urban neighborhoods. If anything, protecting a neighborhood from a highway has tended to facilitate gentrification, which is a process whereby *all* of the residents of an area—and not just those who live inside the highway corridor—are forced to leave. Through gentrification, the neighborhood is "saved" only insofar as its architecture remains.

Indeed, Liu makes clear that architecture fascinates him far more than do the people inside of it. Certainly this bias would explain why he is able to write an entire article about the role of architecture in the Atlantic Yards development conflict—a conflict which is, ultimately, about housing prices—without even mentioning the word "housing." For Liu, architecture's primary responsibility is not to provide shelter, but rather to project certain images (conveying "history," or "humanism," or the "transformative power" of athletics, or whatever). Such a notion of architecture usually gets branded "postmodern," but to make the definition more relevant to Saval's discussion, we might instead use the term "neoliberal"—since it is a definition that regards society as composed of image-consumers, and not of human beings with a shared fundamental need for shelter.

Liu begins his article by self-identifying as a fan of the NBA. One wonders: is it necessary that such self-identification lead to his thinly veiled pro-corporate political position? Perhaps; after all, above all else sports fans want for their "home" team to win a championship. This desire calls for the best young players, which calls for money, which calls for expensive arena seats and ludicrous amounts of public funding for arena construction. Most fans, whether rich or poor, are comfortable mortgaging their own futures in their longing for that elusive ring.

And yet a professional sports league is by definition limited. The season, the game, the court, the rules—all this is bounded. The whole point, the whole excitement, hinges upon the fact that the competition is sup-

The Kitchen Club

open 7 days a week
for lunch and dinner

30 Prince Street   212-274-0025

posed to be "only a game"—the merciless hypercompetitiveness of which is *not* supposed to spill over into all other aspects of our lives. Liu himself, in celebrating such "old-fashioned" sporting venues as Ebbets Field or Fenway Park, suggests the importance of the stadium as a bounded, autonomous construction (neither ballpark was built as part of a "multi-use complex"). To this end, the proposed Nets arena would be acceptable if it weren't part and parcel of a far vaster corporate building program, one which will annihilate the presence of economically struggling groups as thoroughly as a great basketball team annihilates a lousy one.

Bruce Ratner is using the overwhelming cultural popularity of sports to sell his plan for Brooklyn. He is banking on an uncritical understanding of sports as "justifying" capitalism at its most cutthroat. Yet sports is, and has always been, salvageable for a politics of resistance. Think of Tommie Smith and John Carlos raising the "Black Power" fist during the 1968 Olympic medal award ceremony.

Saval's "renewed attention to and investment in the notion of public development" need not come at the expense of *any* cultural practice, be it architecture, sports, or the celebration of history.

—*Jacob Shell*

Dear Editors,

A glance in the mirror Jonathan Liu offers me in "A Sporting Chance" shows a creature of straw, wearing my name. Liu indulges the same caricature of an anti-Ratner position as Charles "There's this small culture of inertia" Schumer and Frank "They should have been picketing Henry Ford" Gehry—i.e., that to stand against this particular development is to stand, somehow, against progress—and the contemporary city—itself. Hooey. Balderdash. Flapdoodle.

Let's make it simple. A thousand different futures could be projected for that zone (and if you chose from a thousand at random you could hardly do worse than Ratner's top-heavy, over-dense, privatized, underplanned, compromised-yet-railroaded vision). Who ever claimed the only choice was between this and "stasis"? (If you're not for wiretapping, you must be in favor of terrorists.) I like sports too, but when did basketball come to mean towers? Why not ask for better, instead of consoling ourselves in advance for acquiescence to yet another triumph of capital's brain-dead imperatives? "Growth for growth's sake is the logic of the cancer cell." Edward Abbey said that. I don't find anything more persuasive than cancer logic in Liu's elaborate rationalizations.

—*Jonathan Lethem*

GERMAN DOPE FIENDS

Dear Editors:

Perhaps if Johannes Türk ["The Trouble with Being German"] had limited himself to the discontents of Berlin his commentary would be less annoyingly coy. Berlin is a special place and remains oddly depressed—both economically and psychologically—for the capital city of Europe's (yes, still) richest country. Subsidies propped up the city during the cold war, and it was arguably the best place in the West to get good, cheap drugs as well as high culture. German students still flock there in droves for the nightlife and cultural attractions, but finding a living wage is difficult and most never settle permanently. The city relies on an intermittent rush of young foreigners both from within Germany and without to stay fresh. Cheap rents have been a boon to expat artists from Williamsburg, Paris, London, Tokyo, you name it. Cheap flights, cheaper alcohol, and an impossible wealth of grants, fellowships,

Forthcoming in *n+1* Number Six   **(Last Stands)**

SUMMER IN SAMARQAND
LOWER THE VOTING AGE!
BEFORE THE LAW PROFESSOR
OFFICE: A GENEALOGY

NEW YORK BEFORE STARBUCKS
APOCALYPSE AND THE NOVEL
NEW CRITERION AT 25
THE FLIES: A PLAY
HIGH CULTURE OR NO CULTURE

[+ THE INTELLECTUAL SCENE]

Don't wait another six (or eight) months.
New, web-only essays and fiction every Monday at www.nplusonemag.com.

[PHILOSOPHY]   BADIOU: BADASS
[LITERATURE]   ON GILBERT SORRENTINO
[POLITICS]   BUILDING MISS BROOKLYN
[ACADEMIA]   ROBBINS VS. WBM VS. ROBBINS VS. WBM
[FOREIGNERS]   THE UNSTABLE FRENCH

[+ SPORTS, ART CHRONICLE, & ORIGINAL FICTION]

and other stipends help keep it going. The German government wants you to love Germany—and what better way than to present a theme park of trauma, history, and rebirth?

This is the entire point of the newly dubbed "Berlin Republic": lots of communist architecture interspersed with glass and steel, makeshift clubs in abandoned buildings and ethnic restaurants to boot. The '68 generation changed some things for the better (no doubt), but keep in mind Schröder now heads a finance group building an oil pipeline between Germany and Russia, aided by his best friend, the virtuous Vladimir Putin. Principles? The man wants to get paid. To see that the Iraq war was foolish took little political courage or genius, especially in a country where appealing to pacifism is like appealing to God.

I am also surprised to hear that Heidegger isn't being taught at German universities. Really? Countless works on Heidegger have been published in the German language in the last fifteen years. Perhaps Türk should have mentioned Carl Schmitt as one of the doyens of German political philosophy who's getting little exposure in the Fatherland. There are a host of interesting and creative German intellectuals that compete on a much vaster plane—Peter Sloterdijk comes to mind—than many American self-styled intellectuals. And that Germans are embarrassed to speak German outside of Germany (a typical lament of the German university student)? Have you been to Spain, Portugal, or Tuscany recently? Germans are fucking colonizing these places; you can order food there in German, I promise; you may even find a Bretzel or a good Schnitzel if you're lucky.

—S. C. Gummer

(N+1) X 2

Dear Editors,

We were very surprised in discovering some months ago another magazine with the same title we chose in April 2000 (first issue of Italian *n+1*). Now some guy registered as admin. in Italian Wikipedia told us that *n+1* already existed when we made the encyclopedia article. We don't believe that will create an ambiguity, but... damn! Why did you adopt such a title among the millions possible? What does it mean for you? We are interested in the answer, but not for copyright (we adopted a politics of copyleft).

—Alessandro
(for the editorial staff)

Marco Roth replies:

It's one of those strange intellectual coincidences. We chose *n+1* as the working title of our journal. For us, it was a metaphor for the possibility of progress, the infinitely open set, at a time when Americans seemed to have lost faith in both progressive politics and the possibility of individual improvement, in literature and thought, without the aid of capitalism. Only then did we discover your journal. We attempted to come up with an alternative title, but nothing pleased us as much or suited us as well. We hoped the world would be big enough for both *n+1*s: yours dialectical and Marxist, ours progressive and eclectic, both united in a belief that we deserve better than what our governments and culture presently offer. +

Reader—

Has life brought you money? Did you ever think of doing something unusual, by backing a literary-political-cultural magazine? Now's the time. *n+1* is in need of an angel: some one person or organization to help us be really ambitious, to back us, to let us publish more, to encourage us to fight the forces of reaction in the arts and politics, and to publish and sponsor the best new writers and unknowns.

If you'd consider being our angel, contact us at editors@nplusonemag.com. We have much more to talk about, and so much still to do.

WINNER OF THE 2006 UTNE INDEPENDENT PRESS AWARD FOR BEST WRITING
SUBSCRIBE AT WWW.NPLUSONEMAG.COM/SUBSCRIBE.HTML

"Edgily erudite." Times Literary Supplement
"Lively." Boston Globe
"Refreshing." Slate
"Putting the smart in smart-ass." New York

"Pointed, closely argued and often brilliantly original critiques of contemporary life and letters... a generational struggle against laziness and cynicism."
A. O. Scott, *New York Times Magazine*

"They intend nothing less in their periodical than to reimagine and reestablish the world."
Jordan Mejias, *Frankfurter Allgemeine Zeitung*